# SONORAN RAGE

## A COLTON BROTHERS SAGA, No. 2

A Novel

# MELODY GROVES

La Frontera Publishing

Sonoran Rage
A Colton Brothers Saga, No. 2
A Novel
Copyright © 2008 Melody Groves

Cover illustration: "Los Diablos" ©2008 Frank McCarthy courtesy of the Greenwich Workshop, Inc. www.greenwichworkshop.com. All rights reserved, used with permission

Cover design, book design and typesetting by Yvonne Vermillion and Magic Graphix

Printed and bound in the United States of America
First edition
First Printing, September 2008


Library of Congress Cataloging-in-Publication Data

Groves, Melody, 1952-
Sonoran rage : a novel / Melody Groves. -- 1st ed.
    p. cm. -- (A Colton brothers saga ; no. 2)
ISBN 978-0-9785634-4-8 (pbk.)
I. Title.
PS3607.R6783S68 2008
813'.6--dc22

                            2008032975



Published by La Frontera Publishing
(307) 778-4752 • www.lafronterapublishing.com

# Dedication

In Memory Of:

Roy L. Dean (1913-2002)

For:

Colton Dean Saab Montoya

# Acknowledgements

My very sincerest thanks to:

Western Writers of America who have opened many, many doors.

SouthWest Writers who have helped me learn how to write.

# And a huge THANK YOU to:

Myke Groves
Erin Montoya
Haley Crawford
Margaret Dean
Johnny Boggs
Mike Harris

"Thanks for always being there."
-Wyatt Earp, Tombstone

# FORWARD

Apache Pass, southern Arizona in the 1850s, was the scene of one of the bloodiest massacres of Americans in Arizona history. Nachi, the father of Cochise, ambushed a westbound wagon train in Siphon Canyon. More than 30 immigrants, including women and children, were murdered.

By the time Butterfield Overland Stage Line opened a station there in 1858, a large number of Chirichaua Apaches were living throughout the area. Among these was Cochise, with about 700 warriors and their families. Relations between the Butterfield employees and the Apaches were relatively serene, but being surrounded by so many Apaches kept the employees on their toes.

Despite the fact that the Apaches who lived at the pass allowed the twice-weekly stages to rumble though and tolerated the presence of the employees, the Apaches continued to raid Mexican and American ranches. There were several "incidents" that led to open warfare between U.S. troops and the Apaches near the pass.

The Bascom Affair is generally credited as being the spark that set off the hostilities. Second Lieutenant George Bascom accused Cochise of kidnapping a young boy, then seized Apache hostages to assure the safe return of the youngster. Wrongly accused, Cochise retaliated by capturing some white men, including a Butterfield employee at the Apache Pass way station.

Bascom captured Cochise, but the Apache managed to slip out of Bascom's grasp. However, because of his escape, Cochise's brother and two other Indians were hanged. Cochise retaliated and killed the station manager along with two others. The first of two battles between the U.S. Army and Cochise's Chirichaua Apaches in 1861 resulted in many deaths on both sides.

The misunderstanding on Bascom's part halted negotiations with the Apaches and set relations back forty years.

i

Besides the Bascom Affair, the Civil War had much to do with the increase of Apache raids in southern Arizona. The threat of an invasion by Confederate Texans caused the federal command to order the abandonment of nearby Forts Breckenridge and Buchanan. Soldiers were ordered east to the Rio Grande, and the citizens of western New Mexico (Arizona) were left to fend for themselves.

As if adding insult to injury, the Confederates seized all the Butterfield stations and coaches in Texas. John Butterfield, already in ill health, retired, then died in 1869.

Cochise, a man who valued honesty above almost everything, lived until 1874. This Chiricahua Apache leader's reputation was one of skill and sincerity. Known as a bit of a renegade, he along with his father-in-law, Mangas Colorado (Red Sleeve), maintained Apache leadership throughout the tough times as they watched their empire shrink.

Cochise ("Hardwood") was born in Arizona around 1805. Described as a large man with a muscular frame, classic Roman features, and long black hair, which he wore in traditional Apache style, Cochise was the leader of the Chiricahua Apaches, one of several tribes in Arizona. He married Dos-Teh-Seh, daughter of Mangas Colorado, in the 1830s. Their sons, Taza (born 1842) and Naiche (born 1856) grew up to become leaders in their own rights.

While gentle in manner during normal occasions, Cochise was capable of extreme cruelty in warfare, torturing his victims as he and his people had learned to do from their Mexican enemies. But, he was intelligent and sensitive as well, recognizing from the start that peace was the only possible ensurance for the survival of his people—he simply wanted a just and lasting co-existence.

By this time, the United States stretched from coast to coast. California to the west, the Gadsden Purchase south. The Plains filled up. People craved communication. Letters and news took months to reach either coast, since the mail was routed overland by mule train or by ship around Cape Horn, a perilous journey at best. So, when John Butterfield figured out an expeditious way to connect the coasts, he changed history.

In response to demands of people on both coasts, the U.S. Post Office advertised for bids on a new, overland mail route to California. The daunting requirements kept many bidders away: whoever won the contract needed to have operations up and running within 12 months, along a route that spanned 2,800 miles, traversed in 25 days. The winning company would need to hire 1,000 men, build 250 wagons, purchase 1,200 horses and 600 mules, buy 800 sets of harnesses, build 200 way stations, and dig 100 wells—all for $600,000 a year.

John Butterfield—former mayor of Utica, New York, owner/driver of several freight companies, and good friends with President James Buchanan—was awarded that contract and work began.

Most of the work was done on time. There were reports that a few way stations from Tipton, Missouri, to San Francisco, California, were still being built as the first stagecoaches rumbled though. But by and large, things were ready by September 15, 1858, when the Butterfield Overland Mail service launched itself into history.

John Butterfield himself carried the mail on the first leg of the journey, then turned the reins over to his son John, Jr. The stage ran day and night, stopping every 20 miles to change horses or mules, but that was not enough time for much of a leg stretch for cramped passengers. They were afforded two longer stops a day for meals, which cost as much as $1 and usually consisted of coffee, beans, venison, mule meat, salt pork and plenty of mustard. The stage traveled an average speed of 5 miles an hour, making about 120 miles in 24 hours.

The mail was so reliable that the British government sent official correspondence destined for British Columbia via the Butterfield Overland Mail. When it first began operations, the company transported only letters, but later added newspapers and small packages. The stages never hauled valuable freight or payrolls.

While the United States grew, so did Mesilla in southern New Mexico Territory. In 1850, about 650 people called it home. The Gadsden Purchase, which annexed Mesilla to the United States from Mexico and established the current international borders of New Mexico and Arizona, was signed on its plaza in 1854. By 1858, over 3,000 people resided there, making it the largest town between San Diego and San Antonio.

Mesilla flourished as the center of commercial trade and political events. In fact, Mesilla became the capital of the Confederate States of Arizona (1861-62), which extended all the way to California. The Confederate flag once flew high where today's Fountain Theater stands. The San Albino church was built around 1852 on the south end of the plaza, but three years later, it was rebuilt where it stands now, on the north end. Today, 2,000 Mesillans live within the history that is an integral part of the development of the West.

From the 1850s on, the West boomed as it expanded, stretching its wings, so to speak. Mexicans, Indians, European immigrants, Americans seeking adventure and fortune—all found their way to the Southwest. And with them, came trouble.

# PART ONE

# CHAPTER ONE

*January 1861*

James Francis Michael Colton gripped his shotgun tighter and tugged his hat brim down a bit lower, just to where he could still see the desert. The stagecoach wheels kicked up dust as they rolled toward the next way station. He sneezed, then surveyed the horizon from his seat on top.

Like sun-faded pictures, gray saguaro cactus dotted the landscape, waiting for the sun to rise high enough to add color to their stately green shapes. This was James' favorite time of day. In a few minutes, the sun would turn the distant mesas into the orange, rose, and purple of the Sonoran Desert.

His stomach rumbled. It'd been too long since they'd left the San Pedro station. With the taste of coffee and biscuits still on his tongue, James looked forward to the Apache Springs station and Charles Culver's strong coffee and stew.

But they still had a ways to go. And this stagecoach seat was hard. He shifted his weight.

The swaying Celerity coach tempted James to sleep, but he struggled to stay awake, stay on his toes. His job was riding shotgun guard next to his brother, Trace, and he was paid to keep the passengers and the mail safe. Although there was only one passenger today, they were in the middle of Apache country, here in southern Arizona, and reports said that Cochise was tired of stages running across his land. James wanted to get home. Back to Mesilla. This trip couldn't be over soon enough.

James straightened his shoulders, pulled in crisp January air, and studied the scenery passing on his right. Creosote bushes, alligator juniper, a covey of startled quail. Then...

Movement.

A figure crouching behind a bush. A horse? An Indian?

James leveled his new twelve-gauge shotgun shoulder high. "Trace! Something's in those bushes! Over there!" His arms jerked with the coach.

"What?"

*Why doesn't my brother listen to me?*

"Someone's hiding. Right there." James sighted the Belgian double barrel across the mule team's backs. His finger on the trigger, he pulled against the pressure.

Trace squinted where James' shotgun pointed. Then he flicked the black whip over his team, snapping sharper than usual. "Step up, mules!"

James lurched with the stage, and he took a harder look at the offending sagebrush as they neared.

Nothing. There was nothing behind it. In fact, another look as they raced past revealed nowhere to hide. There weren't enough leaves and branches to cover a rabbit, much less an Indian. Only the stagecoach moved.

Trigger finger relaxed, James rested the shotgun by his foot, and then he pried his hat up off his forehead. Tiny beads of sweat had pasted the hat to his skin.

Trace pulled back on the reins.

"Whoa, boys. A nice easy gallop will do now." He glanced at James as he set the whip down on the seat between them. "Every shadow, rabbit, and hawk's got you spooked."

"I could swear I saw a pinto. Or an Indian."

"You just keep those eyes open like you've been doing," Trace said, that big brother baritone more pronounced than usual. "But ever since Tucson, you've seen what? Two dozen charging Apaches? Three runaway freight wagons? A band of renegade Mexican bandits?" He raised one shoulder. "Oh, and a puma ready to attack."

James stared into the desert. "Sure thought they were real."

"Just your nerves." Trace hunched his shoulders, then twisted his upper body. "I'm ready for a get down. My rear end's flat as this board."

James turned his attention to Trace. Driving the stagecoach was a hard and dangerous job. The driver was in charge of everything—the guard, the coach, the mail, and the passengers. It was a job of importance and prestige in the community, plus good pay. The drivers always walked with a bit more swagger in their step than other people. And they should. They deserved respect.

He watched his brother adjust the tightness of the lead mules' reins, making sure they gave the passenger a smooth ride. James remembered the feel of the thick leather entwined between his fingers when his brother taught him to drive a stagecoach, so he could take charge in an emergency. Those reins exuded power, the six Missouri mules pulling together like a well-disciplined army.

Would he want to become a stagecoach driver like his brother? After Saturday, he'd have to think real hard about his future.

Maybe by this time next year he could have his own run— with a shotgun guard at his side, just like he was now with Trace. Maybe one of his younger brothers would want to come west, leave their Kansas home like he did, and join the Butterfield Overland Stage Lines. Andy was still too young, but Luke, at eighteen, was ready.

He allowed a grin to crawl up one side of his face. Yeah. He'd like being a driver.

The Sonoran Desert sky encased James in a blue deeper than he'd ever seen before. Was it his imagination, or were Nature's colors brighter than usual? Now that the sun was higher, the saguaros turned deep green, and off to the south, the sky melted into three flat-topped mesas standing blue and purple in the distance.

Mounds of copper-colored boulders came into view. Those large boulders lining both sides of the stage road were a landmark signaling that Apache Springs lay ahead. James relaxed a little. A couple more hours and he'd be enjoying a cup of Culver's strong coffee.

He reached over and patted the front of Trace's coat. "You still got it, don't you?"

"Ask me one more time," Trace said, "and I'll give it to the next woman I see."

James felt his cheeks warm, despite the January wind.

Trace wagged his head. "In my pocket. Don't worry, I won't lose the ring."

"Hell, Trace. Saturday! That's a week from today!"

"I know."

James couldn't hide his grin.

Trace cut his eyes sideways. "Should be me getting married first. I'm four years older." His eyes widened. "Wait, what'm I saying?"

"If you weren't so blind, big brother, you'd know Teresa's sweet on you." James turned one hand palm up. "She's always cooking your favorite food and laughing at your dumb jokes."

A shrug, then a grin edged toward Trace's ears. "I'm truly happy for you. Lila's a great gal. And, it's not every day I get to stand up for my kid brother."

James returned the grin. He caught a sparkle in his brother's brown eyes.

*Boom!*

Rifle shots echoed off boulders. James shouldered his shotgun, swinging it left then right. Where were the shots coming from?

To his right. A puff of smoke.

*Boom!*

Trace pitched sideways off the stagecoach seat. James grabbed the reins with one hand and yanked. Then he glanced over his shoulder. Trace lay on his side in the desert sand.

*Boom!*

A fireball seared James' forehead, branding iron hot. A shocking white flash. He released the reins to grab at the pain exploding in his head, rippling down his body.

Rocked back and then sideways, he grabbed for the edge of the seat, but his hands grasped only air.

He hit the ground. Hard.

Somersaulting across the desert, he rolled to a stop, his face digging into sand. It filled his mouth, clogged his nose. He couldn't breathe.

James forced his head up, spitting out dirt. Trace? Where was Trace? Agony spiked down his body, but then he spotted his brother.

There, just a few yards away. Motionless.

Head too heavy, it thudded back to the ground.

Hooves thundering. Men shouting. Rifles booming.

Swirling blue. Spiraling white. Spinning black.

Silence.

# CHAPTER TWO

Lila stood behind the counter, waiting for the woman to choose. Please hurry, she thought. I've got a million things to do.

"I'll take two yards of this yellow calico." The woman handed the bolt to Lila. "And ten buttons. That should do nicely." Her gaze roamed over the material stacked behind Lila Belle, who set the bolt on the wooden counter. The Mesilla Mercantile was famous for its selection of cloth.

Lila nodded, her thoughts elsewhere—out in the Sonoran Desert. With James. As she unrolled the material she thought about her wedding dress. Lacy white, big puffy sleeves. In fact, she and Teresa had spent hours sewing it meticulously—with lots of love thrown in for good measure.

While she measured the cotton calico and cut it, Lila mentally busied herself with the last-minute preparations. Here it was Saturday, only one more week. So much to do. She and James would have the perfect wedding. All their friends at the church, her new dress, James, smelling of soap and his special sage aftershave, all dressed up in his dark blue Sunday suit. Teresa and Trace would stand up for them in front of God and everyone.

Perfect.

"And a yard of ribbon."

Lila focused on the customer in front of her. As much as she enjoyed her job, today her heart wasn't in it.

She surveyed the inside of the Mesilla Mercantile, by far the busiest store in this New Mexico town of over three thousand people. Barrels of flour, sacks of sugar, bundles of material, boots and shoes all lined the back wall. Since today was Saturday, there were plenty of shoppers. Children too. They gathered around the jars of penny candy, which beckoned to them like the promise of a hayride. There were too many customers to allow her time to just think.

Hundreds of things to do. Mrs. Grey, her employer, had given her the week after next off as her wedding present. A couple of those days would be spent in Franklin on their honeymoon.

Lila's cheeks warmed.

Then, she and James would settle down in Mesilla and begin their lives as husband and wife. She'd decided to write her new name as *Mrs. James F. M. Colton.* Her favorite part was the *Mrs.* That had a special ring to it. As special as the ring James had promised to get in Tucson.

"I don't deserve to be so happy." Lila spoke to no one in particular in the store. Saturday shoppers always lingered. People chatted with friends and dallied longer over pieces of calico and bonnets than on regular days. Lila wished all these customers would go home so she could finish her 'to do' list.

The bell on the door jingled—again. This time Lila smiled as she spotted her friend.

Teresa held the door for an older couple going out. Then she stepped in as graceful as a deer. A tall deer.

"Teresa!" Lila's southern melodic drawl was even more pronounced than usual. She walked toward her. "I was hoping you'd come by today. How are you?"

Teresa's grin spread across her pink-cheeked face. "Question is, how are you, Miss Almost-Married Lady?"

Lila led her friend across the store, away from a clot of shoppers, so they could talk more privately. They hid behind a pot-bellied stove and lowered their voices. The butterflies in Lila's stomach fluttered up to her throat, especially as she watched her friend's eyes dance with the shared excitement.

"I'm so excited," Lila said. "I can't sleep at night."

Teresa leaned in close and whispered. "You won't be sleepin' at night for a while anyway. Better get all the rest you can now."

"Teresa, how you talk!"

"I know. Ain't it fun?"

Both women giggled and blushed, then giggled again.

Lila nodded, but her joy faded. "Wish the boys were home right now. Wish they didn't have to make that Tucson run any more. Not when there's so much talk of Indian trouble over there."

"I'm sure they're fine." Teresa's voice tensed. "They can take care of themselves. We've got the best men in the whole world.

Nothing's gonna happen to them."

Lila realized it was good to have someone to worry with.

"All I know is they're comin' in Tuesday night, but that's a long ways away." Lila wanted to pout, but knew she was too old for that.

"It'll come soon enough." Teresa leveled her gaze on Lila and grew serious. "That'll only give James what? A couple of days to take a bath and get a haircut before the wedding?" She raised both eyebrows. "You think three days will be enough?"

Lila considered. Would it be enough time for *her*?

Teresa examined a shoe on the shelf. "Just 'tween you and me, I wish it was Trace and me getting hitched, too." She looked over at Lila. "Suppose we ever will?"

"I don't see why not. Trace'd make any woman proud, and you'd be the perfect wife." Lila nudged her best friend. "Give me two weeks...then we'll be sewin' *your* wedding dress."

"That's fine." Teresa lowered her voice. "But I'm gonna need more than three days to get ready." Her laughter soaked into the walls. "In the meantime, let's get you married. I've got to get going, but I'll stop by your room tonight. We'll do the final fitting on your dress."

Waving over her shoulder, Teresa shut the Mercantile's door. Lila walked back toward the counter as she thought. Would they ever be sisters-in-law? It would be a fine thing. James, Trace, and Teresa were as close as she would ever get to having a family. Until children came along. Those stomach butterflies returned.

"Excuse me, Miss." A man's deep voice behind Lila spun her around. He held up a pick ax. "This the only kind you got?"

Lila pointed to the back wall. "There's some others." She walked him to the mining supplies. "Going prospecting?"

His bushy beard spread out at his shoulders, same length as his hair. Somewhere behind all that hair was a mouth. "Up around Santa Rita and Pinos Altos. Hear there's quite the silver vein up there."

*Santa Rita. Pinos Altos.*

Lila Belle's breath caught in her chest, wedding plans replaced with memories. "Just be very, very careful." She looked down at her trembling hands. "Don't play cards with strangers."

"Why?" The man frowned into her face.

"My fiancé was almost killed playing poker up there." She

9

couldn't look at him, but the story poured out to this total stranger. "He was winning. Big. They took losing hard and—"

"Let me guess," the man said, his voice turning soft, velvety. "They beat him up and kept the money."

"He nearly died." Her words spun just above a whisper. Images of bloody, battered James being carried to her tent by the Santa Rita deputy flooded in. A tear perched on a corner of her eye. She sniffed back more tears, then turned to the man. "Just be real careful."

"I'll mind your words, ma'am." His gray eyes lit up. "You said you're getting married to him?"

Lila nodded. "A week from today." The horrors of last year lifted from her shoulders. Images of her dress, her friends... James...filled her mind. Lila Belle Simmons smiled. Marrying James was meant to be.

# CHAPTER THREE

Cold. Trace was cold. Now warm. Cold and warm at the same time. His right side burned. And something tickled his cheek. He waved it off, but then it was back again, this time on his ear, buzzing.

Too much light. He draped an arm over his face, but the glare wouldn't go away. It dug into his eyes until they watered.

*Where the hell am I?*

From the sky to the sand, his eyes trailed along the desert spreading out before him. Boulders... Two saguaros a few yards away... Clumps of brown scrub grass... Barrel cactus...

His brother, crumpled in the dirt.

"James?"

It took longer to get to his brother than Trace wanted, and it took more effort than it should have. He was hurt bad, but he'd worry about his own wound later.

"James?"

Trace pushed his rag doll brother over onto his back. Sand coated James' cheeks, and his brown hair, stiff with dried blood, stuck to his forehead. When Trace peeled the hair away, it revealed a ragged gash running from James' temple to the top of his head.

The bullet's path.

"James?"

*Was he dead?*

No response. No eye blink. Not even a twitch.

Trace's trembling hand searched his brother's neck for any sign of a heart beating in his twenty-year-old chest. There—faint, but regular. He allowed a sigh.

But it couldn't be happening again. Last year, he and his brother had been robbed on this same run. They'd been separated, and Trace spent six weeks finding James. This time, they would make it out together. And, Trace vowed, they would make it out alive.

The stagecoach was gone. The six mules, the passenger, even the people who shot them—gone. There was nothing but yucca, cactus, and blue sky.

With his brother alive but still out, Trace focused on his own wound. His side throbbed and something wet trickled down his skin. He pulled up his shirt and inspected the hole in his side. Blood seeped through his fingers.

*If I don't get to a doctor...*

His world grayed, and Trace folded onto the ground next to his brother.

* * *

Trace blinked awake. Dry. His mouth clicked and popped as he opened and closed it. He ran his tongue around his chapped lips. A drink. Water. He needed water right now. He pulled in a lungful of desert air. His side throbbed and burned, but the pain stayed in his gut, in his chest, and didn't rampage throughout his body as it did earlier.

Pushing himself up, he sat on the sand and surveyed his surroundings. The sun was headed toward its plunge in the west, but not for a few more hours now. And it was getting chilly. Trace pulled his coat tighter around his body.

A twig snapped behind him.

"James?"

*Was James up and gathering firewood? Or maybe he found water.*

No response.

"James?" Trace swiveled around and stared into nothing. One lower mesquite branch shook.

*Probably rabbit ran in there.*

"James? Where are you?" His words rippled across the sand.

Silence.

"Where the hell are you?"

Panic pressed against Trace's chest. Images, memories crowded in. He pulled fuzzy pictures forward. James on the ground, a bullet creasing his head. He'd been out cold, lying right over there. A mere five, six feet away.

As much as Trace tried, he couldn't get to his feet. Trace settled for crawling.

He spotted swirls in the sand, like hands had scraped against desert dirt. Knee prints. Further on, boot prints.

Leading away. Off into the Sonoran Desert. Toward nothing but sage, sand, Mexican bandits, and Apaches.

Trace sat back on his knees.

*Panic won't help right now. Think, Trace, think.*

"All right. Let's see where we stand."

Somehow talking out loud brought the panic down.

"No water. No food. No gun. No blanket. No matches." His shoulders slumped. "No brother."

*We're in one helluva fix.*

Another look around.

"Hell. I don't even know where we are."

But he knew his first task was to locate James. He couldn't have wandered too far, could he? As soon as they got back together, they'd try to build a fire, stay warm until morning. They could survive a few days without food.

Water was another matter.

Getting to his feet took more strength than he thought possible. Exhausted, sunburned, thirsty, he set out south following his brother's dragging boot prints. They meandered around a piñon tree, down a shallow draw, through grama grass. Then back into dirt.

Trace stopped. "James?" He hollered louder. "James?"

No response.

He stumbled on, past a jumble of boulders, around a jojoba bush, up a low rise. Stopping, Trace bent over, pulling in as much air as his taxed lungs allowed. His boots sunk into James' boot prints. James had to be close.

While he stood there panting, images of the stagecoach shooting paraded across his mind. Who shot them? Mexican bandits? He'd heard of a couple groups of renegade Mexican soldiers marauding anybody who crossed their paths. Then there were the Apaches... and the Pimas. The Apaches had been peaceful for the most part, letting immigrants pass over their land.

Had something changed?

Other questions crowded in his mind while he fought to put one foot in front of the other. He licked his lips, praying a spring would appear—like magic. Like in some of the storybooks his ma had read when he was young. Where were the magic words now that would bring his brother back? Give them water? Food?

More swirls in the sand, obvious handprints. James had fallen, lay there awhile, then clambered up to his feet. Trace could read those marks with his eyes closed. The boot prints dragged longer. James was tired, real tired.

*Then why didn't he just sit down and rest?*

Another rise, higher than the last. Trace gritted his teeth, gripped his side, and pushed on. He stood at the top and squinted into the setting sun.

There. Off to his right. Was that a large shadow or something big curled under a bush? He focused. Something big. James! It had to be.

Trace rushed down the hill, stumbling, picking himself up, loping on while fighting fear.

"James?" Trace knelt by his brother. "Thank God." He shook his brother's shoulder. "James?"

Nothing. No movement.

Trace shook him harder. "You can't die. Not now. Not here." His words turned into sobs. "No."

He sat back in the sand and squeezed his eyes shut, tears threatening to cascade down his cheeks. No, his brother wasn't going to die out here. Not if he could help it. Trace's world blurred. Wet plastered his shirt to his side. He took a deep breath, despite the roaring pain.

"All right. Let's think this through."

He put his hand on his brother's chest. Was that a beating heart? He cradled James and shook him.

"James? Wake up. Please. Wake up."

Wrapping his brother in his arms, Trace pulled him against his chest. Was that a sigh?

"James?"

An arm twitched. A moan.

Trace let the tears flow. "Thank you, God. Thank you."

He rocked his brother back and forth until James' eyes opened.

Trace smiled. "Welcome back." He laid James back on the ground, took off his own coat, and draped it over his brother. "Gonna get cold tonight."

A longer look at the horizon revealed a couple of boulders leaning together to form a natural shelter. If Trace could get James over there, then maybe they'd have a chance to survive.

He wanted to swallow, but his dry throat produced nothing but a grunt. How could he get James over there? It was what... a hundred yards away. Maybe James could walk. He'd have to. Trace's throbbing side oozed blood. It would be suicide to try to carry his brother.

"There's a place over there to hole up, James." Trace waited for his brother's brown eyes to focus on him. "I'm gonna go take a look." He pushed up to his knees. "You stay here. Don't move."

A nod from James then he closed his eyes.

By the time Trace inspected the rock shelter, the sun sat on the horizon. This time of year, sunsets came early and cold. He shivered and wished he'd brought an extra coat. And water. And food. And...

This boulder lean-to would do for tonight. The way it faced would keep the wind off and hopefully, with their combined body heat, keep them from freezing to death. Trace knew it would be hard to get James over here, but it was probably their only chance of survival. He walked back to his brother.

* * *

Trace hugged his brother as they lay shivering on the cold ground in the pre-dawn light. His coat covered only his shoulders; his back felt like ice. At least James was warm. Trace could feel the regular breathing of his little brother. Still alive.

They'd both spent a restless night, but today held hope. Maybe today his brother would come to his senses. Maybe today he'd find water and food. Maybe today they'd find a way out.

Wind whispered through the boulders. Was that a voice? Trace listened harder. No. He'd listened to small animals darting here and there throughout the night, but nothing larger than a rabbit. No coyotes, nothing that would try to eat them—or rescue them.

Early dawn images played with his imagination. Was that a man's shadow on the rock above his head? It moved ever so slightly. Back and forth. It disappeared then reappeared as if deciding to attack. Trace eased away from James, rolled up to his knees, and peered out across the desert.

15

A leafless piñon tree waved back and forth in the occasional breeze.

Disappointed it wasn't a man, Trace still was glad it wasn't attacking. Apaches didn't hunt at night, he knew—their beliefs forbid it—but they sure attacked at first light. He'd heard stories.

*Water. Need water.*

Trace looked over his shoulder at his brother. Still asleep. The aching in his side reminded him he needed help, too. But not now. He couldn't afford it now. He'd have to push on until there was time. Then he could be injured.

"James?" He rocked his brother's shoulder until James' eyes opened. "You awake?"

A nod. James ran his hand across his mouth.

Trace cocked his head toward the opening. "I'm gonna see if I can find water. Or help." He tucked the coat in around James. "You stay here. I mean it. Don't move."

Another nod.

"Promise?"

A third nod.

James closed his eyes.

Outside the rock shelter, Trace squinted into the rose-hued sunrise. Way off to the east, the Dragoon Mountains' jagged peaks pointed to the cloudy sky. To the south, the desert of Mexico beckoned. West promised sloping hills. Maybe water would be that way. He headed west.

Step after step, yard after yard, Trace spotted nothing but ever-expanding desert. His thoughts turned back to his brother.

*What the hell was I thinking going off like this? James wandered away once before. How do I know he won't again?*

His brother wouldn't just up and leave again, would he?

*One step. One more. That's it, like that. One more. Now another one.*

Trace sloshed through the desert sand, his boots creating little sand dunes with each step. He stopped. A panoramic view revealed no green growth, no hint of a stream or spring.

He dropped to his knees and gripped his side.

*What'm I doing out here? It's hopeless. A fool's errand. I'm on a fool's errand. I should be back with James.*

Could he even make it back? He turned around to look at the way he'd come. His boot prints marched over hills and around bushes; a few marks even dragged through the sand.

*Tired. Too tired.*

Eyes burning, he rubbed them and was surprised to find himself lying in the sand. From his vantage point, the desert spread before him. Then he saw it.

Movement.

Something in the distance moved. Something bigger than a rabbit or coyote. Something not too far away.

A man. A man and a mule.

Trace pushed to his knees, but the pain in his side doubled him over. He clutched the newly wet material with one hand and used his other hand to wave.

"Help!"

Did words even come out? His throat was too dry, his tongue too swollen to produce sound.

Staggering up to his feet, he stumbled forward, toward the movement. "Help!" He waved again.

The man slowed his pace, then turned toward Trace.

"Help!" Trace flailed his arms in the air and prayed the man had seen him. He didn't appear to be an Apache, but at this point, Trace didn't care. As long as he had water and could help save his brother.

Staggering, Trace plowed ahead. Waving, holding his side, shouting. The man stopped. More steps. Trace counted.

*One step. One more. Another one. I can do it! Have to. Save James.*

Another wave, then his world spun. He sunk to his knees.

"Help!"

As much as he wanted to get up, or even crawl toward the silhouetted figure, his energy drained.

Too much.

A boot nudged him. Trace grunted. Thoughts forced into focus, he knew the pushing foot belonged to James.

"James?" Had he produced sound?

Strong hands grabbed Trace's shoulders. They shook him.

"Wake up! Snap out of it!"

His mouth opened and closed, desert dry. Trace fought to swallow, but nothing trickled down his throat. He pried one eye open, then the other. Dusty scuffed boots stood next to his face. His gaze trailed up over heavy canvas pants, past a plaid shirt, and into a sun-browned, rosy-cheeked, crinkle-eyed face. Definitely not James.

Was he dreaming? Trace tried speaking again.

"Who...?"

"Bet you're needin' some water, aren't you?" The man disappeared, then just as quickly reappeared with a canteen.

Trace drank until he couldn't breathe, then he drank some more. Sated for the moment, he pushed himself upright and came face to face with the man.

"Thanks," Trace said.

"Thought you were a mirage, the way you were carryin' on when I saw you." The man chuckled. "A mirage. You know, something that isn't real."

"I'm real all right. Thanks again." Trace felt life seep back into his chest, into his soul. "I'm Trace Colton. Drive stage for Butterfield."

The man's green eyes examined Trace head to toe. "Appears you're built like a stage driver. But if you are, where's your stage at?"

*Good question.*

Trace shrugged. "James and I were ambushed a few miles from here. Guess they took the stage and the mules."

*James! Where was James?*

"I gotta get back. James, my brother, he's been shot."

Standing, the man offered a hand to Trace. "Why didn't you say something before now? Where's this man at?"

"Back this way." Trace turned, putting one foot in front of the other. He stopped, pivoting around to the man. "What's your name, anyway?"

"Henry Alonsis Mancuso, the Third." He stuck out a hand. "Just Henry. Only name I use." A smile turned his thin lips into an "o."

Trace regarded him again. He was young. Not as young as Trace and his brother, but probably mid-thirties. Dark blonde hair hung under his hat at his shoulders. No beard blocked a pockmarked face. And he was much shorter than Trace, hitting him at the shoulders. But still, Trace owed him his life.

"This way, Henry. And thanks." Trace nodded then trudged over the desert, retracing his tracks. Henry and his mule followed alongside.

As they walked, Trace considered. With Henry here to help, they just might make it out alive. Out of this Sonoran Desert. Out of certain death. Now, if James was where he promised he'd be, things would work out. They'd have to. Trace would have water, shelter, his brother, and more than likely food. And surely Henry knew his way around the desert. He could point them in the right direction. They would find Apache Springs, borrow a horse or mule from Charles Culver, and be back to Mesilla in time for James' wedding.

Life was looking up.

\* \* \*

He'd gone much farther than he'd thought. Trace followed his tracks well over two, maybe three miles before spotting the boulders leaning together. His pace picked up, and Trace lurched to the boulders.

"James?" Trace crawled inside.

Empty.

"James? Where are you?"

Trace scrambled out of the makeshift shelter and examined the landscape. Mountains to the east, rolling hills to the west, flat desert behind him, a gully to the north. He turned in a circle.

"So where's this James?" Henry peered inside the boulders, then straightened up. "Where'd he go off to, you reckon?" He ran his hand down his mule's muzzle. "Maybe there isn't anybody named James here. What d'you think, Mule?"

Trace lashed out. "He *was* here. Right here." He funneled his hands around his mouth and shouted. "James?"

Silence.

*Not again. This can't be happening again.*

Then he spotted them. To his left, unmistakable boot prints heading north. He waved to Henry. "This way!"

Down the gully, around a sage bush, Trace followed the tracks. There. Just ahead crouched his brother behind a larger sage. Trace frowned.

"James?"

"Shhhh..." James lurched up and grabbed Trace's vest front, pulling him down. "They'll find you."

"Who?" Trace glanced around. Just Henry and his mule.

19

"What's going on?"

James bear-hugged Trace, then released him. James sank down to the desert, Trace's vest still gripped in his hand.

Trace pried his brother's hand off, retrieved Henry's canteen, then helped James drink.

"I thought you'd been killed," James said. He finished a third long drink, then rubbed his head. "You didn't come back, then they came."

"Who?"

"Them." James turned his brown eyes on Trace. "Indians, that's who."

"Indians?" Henry squatted down by the brothers. "What Indians?"

Voice just above a whisper, James spoke each word as if explaining to a child.

"The Indians that attacked me. Think they were Apache. Couldn't be sure. But I ran and hid here." He turned to Trace. "They're coming back. I know it."

"I didn't see any tracks," Henry said. He half turned in the late afternoon light. "Did you, Trace?"

"No."

"You're both blind. They were *there*." James pointed toward the boulders and then pushed up to his feet. "I hid real good. That's why they didn't find me."

He swayed.

Trace regarded his little brother. That face that had just started shaving a couple years ago seemed to have aged since this morning. He looked ninety instead of twenty.

"You all right?" Trace held his side as he stood.

"Terrible headache." James took the canteen from Henry. After another long drink, he licked his lips. "Who're you?"

"Henry." He extended a hand. "And this here's Mule."

"Funny name for a mule." James ran his hand over the animal's neck.

Henry nodded, spit, then nodded again.

"Damn Apaches keep takin' my mules. Lost eight just last year. They like to eat 'em. A real delicacy." He shrugged. "So after a while, I ran out of names, and now I just call each of 'em Mule. Saves effort."

Trace didn't bother to hide a chuckle. "Guess it does." He

headed back toward the boulders. "Best set up camp for tonight, then first light head off for Apache Springs."

With his side throbbing as bad as it was, Trace knew he had to lie down before he fell down. Maybe Henry could poke around for that bullet. Otherwise, Trace knew he'd be dead inside a week.

"Apache Springs?" Henry frowned. "You know how far that is?"

Trace nodded. They had no choice. Tucson was too far west to even consider going back. They'd have to head north and east.

"Four days' walk from here," Henry said, as he fell in behind James.

Glancing over his shoulder, James walked with Trace but spoke to Henry.

"Keep your eyes peeled for Indians. They're here. I'm not lying." He steadied Trace who sagged. "And I'm not crazy. Just this damn headache."

Trace hoped he would make it to the boulder shelter before he collapsed. Each step was becoming harder and harder to take.

*One step. One more.*

But, had the Indians actually come by or was it his brother's imagination playing tricks?

Either way, they were in trouble.

# CHAPTER FOUR

Cochise threw aside the deer hide covering his wickiup entrance and greeted the new day in his usual fashion. He saluted the sun, earth, and all living beings. The rising sun warmed his body and his spirit. Ritual finished, his long strides took him to the communal fire pit, where a woman handed him a plate of stew and a gourd container of water. He nodded at the woman and pulled in the aroma of deer and herbs.

Cochise perched on a rock near the campfire. As he ate, the mountains changed from gray to dark purple. Sacred mountains. Mountains of his ancestors, the Chiricahua Apache. His gaze flew across the meadow full of sage and mesquite. The stream that ran full in the warm days was now a trickle. But the hills covered with cactus and sage held the promise of life. Deer, wild turkeys, rabbits, even pigs provided food for his village, his tribe.

His people.

Smoke from the village fires wafted across his face. Stew, bread, cooking rabbit melded into one aroma. The aroma of life.

A man sat down a respectful distance from him.

"The gods are truly smiling on us, Cochise," the man said. "Our raids have been successful, and not one of us has died. We are invincible warriors."

"Be careful, One Wing," Cochise replied. "If we think we cannot die, that is the time we will. We must remember, always, the Old Ones who have gone before us. The Old Ones tell us now to push back the settlers."

One Wing sipped from the gourd and spoke over the top. "The Old Ones are wise. Not only should we push back the Americans— we must kill them all."

A green and blue striped lizard scurried under a creosote bush, startled by the two other men who joined Cochise at the fire. Cochise shook his head.

"In my heart, One Wing, I don't wish for them to die. I wish for them to leave us alone."

"It is our way." One Wing snorted. "Killing is the only answer."

Cochise watched the women cooking over the open fires, the children busy at chores. "You lust for blood too quickly," he said.

He stretched, and with it his chest swelled as he surveyed the endless sky, the hills brown with spring yet to come, and the rugged boulders.

"And yet," he said, "I would kill for this."

A young warrior rushed toward the circle of men and pointed behind him.

"Cochise? A rider comes from the east. He rides fast."

Cochise and One Wing left the fire pit to meet the rider, and every Apache warrior had gathered with them by the time the man reined up. He slid off his pinto, dust dancing around his moccasins, then stood in respect, waiting for the invitation to speak.

The crowd of warriors parted to give their leader access to the visitor, and Cochise recognized the man standing before him. Dancing Hawk, of the Bedonkohe tribe. He was out of breath, had ridden hard.

A quick nod and Cochise spread his arms. "Welcome to our camp, Dancing Hawk."

The Bedonkohe nodded. "I bear news for your tribe, Cochise."

Cochise pointed toward the fire pit in the village's center. "Let's sit by the fire and hear this news," he said. He led the procession through the village and then perched on a nearby rock.

With everyone seated, Cochise motioned to the visitor. "Speak."

Dancing Hawk's eyes slid downward, and his shoulders rose with a deep breath. "Two days now, we raided a large ranch of white settlers. Killed them. Only two escaped."

The warriors hooted at the victory. Cochise gestured for silence.

"The raid went well," Dancing Hawk said, "until we returned to our camp and discovered..." He glanced at his friend, One Wing, and then frowned.

Cochise leaned forward. "Speak."

Dancing Hawks' eyes darted from his friend to Cochise and

23

back again. He straightened his shoulders.

"Cochise, your brother has been taken captive."

Impossible. Coyuntura was too smart, too quick to be captured. But, his warriors didn't lie. Dancing Hawk wouldn't either.

"My brother's family? Are they safe?" Cochise asked.

"His small children escaped, but his wife, his son Lone Fox, and three other warriors were captured."

"Who did this?"

"The United States Army."

A collective gasp from the crowd. Two of the men turned to each other, their conversation too low for Cochise to hear.

Soldiers! Cochise unfolded from his seat. What right did they have taking prisoners? White Eyes. Men he'd allowed to pass on his land. Men who'd brought cloth for his women, whiskey for his men, sweet candy for his children. He glared into the mountains. All right. If the White Eyes wanted war, then they would get it.

One Wing jumped to his feet. "I swear we will bring Coyuntura and his wife back to his own people." He turned to Cochise. "There is a way to save them. A few suns past, Standing Pony and I captured a stagecoach."

Cochise nodded. "I remember."

"We chased the passenger over several hills until he could run no longer. It made good practice for our younger warriors." One Wing pointed toward his own wickiup. "His scalp hangs by my door."

One Wing's gaze ran across the warriors gathered around the fire and landed on Standing Pony, his brother.

"The passenger ran like a scared rabbit," One Wing continued, "and our warriors chased him. We left both drivers for the coyotes. They were already dead and did not present enough of a challenge for our young braves to scalp." He stood by Cochise. "But now, let us return for their bodies and trade them to the Army for Coyuntura."

"They will not trade for dead men," Cochise said. He folded one arm on top of the other. Then he turned his gaze to One Wing. "Bring me two men alive."

One Wing whooped with delight. "After capturing those men, we'll kill all other White Men within a four-day ride."

The crowd mumbled their agreement.

Cochise watched his people. His tribe. If he wasn't victorious now, they would lose more than their hope. They'd lose their home.

Cochise held up his hand, and the warriors fell silent.

"We can no longer raid one ranch at a time," he said. "We can no longer stand by and watch our enemies take our brothers. My brother." He turned to Dancing Hawk. "Where is he held?"

"Coyuntura is being taken to Apache Springs, then over to a fort many days ride from here. I've been told he will sit there behind iron bars. A place called Fort Bliss." Dancing Hawk shook his head.

"I will not let my brother die trapped in a small wickiup," Cochise said. "One Wing, Dancing Hawk. Gather all the warriors of both tribes, bring them together."

As One Wing and Dancing Hawk nodded, Cochise's gaze wandered up and down his circle of warriors. He met the eyes of each man.

"You must raid, burn, and destroy all the ranches between here and the fort. At every ranch, leave a sign that my brother is to be released."

Cochise thought of his brother. No longer free to roam the desert, to watch the stars at night or the sun in the morning. No longer free to hear the coyotes sing or see the hawks fly. No longer free to go where he pleased. It was hard to imagine that kind of suffering.

The Apache chief looked up at the white clouds pushed by the winds. It would turn cold again. Maybe snow.

"I want my brother free. Now."

# CHAPTER FIVE

James' swollen eyes twitched open then squeezed shut at the blinding sunlight. The aromas of coffee, beans, and biscuits drifted under his nose.

"Trace?"

His pounding head sent lightning bolts into his brain. He grabbed the top of his head and rolled over, the wool blanket bunching under his side.

"He's still sleeping. Best not disturb him right off."

The voice. Whose? The unfamiliarity of it jolted James into full consciousness. Pa? No, too gravely. He stared sideways at a man bending over the campfire. An iron pot perched in the middle of the flames. With the lid gripped in one hand, the man stirred something with the other. James frowned, then pushed his aching body until he could sit up all the way and regard this man right side up.

"Who..."

The thumping in James' temples caused his entire world to pulsate with his beating heart. It hurt just to breathe. Tears clouded his vision. Head cradled with both hands, James closed his eyes. Even that hurt.

A body next to him. A tin cup pressed against his chest. Boiled coffee smells wafted around his head.

"Here, drink this. You'll feel better."

Not wanting to move but knowing he must, James opened his eyes and accepted the cup. The black liquid went down smooth, warm. He nodded. His head already felt better.

"Where's my brother?" he asked.

The man pointed behind James. "Just over yonder. I got that bullet out last night. Your brother's lost a lot of blood and fair amount of hide." He loaded a tin plate with spoonfuls of beans. "Give him a day or two to rest and he'll be fit enough to walk."

Despite pushing up to knees, then trying to get his feet under him, James couldn't stand. Crawling would have to do. Rocks gouged his knees and a cactus thorn poked his hand. The yards felt more like miles.

"Trace? You all right?"

Trace's image blurred. James fought to stay awake and keep his focus, if anything for Trace's sake. No telling what this man who built the fire and gave him coffee would do. Plus, someone had to fend off the Indians. They were bound to return—and soon.

The man squatted on the other side of Trace and pointed his spoon at James. "Like I said. Best let him rest. He'll be up soon enough."

"Any sign of infection?" James peeled up the blanket covering Trace. A white bandage covered his brother's side.

"Nope. Clean as a whistle." Henry pulled the blanket back over Trace, tucking in the side. "He's gonna be fine, but you're looking peak-ed. You need to rest. Get your strength back." He helped James to his feet. "You sit over here by the fire while I get you something to eat."

Who was this man? A vague recollection pushed into James' memory. Something about a mule. Or was it Indians? He rubbed his aching head, and the agony reduced to mere unbearable pain. Coffee. Maybe more coffee would help jar the brain, ease the pounding. As they walked, he regarded the man.

"Do I know you?"

A chuckle rattled the man's plate of beans. "You might say." He waved that spoon again. "Met you yesterday."

Yesterday. James struggled to bring yesterday into focus. Something about the boulder lean-to, then Indians. Different images melted into other days, other years, other people. He squeezed his eyes shut.

A nudge on his arm opened his eyes. The man held up a whiskey bottle, then poured some into the tin cup he held.

"I use this only for medicinal purposes, of course." A grin took up half of his face. "Makes the coffee go down better, too."

James took the offered cup and downed it in one long gulp. The heat from the coffee ignited the whiskey. Both burned going down. His stomach warmed.

"Thanks." James held the man's gaze. "Thanks for patching up my brother."

27

The man nodded as a splash of whiskey poured into his own cup. "Name's Henry." He sipped his coffee. "And you're welcome."

"Don't know how we'll ever be able to repay you," James said. The fire's flames danced around the pot. The comforting smell of cooking beans married with the mesquite wood. It wafted through the air and tantalized James' stomach.

Henry shook his head. "No need for paybacks. Glad to help. Reckon there'll come a time when you'll help somebody else." He loaded his plate again, then handed it to James. "That'll be payment enough."

He was starved. No, not starved. Ravenous. James hadn't eaten since…since…he couldn't remember when. Probably a few days back. No wonder his head hurt so badly. A cool breeze snaked down inside James' shirt. He shivered despite his warm coat.

"Know what day it is, Henry? I gotta get back to Mesilla before Saturday."

Henry shook his head, then perched on a nearby rock and sipped his coffee. "Why Saturday?"

A smile blossomed on James' face. "I'm getting married."

"Married? Congratulations!" Henry saluted him with his cup, then slurped loud. "I'm thinking it's getting on toward Tuesday. But I can't be sure. No way of telling out here. And I don't keep a calendar. Gave that up years ago."

"Tuesday?" James' chest tightened. "I'm supposed to be back today. Lila's gonna be worried sick when I don't come in." His spoon of beans remained mid-air. "Sure don't want her to worry. She's done enough of that already."

Henry shrugged. "Not much you can do about it now. Might as well relax and heal up. Both of you."

"We're only two days out of Tucson." James eyed the pot. Another plateful would sure taste good. "We can catch the next eastbound stage, be back to Mesilla in two more days. Or take the mule back to Tucson, get a message to Mesilla that we're in trouble."

As he shook his head, Henry's blond hair swept his shoulders.

"Had this conversation yesterday," he said. "I'll tell you again. We're more 'n two days from Tucson. For one thing, you wandered a passel of miles south of the road. And for another, Mule doesn't travel as fast as your stage. Two of us gotta walk to Apache Springs,

28

and with you, and especially your brother hurt, we can't go just yet."

"But—"

"*And* I wasn't heading north, anyway. I'm going south, down into Mexico." Henry leaned in close and dropped his voice. "*But* I'm willing to help you and Trace get back. *Then* I'm heading down to the silver."

Curiosity bested James. Besides, he wasn't winning the argument anyway. "Mexico? Why there?"

"Where've you been? Haven't you heard? Big silver strike south of the Gadsden Purchase. I hear it's just ripe for the picking." Henry's spoon, dripping with bean juice, poked into his own chest. "I'm gonna get rich. See what my family thinks of me then. I'll show 'em." His gaze trailed off into the distance. "Yes, sir. I'll show 'em. Make me go to law school, will you? Hell, I'll do what the hell I please. When the hell I please. Not going to do what they say. Be what they tell me to be—"

Henry jerked back into the present. He lowered the spoon, bean juice now smeared over his shirt. His shoulders slumped.

Unsure what to say, James filled his mouth with beans. The silence gave him time to mull over what Henry had said. Guess Henry wasn't happy with his family. Real different from James' family. The Coltons were a tight-knit group, and his folks let their sons choose their own lives. While Ma fought back tears when James told her he was leaving to come join Trace as a shotgun guard for him, still James knew that Ma wanted only happiness and success for him. Him and his three brothers.

Until a couple days ago, he'd been not just happy, but something close to ecstatic. Giddy with wedding plans. And now... now it looked as if those plans would be put on hold for a while. But just a day or two. Maybe a week.

The mid-day sun warmed James' neck. Despite his stomach now bulging with beans and coffee, his head throbbed and pounded until he knew it would explode. Lying down would have to do. James left Henry to his campfire with his memories, spread out the wool blanket, and lay next to Trace.

James heard nothing further until his brother swore. He rubbed his eyes open, sat up, then followed the gaze of the two men, standing, staring west.

A steady plume of brown smoke spiraled into the sky.

"What's that?" Trace, standing next to Henry, pointed to the western horizon.

"Trouble." Henry turned to James. "Get up."

James elbowed his way between the two men. "Indians?"

Henry nodded. "I'm thinking we want to be heading toward Apache Springs." His slim arm waved to the northeast. "About as safe a place as we can get to right now." He kicked sand over the campfire.

Beads of sweat ran down Trace's face. He clutched his side, then looked at James.

"Think we can make it?"

"We got to."

Henry turned around and spit one long oath.

James followed where Henry pointed west—toward Tucson. A smoky pillar twirled into the clouds.

# CHAPTER SIX

Lila flitted around the store, helped customers, straightened merchandise, dusted anything she could find. She waited for the sounds of a late afternoon stagecoach pulling up to the Butterfield office. That rattle of stagecoach wheels, Trace's "yee haw" ordering the horses to stop, the bevy of excitement always put a smile on her face.

Soon James would jump off the high seat of the stagecoach, sweaty, dirty, smiling—she could smell the miles of dust and mules on him. His arms would close around her, and she would hear his heart beating while she laid her head against his muscled chest.

She checked a watch near the money drawer. Still two hours before he was scheduled to arrive. James. She'd waited so long for him to get around to proposing, and now that he was about to return and make her his wife, she knew if he didn't show up soon, she'd faint dead away.

The few customers in the store didn't do much to distract her. Women were in a hurry to finish their purchases and rush home to fix dinner for their husbands and children. For the first time in her life, Lila Belle Simmons was envious.

Patience was one of her strongest attributes, she knew, but she couldn't be patient today. She stepped out of the store and onto the wooden sidewalk in front. The boards creaked under her as she strolled past a butcher's shop, the San Albino church at the plaza's north end, and a dressmaker's store. After turning the second corner of the square, she stopped in front of the sheriff's office.

"You had him for a few days, but I'll have him the rest of my life," Lila whispered. The memories raced. She'd stepped through that door a year ago to ask Sheriff Fuente if he knew anything about James. She realized much later that her inquiry almost got James hanged. Because of her, the sheriff figured out his identity, tracked him down, and arrested the man she loved.

The image of James on the gallows' platform, the rope around his neck, the executioner's hand on the lever brought new tears to her eyes.

*I've cried a million tears over you. Last ones I cry will be when you slip that gold band on my finger.*

"Anything I can help you with?" A male voice boomed behind her. Lila spun around.

"Sheriff Fuente, you scared the livin' daylights out of me." She grinned, more from relief than pleasure. His smile appeared genuine, sincere.

"I saw you staring at the building, thought maybe it was on fire or something."

She massaged the bare knuckle of her ring finger. "I was just out walkin' around, waitin' on James."

"The usual, right?"

"Yes, sir, the usual." She turned toward the stagecoach stop and offices across the plaza. Fuente stared at the jail.

"You know, I'm glad James didn't hang. I sure didn't take any pleasure in walking him down there."

"But you thought he was guilty, Sheriff. Everyone did."

"Yeah. That's one time I'm glad I was wrong." He patted her shoulder. "After you two get married, you gonna let him climb back on that stagecoach and drive off with his brother?"

"I'd rather have him stay with me," she said, "but he loves his job too much to ask him to give it up. I'll wait for him."

"I hope you don't have to wait too much longer." The corners of his eyes wrinkled with his smile. "If he knows what's good for him, he'll skedaddle on home."

"You can be sure I'll remind him of that, Sheriff." She whipped around at the clip-clop of horses entering the plaza. Two cowboys on old nags. Not James and Trace.

Sheriff Fuente touched her arm, held it for a few seconds.

"He'll be along shortly, Lila. Don't worry. If I know James, he's on the edge of his seat. Never seen anyone wantin' to get married as much as that soon-to-be husband of yours. Probably driving Trace crazy."

Lila smiled. The tightness in her chest and stomach kept her breathing short. Fuente shifted his weight.

"Well Lila, I've got to go shuffle some papers. Lookin' forward to Saturday. See ya then." He tipped his hat, then stepped into his office.

Determined to stay busy until James arrived, Lila marched in a straight line across the plaza, cut around a group of children playing with a lizard, and stepped back into the Mesilla Mercantile. She wrapped and rewrapped the bolts of calico, dusted the shelves for the second time that afternoon, straightened the short row of boots, and rearranged the hats. Again. Anything to stay busy and keep her mind off James.

Shortly before closing time, Teresa stepped into the store and grinned at Lila.

"Any minute now," Teresa said. "I can feel them rounding that big old cottonwood, hear them yellin' at those mules to run faster. They're hollerin' 'Go mules. Got two beautiful women waitin' for us. Gotta get home!'"

Lila laughed at Teresa's silliness, while Teresa searched the store and grabbed two wide-brimmed hats off the closest shelf. She plopped one on her head and one on Lila's.

"Trace is probably sayin' 'I can smell Teresa's fried chicken and beans,'" Teresa said.

She pulled Lila over to two wooden barrels. Each woman sat on top of one, imaginary reins in hand. Skirts spread over the barrels, Lila and Teresa perched side by side on their seats and snapped invisible reins.

"Hurry up mules! Take us home!"

Teresa held the pretend whip above her head and lashed the backs of pretend mules. Lila cradled a pretend shotgun in her arms, then held it against her cheek, sighting it.

"Look, Trace! Off to our left—a charging elephant! Don't worry. I'll protect us. I'm the best shot this side of the Rio Grande."

"Best shot in the whole world, James, next to Grandpa." Teresa snapped the reins over the Missouri mules.

Lila squeezed the trigger, jerked back with the recoil, and grinned. "Got 'im."

"One more mile to go," Teresa said. "There's Mesilla and our beautiful women!" She glanced at Lila, then back into the distance. "There's Teresa. Ain't she a looker, James? Think I'm gonna marry her."

"Not before I marry the most gorgeous creature on God's green earth, big brother. My Lila's been waitin' a long time." Lila leaped off her cracker barrel and pranced around the empty store. "Giddy up, mules. Giddy up!"

Doubled over with laughter, Teresa held her side and struggled to catch her breath.

Lila leaned against the counter until she could breathe without bursting into more laughter.

Giggles quieted into conversation.

"Where are those men of ours?" Teresa asked. "I thought Trace'd be back at least an hour ago."

Lila's voice dropped to a whisper. "I've heard about the Indian problem, heard it's gettin' worse. You don't suppose—"

"I don't suppose anything. They're fine. Might've had a broken wheel or a passenger got sick or something as simple as that. Let's not get worked up over nothing."

"I sure hope you're right. Don't know what I'd do without James."

Teresa jumped to her feet and grabbed Lila's hands. "Let's not sit here and wait for those late men of ours. Close up this place and let's go get something to eat. The boys can catch up with us when they get here."

At the restaurant, both women glanced up every time the door opened, and their disappointment grew with each person who stepped in and wasn't one of the Colton boys. As the minutes dragged by, the lump in Lila's stomach knotted tighter and tighter. Supper became an endurance test.

After a third cup of coffee and a couple bites of pie, Lila and Teresa paid the bill, then stepped into the crisp night air. Stillness shrouded the plaza.

Teresa sighed and turned to Lila. "They're simply late. They're fine."

"Hope you're right. If they're not back by mornin' I'll go over to Butterfield's office and see what they know. Don't you think they're as worried as we are?" Lila knew the answer, but asked the question anyway. It made her feel a little better thinking someone besides Teresa would be concerned.

Teresa gave Lila a brief hug. "Gotta go. Don't worry and get some sleep. See you tomorrow." She walked across the dusty, leaf-littered street and disappeared around the corner.

Now alone, Lila's tears blurred the buildings of the plaza. A drop trickled down her cheek.

*Is this the way life with you is goin' to be, James Colton? Am I up to the challenge of worryin' about you all the time? Could I possibly go on without you?*

# CHAPTER SEVEN

James, Henry, and Trace trudged over cactus-strewn hills, down gullies, and around stands of piñons until Trace knew he couldn't put one more foot in front of the other. Couldn't take one more breath. Couldn't squint any harder to keep the setting sun out of his eyes. And it was getting cold. Without a cloud in the sky, the desert would turn ice cold tonight. Good thing Henry had matches. They'd light a fire and stay alive.

Would there be a cave up ahead? Maybe another rock outcropping where they could hole up until morning. Was that too much to wish for? Trace thought back to his childhood when Ma would point to the first star of the evening and together they'd make a wish.

Star light, star—

"Indians!" James shouted. He grabbed Trace's coat sleeve and dragged him toward a sage bush. The men stumbled and ran until all three crouched behind the shrub, its spindly arms providing little concealment.

"Where?" Henry gripped Mule's reins.

"Shhh. Keep quiet." James pointed east. He rubbed both eyes.

They waited. Trace sank back onto the desert sand. James stared straight ahead, his head following movement. Henry kept his hand over Mule's muzzle, despite her attempts to munch on the tiny sage leaves.

They waited.

Trace's legs cramped, and his side throbbed. He eased his body to his feet. A long, steady survey of the area revealed no Indians. No moccasin tracks. No sign they'd been close.

*Gotta get James to Apache Springs. Culver's coffee and stew will fix him.*

At least he hoped it would.

"Let's go." Trace tugged on his brother's coat. "Indians are gone."

Henry nodded. "Sure are. And, I think there might be a place to hole up not too far from here." He pulled a reluctant Mule away from the sage.

* * *

Trace jerked awake every fifteen minutes. Stars migrated across the heavens, coyotes sang long, sad tales, and cold breezes brushed his face. Moonlight shafts threw eerie shadows on his sleeping companions. Trace wrapped himself tighter in the scratchy wool blanket and fought to stay alert. As soon as his eyes closed, a noise would startle him awake. A creosote bush rattled. A rabbit? An Apache? James?

No, James slept right here next to him.

Trace rubbed his fatigue-burned eyes. Instead of sleeping, he plotted and planned how they would hide from the Indians or Mexicans while making their way over to the stage station. Maybe the three of them had something to trade with. Something of value besides their lives. Nothing came to mind except Mule. And she was needed to help get them out of this desert.

By the time Trace could make out gray features around him, Henry stirred, then sat up. A yawn, a long stretch, a good scratch, then Henry stood.

"Best be getting a move on if we're gonna get to that station," Henry said as he buttoned his shirt, then scooped up his hat from the bedroll and fit it tight down over his hair. He reached over and shook James until muttering came from under the blanket.

Then he stood and searched through one of the mule packs. He extracted a can from the canvas pouch, and used his Barlow knife to pry open the lid.

Trace tasted the peaches before they were even out of the can. Henry stuck his knife into one peach and offered it to Trace. "This'll have to do 'til we get some miles under us," Henry said.

Remembering the sweet taste, Trace eagerly slid the fruit off the tip. "Haven't had peaches for ages." His tongue caught a trickle of juice on the corner of his mouth. "Last time was at home."

It went down smooth. The sweet flesh melted on his tongue.

James threw back the blanket, then struggled to his feet. "I

37

remember." He swayed, holding his head.

"Ma made a pie," Trace said. He tasted those peaches, that flaky crust, smelled the pie cooking.

James snapped his fingers. "For Andy. Right?" He pried the fruit from Henry's knife.

A nod from Trace.

"Andy's our littlest brother, Henry. He's about sixteen by now." Trace spoke around the peach, this piece of heaven in his mouth. To the east, crimson melted the gray sky. Fingers of gold-red carpeted the desert. Trace turned to Henry. "Ma always wanted a girl, but after four boys, I think she gave up."

"Four, huh?" Henry chuckled. "There were only two of us." He looked away. "Bet your pa taught you how to chop and plow real quick."

"Sure did," James said. "But Ma kept us in line with her wooden mixing spoon." He held up the imaginary utensil and whacked at the air. "You know, Trace, it's amazing something that hurt so much then is so funny now."

"Especially the time you got it for dipping into the sugar when Ma was out getting eggs for Pa's cake." Trace chuckled, then clutched his side. It hurt damn bad. He hoped he'd hide the grimace. "Where'd you end up hiding out?"

James studied his hands. "Little cave down by the creek."

"But Ma found you."

"Sure did. Right before Pa—"

"Look. I love hearing good stories," Henry said, "but we gotta go. No telling what those Indians got a hankering to do. I don't aim to wait around and find out." He turned to James. "You're fit to walk, but your brother needs to ride Mule. Trace won't make it too far on his own feet."

Did Trace look as bad as he felt? Apparently so, if Henry said he should ride. Trace helped move a couple of the packs and did his best to clamber up onto the mule's back.

James walked next to his brother. "Shouldn't we look for the stagecoach? Isn't that our first responsibility? I mean, besides getting out of here in one piece?"

He frowned toward the west.

The stage, the passenger, the mules were gone. Trace realized for the first time that his brother didn't fully understand their dire situation.

"Leave the stage be," Trace said. "Nothing we can do about it now. We gotta save our own hides and then later we'll see what we can do." The wound throbbed. Was that blood he felt oozing between his fingers? "Besides, that Celerity stagecoach is expensive. Mister Butterfield'll want it back. He'll come looking for it."

James bit his lower lip. "Hope he comes soon."

* * *

The warm January sun threw no shadows by the time Henry ordered a rest stop. Trace's stomach rumbled and growled. More peaches would taste good about now. While James helped Trace off the mule, Henry rummaged through a canvas sack for a wrapped piece of meat and another tin can.

Trace stared at the cactus and watched it grow blurry around the edges. He hoped he could get off the mule and into shade before he passed out. James' sturdy grip was comforting. To his left, a mesquite bush and the small patch of shade it cast would have to do. He dropped to the shade and eyed his brother squatting next to him.

"I'm all right." Trace pointed toward the mule. "It's your turn after we eat. You're turning a strange shade of white."

"Just tired. Soon as we get some food, I'll be fit." James turned half a smile on Trace.

His brother was putting up a brave front, Trace knew. James probably felt as bad as he did. Trace touched James' head. "How's it feel? That bullet almost scalped you."

"Pains me some, but nothing I can't handle. Don't worry. I truly am fine." James ran his hand through his hair, his fingers following the bullet's path. He picked out bits of dried blood.

Henry knelt in front of the men, handed each a cup of green beans, and tore off pieces of venison jerky. The three men ate in silence, first wolfing down the food, then slowing when their bellies stopped growling.

"Green beans taste just like they were picked yesterday." Trace shoved another bean in his mouth. "Sure do thank you."

A nod from Henry. "Right now, nothin's better than venison and green beans." He stopped chewing and raised both eyebrows. "Suppose they got green beans down in Mexico?"

# CHAPTER EIGHT

The front office of the Butterfield Stage headquarters was deserted. Inside the room, streaks of early morning sunlight slid down the mud-plastered adobe walls, pooling on the floor, but the main desk stood empty. No employees called out to other men in the back. No one checked and double-checked the bills of lading and passenger lists. And no one appeared at the sound of the door opening or slamming shut.

"Hello?" Lila called.

Her stomach turned at the emptiness of the office. Papers were scattered haphazardly on the main desk, and its drawers were in disarray. When there was no response, she walked down a short hall and peeked into an empty back room, but she stopped short at the sound of male voices. They were coming from the drivers' sleeping area farther down the hall.

"What exactly's going on here, Bill?"

"Read that letter again. How can they do that?"

"You've gotta be kiddin'."

An authoritative voice rose above the others.

"Calm down, men. Let's not panic—yet. Here, I'll read it again."

A paper rustled. Men mumbled. The same man spoke again.

"All right. Word for word. It says, 'Operations of Butterfield Overland Stagecoach Company are to cease and desist immediately. Mister Butterfield regrets his decision to close the company, but the increasing possibility of war between the states, and the Indian uprising in the West have necessitated this move. A twenty-five dollar bonus will be paid to each driver, and a fifteen-dollar bonus to each shotgun guard.'"

A pause, then murmurs. "Signed 'A.J. Milton, Vice President, Butterfield Stagecoach Company.'"

Lila's hand flew to her mouth, covering a gasp.

What will James and Trace do now?

Without thinking, Lila stepped into the room, and all eyes turned on her. She gazed back, recognizing many of the drivers and freighters. Anger etched each man's face. Where was Bill Walters, the man in charge of the Mesilla station?

There he was. Across the room, with a letter clutched in his hand. Lila pushed past two men in the back.

"Mister Walters, what's goin' on?" she demanded.

"Miss Simmons."

Walters picked his way through the gathered men. "This ain't the best time for you to be here," he said. "You best come back later."

"I won't come back later, Mister Walters. James and Trace haven't come back from their run yesterday. Or haven't you noticed?" Her anxiety overrode politeness. She didn't care what she sounded like—she just needed answers.

"We noticed, Miss Simmons. Haven't heard from them, yet. Probably broke a wheel or something."

"Don't patronize me, Mister Walters. You and I both know something's seriously wrong."

She studied the faces of a driver and a shotgun guard standing near her and realized they were close friends of James and Trace. Sunny Williamston and Clay Arrington. They tipped their hats at her.

Walters slid a protective arm around her shoulders and nudged her toward the door. "When I hear from them, you'll be the first to know, Miss Simmons. Now, if you'll excuse us, we have more important matters to discuss."

Lila exploded.

"More important? *More* important? How can you say that? How can your job be more important than the lives of two men?" She wrenched away from his grip and stared into his hard brown eyes. "Just what are you doing about finding James and Trace?"

Walters' arm again wrapped around her shoulders, stronger this time. He guided her down the hall, but didn't speak until they pushed through the front doors and stopped on the boardwalk.

Lila adjusted her hat. "I'll ask again, sir. What are you going to do about James?"

He sighed, then swiped his hand over his mouth. "Do? I ain't gonna do nothing right now. Butterfield Stage Lines doesn't exist

41

any more. At this point, the Coltons are on their own."

The lump in Lila's throat wouldn't allow any words to surface. No, she wouldn't cry. Wouldn't do her any good. Tears wouldn't help her man right now.

With both of Lila's shoulders in his hands, Walters looked into her eyes. "I'm sorry for my harsh words. It's just not a good time for any of us. I'm as upset as everyone. But, I've gotta deal with the men, all the details in closing this business. On top of that, I'm out of a job. I have a wife and four kids to feed. And now Trace and James are mis—Overdue."

Tears brimmed, threatening to overflow.

"Look, James is a nice kid. I like him and his brother. They're both good, hard workers. If I could, I'd go looking for them myself. But, Miss Simmons, I've got a business to deal with and other drivers to supervise. I'm sorry."

Tears spilled over.

"They're fine, I'm sure." Walters looked over Lila's shoulder. "Just ran into a delay is all."

Lila jerked away from his hold.

"We both know they're in trouble," she said. "Bad trouble. I can feel it in my heart. If you don't do somethin' about findin' them, I will."

Lila wheeled around. She marched down the street, crossed the plaza, and shoved open the Sheriff's door. Its slamming pushed more tears down her cheeks.

# CHAPTER NINE

The sun's glare reflected off the sand, turning the light brown into shimmering white. James shielded his eyes. The Apache faces blended in well with the desert. He continued to march behind Trace on Mule. He dragged one foot in front of the other, knowing that any second the ragtag party would be attacked again. They had barely made it past the last group of Indians.

He froze. Smoke. He smelled smoke. The distinctive odor of burning wood circled his head, and the stench of dead livestock turned his stomach. James pinched his nose.

"What?" Henry nudged him.

A survey of the desert revealed no smoke, no burning nearby. Not even a smoke plume in the distance. James pulled in more air. Something smelled like mule. He frowned.

"Nothing. Thought something was on fire."

Henry sniffed. "I don't smell anything. Just dust." He nudged James harder. "Get a move on. Your brother's way out in front. Gotta catch up."

Less than half a mile later, James heard bushes rattling. Turning, he spotted an Indian hiding behind a saguaro. Parts of the Apache's elbow and head were out in plain sight.

"Watch out! Behind you!" James shouted as he dove under a sagebush.

Trace whipped around on the mule.

"What?" He slid off Mule's back and rushed toward James. "What? Did you see something?" Henry hunkered down next to the brothers.

James jerked Trace's gun from its holster and fired into the cactus.

*Bang!*

"What the hell're you doing?" Trace grabbed for his gun. "Give me that."

*Bang!*

James pushed his brother's hand away and held the gun out of reach. "I said stay down." He fired again.

*Bang!*

The gun clicked empty. James glanced sideway. "More ammunition. I need more." James reached over and grabbed at his brother's coat pocket. "More cartridges."

"I'm out." Trace gripped his side. "Yours are gone?"

"Yeah." James grabbed Trace's sleeve, knowing they had just seconds before the Indians attacked. He met his brother's wide stare. "Don't let 'em take me alive. Please, Trace. Don't."

"It'll be all right, James." Henry laid a hand on his back. "They're leaving now."

"No, they're still here." James rubbed his eyes, the burning in his head making things blurry. The cactus to his left grew and shrunk every time his heart beat.

Trace's voice turned soft. "They're gone, James. All gone. See for yourself."

No shadows. No hulking Apaches. Nobody ready to attack. Just his crazy head. James picked up a rock and tossed it.

"Never were any, were there?"

Two heads shook.

"Dammit, Trace. What the hell's wrong with me?"

Henry plucked the Colt .36 from James' grip.

"I'll just keep this in a safe place," Henry said. "Don't want you shooting one of us. Accidental or otherwise."

Trace slid an arm around James' shoulders. "What's wrong? I'd say nothing that won't go away once we get to Apache Springs." He nudged James toward Mule. "How about some water? You'll feel better."

\* \* \*

James stared back at the drag marks his feet left in the sand. Exhausted. They were no closer to that way station now than when they left before sunrise. Or so it seemed. Hours turned into years while they trudged across the barren wasteland of the Sonoran Desert.

The incessant throbbing on the left side of his head intensified until all he heard was his own heart beating. Tears poured down his cheeks with every pulse. He rubbed, thumped, and cursed the wound. Planting his hands on either side of his head, and pressing hard, was the only relief he found. He pressed harder. If he didn't, he knew his brains would leak out.

More Indians. Now fierce wolves. Or were they bears? The sparsely leafed Palo Verde trees hid the attackers well. Overgrown prickly pear cactus and mesquite bushes served equally well as cover for the assailants. Painted Indians sprung up from behind every boulder. They whooped and hollered, then attacked the small party.

James threw himself behind an alligator juniper, cursing Henry for taking his gun. He waited. Silence. He buried his face in his hands.

James jumped at the grip on his arm.

"At it again?" Henry helped him to his feet, dusted him off, and then plopped his hat back on his head. He shrugged. "No Indians around here."

Henry. Trace. Mule. James' world pulled into focus.

"I'm sorry." He hung his head.

A pat on his back, then Henry walked off. "No harm done."

One step. Another. James marched in silence, demanding the images to go away. To just disappear. But they didn't. Without paying close attention to his route, he tripped into a mesquite. He froze. Ear-shattering buzzes. Pig-like squeals. Brass bells clanging. He watched Indians spearing, stabbing...killing his brother and Henry.

*Isn't real.*

He rocked back and forth, the arms of the bush cradling him.

*Can't be real.*

A hand grabbed his shoulder and tugged. "Come on out. Nobody's gonna hurt you."

*Apaches!*

James curled into a tighter ball and scooted farther under the protective covering of the mesquite. Screams. James waited for the arrow to slam into his chest. The arrow that would take his life.

Hands clutched both shoulders and his arm. They tried to pry him from the bush, but he clung to branches and twigs. The hands tugged harder. Small branches snapped and broke. Despite his best effort, he slid out and into danger.

James' strong fingers clawed at dirt and rocks.

"No. Can't get us! Help! Trace. Help!"

James still was no match for the four hands and arms surrounding him, pegging him to the ground.

On his back now, arms pinned over his head, someone on his chest, James twisted like a captured snake. He squirmed until all his strength drained. Exhausted, he lay gasping for breath. They would win. Within seconds he would be dead.

"James." Soft words from above. A familiar voice. "Open those eyes." That same worried voice. "No one's gonna hurt you."

Did he dare believe? One eye opened. Two brown ones gazed back. Grave concern lined a face that bore a striking resemblance to his own.

After a lungful of air, James recognized his brother perched on his chest.

"That's it. Relax." Trace loosened his grip on James' arms, but he didn't let go. Henry knelt, canteen in hand.

"Where're the Indians?" James asked.

"Gone. You're safe." Trace cocked his head at James. "Where are you?"

If James joked, would he be normal again? "Let's see. Plenty of sand. Could be the Pacific Ocean?"

Trace's face clouded.

No, kidding wasn't good.

"Lying here in the damn desert with you on top, big brother. Sand's awful hard. And you're kinda heavy. Teresa's fried chicken's added a few pounds." He squirmed. "It's hard to breathe."

For the first time today, Trace smiled. James studied his brother's face. Concern and confusion dulled Trace's eyes, worry lines jutted out from the corners. Even Henry appeared to have aged just in the last few minutes.

With his brother off his chest and Henry bracing him, James sucked down water. He knew to make it last, but he needed it. At last sated, he grew serious.

"What happened, Trace? What's going on?"

With mouths opening and closing like dying fish, Henry and Trace shrugged.

"That head of yours isn't quite right." Henry sipped from the canteen, then used it to point to James' head. "Guess that bullet did more damage than we thought."

Getting to his feet took some effort, but with Trace's help, James stood. "Those Indians were so real I swear I could even see their faces. Clear." Another deep breath, then James flashed his family smile. "What are we waiting for? Let's see what ol' Charles Culver is serving up at Apache Springs."

Armed with determination, James marched on.

# CHAPTER TEN

James smelled it before he saw it.

Smoldering timbers splayed out in a large rectangle, and a brick chimney stood like a blackened sentinel. Puffs of smoke from the fence curled up into the air. The barn groaned, ready to cave in with the next light breeze. Acrid smoke assaulted his nose. James sneezed. Twice.

Eyes watering from the smoke, he joined his brother and Henry. The turquoise sky hid behind the last gasps of brown smoke snaking up from the ashes. The stench of burning animals and wood combined with the lack of familiar noise spun James' stomach.

"Told you I smelled something," James said as he stood between the men. "Just didn't think it would be this."

Together, the three men skirted the ranch's perimeter. Step after step unearthed another terrifying clue to the final moments of the family and ranch hands who'd lived there. Pieces of material, tools, even animals lay in disarray.

Revolver aimed waist high, Trace peeked into the swaying barn. Within seconds he reeled back into the fresh air, dropped to his knees, and vomited. Uncontrollable spasms kept him on the ground.

James kneeled next to him, waiting until he could speak.

Trace wiped his mouth. "Don't go in there."

The tightness in James' chest threatened to block his breathing.

"This whole thing's terrible," he said. "Much worse than I'd ever imagined." He watched Henry walk toward them. "I mean, you read about it in the newspapers, but you don't realize...this... is...terrible."

Henry pointed over his shoulder. "Appears these good people were killed early this morning." He handed James his Colt .36.

"Might be needing this. Loaded it for you." He ran a trembling hand across his mouth. "Bad ending to the start of a pretty day."

"Yeah." James checked his jacket for more balls and caps. "You think those Indians are still close by?"

Henry shook his head, the hair brushing off two flies attempting to land on his shoulder. "Tracks lead off to the south. Don't seem to be heading back. Probably twenty in the war party."

"Damn." James stared where he imagined the Indians had headed. He weighed his gun in his hand, the cold steel powerful and deadly. He was glad it was back, this old friend. It slipped like butter into his coat pocket.

"Gotta get these people buried soon," Henry said. "Not too much left. Probably dig one big hole." He glanced toward the barn. "Suppose they left a shovel?"

*One big hole for a lifetime of work. For life itself.*

James wagged his head.

Trace stood, gripping the front of James' shirt. "What in the hell are we doing out here in the middle of nowhere?" His arm flailed toward the barn. "That could've been me and you. Why they didn't do that to us when they had the chance..."

"We're just—"

"Soon as we get to Mesilla," Trace said, "I'm gonna marry Teresa, settle down in town and give up this stagecoach business. I wanna live a while longer, James." He words dropped to a whisper. "I wanna live."

Silence. Something skittered from a bush.

"Gotta get that hole dug." Henry started for the barn.

"Make it *four* graves. Three for the men and one for the mom and kids." As much as he wanted to dig one for each person, James knew they had time and energy for only four holes. Even so, it was the right thing to do.

The afternoon dragged out as graves were dug, bodies buried, and rocks packed on each of the four mounds. Final count was ten dead—one woman, three children, and the rest men. All of the animals were either killed, run off, or stolen.

James spent time whittling out wooden crosses for each hole. Four lay side by side that crisp winter afternoon.

"What'll I put on these crosses, Henry? You know their names?"

A long shake of the head.

Creaks, groans, branches snapping. With each noise James froze, searching, waiting for the Apaches. Finally, he finished carving the crosses: **January 1861**.

Henry, Trace, and James stood side by side in the twilight. James offered prayers both for the people whose lives were lost and for themselves. They'd need all the help they could get to survive the rest of their trip.

The sun's rays spread across the horizon, leaving the men in grayed shadows. They stood amid the rubble of lives lost. Henry kicked at the pile of ashen wood.

"Those Apaches most likely won't be coming back," he said, rubbing his arm. "At least not tonight."

"We could still get a few miles away, Henry." James wiped his sooty, dirt-caked hands on his shirt. "Away's better than here."

Far from here and closer to Mesilla. Even half a mile would help.

Trace squatted by a grave. His shaky hands wiped his forehead, then ran across his lips.

"You gotta rest." Henry squeezed Trace's shoulder and met James' gaze. "You could use some, too. Fact is, we all need to."

Trace wasn't strong. James knew that. He stared down at the graves.

*Don't want this happening to Trace...or Henry and me for that matter.*

The fading desert turned purple with the sunset. As much as he hated the thought of staying here, it was the prudent thing to do. He nodded.

Henry headed for the mule. "First we eat. Got another can of green beans just waiting for our stomachs. Might add some jerky, too. Then we sleep. As soon as we can see our hands in front of our faces tomorrow, we'll head on out. Get to Apache Springs maybe in one piece."

Night brought no rest. Henry tossed and turned, thrashing on the hard ground, rolling back and forth, muttering warnings to the world.

James fought the bindings around his wrists. After much discussion and argument, James had agreed to be tied to his brother. He'd wandered off once before and no telling what he'd see tonight. They couldn't afford to have him wandering around in the desert again. He knew he'd have an icicle's chance in hell of surviving another solo trek across the desert. Sleep stayed out of reach.

During the few minutes Trace slept, nightmares attacked. Images of James' agonizing death, Teresa's disappearance, his youngest brother's capture by Apaches jerked him awake. Added to that, the bindings around James' wrists were tied around his waist, the brothers bound together with a rope lifeline. If James would just settle down, Trace could get some sleep.

\* \* \*

Shadowed images took shape as false dawn approached. Henry stretched, then stood and stretched again. With a third stretch, he rethought his crazy idea of showing his family who was in charge of his life. He ambled away from the snoring brothers.

What would they do after arriving at Apache Springs? With the two men safely on their way to matrimony, where would he go? Was this really what he wanted? Why did he have to prove himself this way? Sure, loads of silver would be great—he'd be rich...richer than his pa and brother. But at what price?

He turned around to his sleeping companions, now many yards away, and studied the two brothers. So much to live for.

Then it hit him. He was jealous. Truly jealous. Hell, maybe he'd go back to Mesilla with them, catch the next eastbound stage and go home. Back to Boston. Back to his family.

Henry stood by the side of the tilting barn in the early morning light. A gray silhouette lurched toward him.

Before he could scream, the upraised hand slit his throat.

# PART
# TWO

# CHAPTER ELEVEN

"I've already told you, Lila, there's nothing I can do right now." Sheriff Alberto Fuente threw his hands up. He shook his head for the seventh time that minute.

Lila turned her back to the sheriff and stared at the closed door. The door she'd slammed just moments ago. Hands fisted on her hips, she spun back around. "You wouldn't say that if it was somebody other than the Colton brothers, Sheriff. You've never liked them."

Fuente jumped to his feet. His words rang strong, definite, loud. "Lila, you know that's just not true."

"No, I don't know that." She gripped the back of the wooden chair in front of Fuente's desk. "It just seems that you're not—"

"Not what? Running off to God-knows-where looking for two lost stage drivers? Not concerned, not worried? Not doing my job?" He smacked the top of his desk, and papers sailed to the floor.

Lila's mouth curved into a frown. "Not...not helping."

Fuente stepped from around his desk and held Lila by her trembling shoulders. "I didn't want to tell you. Not yet."

He gazed deep into her fiery blue eyes, searched her face. What were the magic words to soften the blow? What could he say to ease the pain? Nothing came to mind. He lowered his voice. "All wagon trains and mail service between here and Tucson are stopped. Apaches are attacking everything that moves."

She stood still, breaths shallow. Fuente tightened his hold on her shoulders, afraid she'd faint. As if all life had been sucked out of her, she grasped his shirtsleeve, then leaned into him. He pulled her in close against his chest, wrapping her in his arms.

He understood her pain. Felt her pain. Knew her pain. His wife had died a short three years before, and the agony was still keen. The numbness that followed those first few weeks still played on his mind. But now, he held this woman who needed his strength and support, so soft and vulnerable in his arms. He closed his eyes. He vowed to give her everything she needed.

Lila pulled away from his grasp, a final tear trickling down her dark pink cheeks. "I'm sorry, Sheriff. It's just that I've waited so long and James is such a wonderful man...I don't know..."

She lowered herself into the nearest chair and gazed out the window.

Fuente returned to his chair behind the desk. He picked up a wanted poster, glanced at it, riffled through a few more, and then tossed them back onto the desk.

Awkward silence filled the small office. What was he supposed to do now? He had no clue as to the men's whereabouts, no idea where to look for them even if they were still alive.

Still alive. He pinched the bridge of his nose and closed his eyes. It hadn't surfaced until now, but the possibility that the Colton boys were dead was very real. Fact was, there was no chance in hell they were alive.

He'd read the reports coming in from the few soldiers and ranchers who'd escaped the Apaches' raids in that area. He wouldn't tell Lila their stories. He couldn't. She'd be hysterical if she knew the truth. No, best leave the details untold. Save her from some of the agony she'd have to endure soon enough.

Lila wiped a final tear and stood, straightening her long blue skirt. "Sheriff Fuente, I have to find James. He's everything to me." She started for the door. "If I have to, I'll ride out there myself."

Fuente shot up and wedged himself between her and the door. "You can't," he said. "It's not safe. Not for anybody. Tell you what, I'll check around, get a message down to Fort Bliss and Fort Fillmore asking if they're sending a company out that way. If they are, they'll look for the boys."

The right words. Fuente searched his thoughts. He stared at Lila's face, her blue eyes ringed in red.

"Lila, James would want you to stay here and be safe. To wait for him. You know that, don't you?"

She nodded.

"Do what James would want. Be here when he gets back. Whatever has happened, he'll need you. More than he's ever needed you before. Understand?"

Again Lila nodded.

"That's all we can do now. I'll get right on that message."

Fuente gazed down at the woman who was at least half his age. Did she really believe him? A woman alone in the Sonoran Desert had no chance of survival. He wanted her safe, too. More importantly, he wanted her here.

Lila gripped the door handle. She spoke over her shoulder, more to herself than to Fuente. "He's dead, isn't he, Sheriff."

What should he say to this beautiful woman? Should he raise her hopes when the chances were doubtful? Or should he lie and tell her everything would work out?

He eased his arm around her shoulders again, reeling in the softness against him. "There's always hope, Lila. Don't give up. You may get what you want some day."

*We both may.*

Lila pulled away and smiled at him. "Thank you, Sheriff. I'm sorry I came in so angry. You'll let me know the minute you hear from the army?"

Fuente nodded and held the door for Lila. Her slim figure glided across the plaza, her blond hair bouncing with her stride. He muttered once more.

"Yeah, we both might get what we want."

# CHAPTER TWELVE

Warm fingers of light draped over the Dragoon Mountains. Like a bear coming out of hibernation, Cochise emerged from his hide-covered wickiup and faced the gold-orange rays. The warmth felt good this cool morning. He thanked the spirits for another day of life.

As the sun rose, his thoughts turned to the recent raids. A half smile pulled up the corners of his mouth. Victory was exciting. The enemies stealing his land needed to be wiped out, exterminated. Even children. If he spared them, they would grow up, return, and take his land. They, too, must die.

"Cochise, there is news."

He turned at a voice behind him. "I trust it is good."

A young warrior, his chest heaving up and down, waited. He sucked in a lungful of air.

"I ran a long time to tell you," he said. "Three white men stopped at a ranch near Sleeping Woman Mountain, one of the ranches we had destroyed earlier."

Cochise focused on the sweat-glistened warrior. "What of these men?"

"Sitting Eagle proved his bravery. He will be a good warrior. He cut the throat of a man who was standing, guarding two others. The White Eyes never knew Sitting Eagle was there."

Cochise nodded. "Very brave."

"The man fell, but Sitting Eagle caught him, wrapped him in a blanket near the other two men, then laid him quietly—as if he was sleeping. Sitting Eagle did not awaken the other men."

"Did he kill the others?"

"No. Anyone can be killed when they sleep. He waits until they are awake and then hunts them when they're more difficult to kill. Anyone who slits the throats of sleeping enemies is no man." The warrior paused and glanced toward the north. "He stays now to watch."

Cochise raised an eyebrow. "Sitting Eagle is not only brave, he's also wise."

"One of the men must be a prisoner." The Apache brave rubbed his wrist. "His hands were bound, tied to the other sleeping man."

"Bound and sleeping. It *was* too easy." Cochise stared into the awakening sky, then ran his gaze across the camp. "I'll send my war chief, One Wing, to lead. I look forward to his stories."

Cochise turned his back on the man and walked to the fire in the center of the encampment full of activity. A few warriors ate around small fires, and children played with the camp dogs while women poked twigs into the flames. The older girls stirred pots of venison stew and commanded smaller children to help with chores. His tribe. Soon the boys would be warriors and the girls would be wives and mothers. Cochise smiled.

After finishing a bowl of venison stew, Cochise gathered his warriors. He listened to stories of the previous day's burnings and killings, recitations of the raids on their enemies. More than once a nod of his head caused warriors to lift their chins and straighten their shoulders.

As the stories continued, the tales grew in volume and magnitude.

"Our land!" One warrior, his buckskin pants and shirt the same color as his golden tanned skin, rushed to his wickiup and returned with a drum. He thumped it in rhythm to his beating heart.

"Our people forever!" Another Apache jumped to his feet, encouraging the other men to join the revelry. The rest yelled, chanted, prayed for strength in battle.

Amid the din of crazed men preparing for war, Cochise raised his hand and waited for his warriors to hear his words. Once they quieted, he said, "We must keep what is ours! Keep it from the White Eyes who have become our enemies."

"Death to the white man!"

"Kill! Kill! Kill!"

Yes, his warriors, his people, would drive out the enemy. He breathed in their fervor. It was contagious. Men dancing in time to the drum, others holding up their lances like hard-won trophies, women smiling, children hopping up and down in imitation of their fathers.

Cochise waited for chanting to subside. Again, he held up a hand until they had quieted. "But we must also free my brother," he said. "He must not remain in white man's prison." Cochise met the eyes of each warrior.

He drew a breath and continued. "Kill every Mexican and white settler, every man, woman and child who doesn't belong to the Apache. Kill every enemy until there are none left."

Cochise raised his face to the sun. Caught up in the moment, he chose to ride with his warriors. Now he would witness another victory. His warriors would be brave and successful.

"Kill! Kill! Kill!"

The chanting reached a crescendo, words radiating like heat waves across the desert. Warriors and young braves alike raised their weapons to the sky. Knowing they had far distances to travel, the men mounted their horses and kicked them into hard gallops.

\* \* \*

Trace raised one hand, shielding his eyes from the bright morning sun. Sand sprinkled from his cheek as he yawned and ran a hand over his face. He cleared his lungs of sleepy air and twisted, careful not to reopen his wound.

Then he untied the tether knotted around his waist and followed the rope to where it bunched under James' shoulder, who, for once, lay still. He reached over and shook his brother.

"Up and at 'em James. Let's go."

James' tied hands flew up to his face, protecting him from unknown attackers. Both hands formed into fists.

"It's all right," Trace said. "Just me."

James' confused, startled eyes stared back. One side of Trace's mouth curved upward. Was James rational or did he still see imaginary critters and Indians? He untied the rope around his brother's hands.

James massaged his wrists and nodded toward the rope. "Guess that worked."

"Yeah. You stayed right here."

Trace's grin widened. No cougars, Indians, or anything else seemed to be on James' horizon—only open desert. Two pats on his brother's back then Trace glanced toward Henry rolled up in a blanket only a few feet away.

"Henry, time to get going," Trace said. "Gotta get a move on. Sun's already up."

James coiled the rope, the life-saving bind, while Trace fitted his hat and eased to his feet. He felt better than yesterday. Definitely better than the day before. He was still sore, real sore, but he could feel the healing taking place in his body. Was James healing as well?

Crisp golden rays lit the nearby saguaro cactus. Trace surveyed the cloudless sky. Would this be the day they'd be rescued? Or get to shelter?

"Go wake Henry," Trace said. "I'll water the mule."

James stretched and scratched his chest. "Suppose there's more peaches for breakfast? I'm starved."

Trace glanced around the campsite and massaged the holster on his right hip. "Damn. Mule's wandered away. I swear. If it isn't *you* taking off, it's the mule. I better go find her."

He shook his head and followed obvious hoof prints zigzagging into the distance. Trace glared out over the awakening desert and grunted. He followed the tracks into an arroyo, an oath forming under his breath.

Suddenly, his brother's shout spun him around. Something was definitely wrong. Trace ran back toward camp.

"Trace!"

"I'm comin'!"

"Trace!"

Trace slid to a stop and knelt by his shaking brother. "What...?" He frowned down at Henry, blank eyes staring around caked blood. "What the hell? What happened?"

"Don't know. Found him like this." James bit his lower lip. "Think it's Apaches?"

Trace nodded.

"Why didn't they kill us, too?" James pulled his coat tighter around his chest. "We made easy targets."

"Maybe that's why. Too easy." Trace pulled the blanket over Henry's body and mumbled a quick prayer.

James trembled as he spoke. "We're next."

Trace eyed his brother. Would James bolt into the desert, straight into the jaws of hostile Apaches? He gripped James' arm. "Not if I can help it."

"We gonna run?"

61

"Yeah. And I mean *run*."

Trace pulled James to his feet and held both arms. He glanced over his brother's shoulder. The stark desert stared back. "We're awake now, so they're liable to come after us. I don't want to stay and find out."

James turned back to Henry.

Trace scooped up the canteen and slung it over his shoulder. Then he cocked his head toward the east. "They took Mule. We'll have to hoof it. Let's go."

"Henry," James said. "Gotta bury him first."

"No time."

James wrenched his arm from his brother's tight grip and headed for the makeshift cemetery. "I'll get the shovel we used yesterday."

Trace grabbed the back of James' shirt and hissed in his ear. "I said no time. They're probably waiting to kill us right now. Use your head."

James spun around and glared. "Dammit, Trace. I owe him. Hell, he saved our lives. Burying him's the least we can do."

"No ti—"

"It'll go faster with two." James spoke over his shoulder as he marched toward the other graves.

\* \* \*

Apache warriors scouted the area around the burned ranch. Some danced, hooting and hollering on top of the fresh graves. One yanked up the wooden crosses, flinging them across the desert.

Cochise surveyed the destroyed area, a sneer crawling up one side of his mouth.

*Those invading settlers will be wiped out. This land will once again belong to my people, our ancestors and children yet to come. It will always be home to the feared Apache.*

Cochise's appointed war leader, One Wing, approached the Chiricahua Apache leader.

"Sitting Eagle says the two white men are gone only one, maybe two hours."

"Find them, but don't kill them," Cochise said. He peered into the desert. "I want them alive."

# CHAPTER THIRTEEN

Conversations in the Mesilla Mercantile more and more often centered on the increased Apache raids. Men and women spoke of cattle run off, distant brown smoke, and the fear. Always the fear.

The waiting was intolerable. Hours dragged into days. Lila jumped each time the store's door opened and the silhouette of a man appeared. Each time her heart pounded and her breath caught in her chest as she prayed her James Colton was finally home.

A long, lonely evening was once again at hand. Lila locked the Mercantile's door and stepped onto the wooden boardwalk. She navigated around two ranchers swapping stories. Their conversation stopped her.

"I'll tell ya, Jim, I ain't never seen nothin' like it." The man removed his hat and raked his graying hair with thick fingers. "I'll be the first to admit I was scared to death on the trip over here. Not sure I'd even make it."

"Me, too. Hell, nobody, not even all them soldiers, can patrol the hundreds of square miles 'tween here and Tucson." Jim shook his head, leaned over, and streamed brown tobacco juice onto the dirt.

The rancher glanced around Mesilla's plaza. "Yep, hundreds of hiding places. That old Cochise and his braves could be anywhere. I hear tell the army's never gonna find him."

"They run off all my livestock and tried to burn down the barn, but my foreman killed three of 'em before they torched it. I hired ten extra hands to protect me and my family."

Jim glanced at Lila, then tipped his sweat-stained hat.

"Excuse me, gentlemen." Lila stepped in closer. "Didn't mean to interrupt your conversation, but are you by chance from around Tucson?"

"No, ma'am," Jim said. "I'm from the Crazy S Ranch 'bout fifty miles west of here. Why you askin'?"

63

"I'm tryin' to find out about any travelers between here and Tucson. See if anyone knows about the stagecoaches goin' through there." Lila knew her voice quivered, but she couldn't help it. She wanted to be strong, but it was so hard. The second man wagged his head.

"Ain't no coaches gettin' through from Tucson east, ma'am. Or west. Cochise declared war on all the settlers around there, and nobody's gettin' out alive."

Lila fought tears through her clenched jaw.

"Ma'am, some people *might be* gettin' through. And I hear tell the army's gonna send a patrol out to help the ranchers."

The other man spoke up. "Who you know out there?"

"The man I was supposed to marry today." Lila swiped at a tear sitting on her cheek. Her words sounded hollow, strange. "He rides shotgun for Butterfield Stage. Supposed to be back last Tuesday."

She studied the ground, the twilight sky, the Mercantile key still gripped in her trembling hand.

The first man lowered his voice. "Just because Cochise stopped all stages doesn't mean your man ain't comin' back. Just means he may have to walk."

"He's probably just fine, ma'am." Jim glanced at the other rancher. "Could be a bit foot sore, but he'll be back, if he can."

*If he can.*

Those three words spun her world into further despair. She'd lied to herself that James was all right, that he would come back to her. She knew the chances were next to none he would ever come home, marry her, and raise a family of his own. But still she believed. She had to. The key slid from her grip and bounced on the wooden sidewalk.

"Ma'am? You all right?" Jim picked up the key and handed it to her.

"Thank you." Lila ducked her head. "Excuse me."

Gathering her long, green skirt and hurrying across the plaza, Lila ran past the stately white-plastered San Albino church. She refused to think that if James had been here today, the church would still be full of their friends, wishing them well for a long and happy married life.

* * *

Sunday morning ushered in a cold, biting northwest wind, typical of late winter in southern New Mexico Territory. Lila bundled up and left her small boarding house room. The icy wind billowed her swirling skirt as she scurried across the plaza toward Maria's Cocina, a cozy restaurant tucked away in a courtyard around the corner. It was James' favorite place to sit and talk, just relax. They came here often when he was in town.

She took a seat at a corner table, warming with familiar surroundings and the comforting smells of beans cooking in the pot, the sizzle of tortillas on the stove, coffee ready for an empty cup. Her waitress, a slim Mexican girl with four younger brothers to help feed, smiled at her. Lila envied the activity and love of a family. That's all Lila had wanted in life and now it looked as if she would never have it. It was always just out of reach.

Lila drew a deep breath. She couldn't give up hope. There was always a chance James and Trace had made it out alive. Maybe they would ride in today, tired but in one piece.

Maybe.

She stared at the breakfast plate in front of her. Bean-covered tortillas swimming with enchilada sauce and eggs on top. Huevos rancheros. James' favorite breakfast. She picked at the pieces of chicken and one or two beans. There was no way she could eat this. Not today. Not with James and Trace gone. Not with that lump in her throat.

The door squeaked open, then banged closed, and heavy boots walked over the floorboards. Lila looked up. Two of James' friends had stopped at her table.

"Howdy Lila." The dark-haired man flashed a wide smile, then pointed at her plate. "We're just gettin' ourselves some breakfast, too. Mind if we join you?"

"I'd be honored if you did, Sunny," Lila said. "You and Clay sit, please."

It would be good to have them sitting with her. In fact, it felt normal, except James and Trace were absent.

Clay sat across from her. Tom Williamston, called "Sunny" by everyone, took the chair next to him. He set his wide-brimmed black hat down on the table.

Lila looked from man to man. "Last time I saw you was over

65

at the stage office when you got the news Butterfield was shuttin' down. Sure sorry to hear it."

Of the two men, she liked Clay the best. His red hair and freckles reminded her of a little boy. He was very easy going unless something made him mad. When that happened, his green eyes and Irish temper flared. She'd heard he was unstoppable. James shared Clay's temperament.

James once told her about an incident in a rowdy Tucson saloon last summer, when Clay had single-handedly broken up a fight between five muscle-laden wranglers arguing over a barmaid's attention. James said they never knew what hit them.

Lila smiled at the remembered sound of James' voice. He was next to her. His hand holding hers, his arms—

"We're sorry about James," Clay said as took her hand.

He held it longer than he should have. Lila eased out of his grip, his sympathy making it difficult to maintain her resolve. She had to be strong. Sunny cocked his head, a corner of his mouth pushing up his mustache. She returned the grin. It felt good to be with these two men and to smile again.

After ordering, Clay picked up a fork, played with the tines. "Sunny and I been talking." He waved the fork at Lila and then at Sunny. "Now you know those Coltons are about our best friends in the whole world. Trace and me've been drivers since old man Butterfield first hitched a team."

The waitress brought a plate of steaming tortillas, and she set them in the center of the table. Clay picked up the top one, rolled it like a cigar, and bit the end.

While his friend's mouth was full, Sunny jumped in the conversation. "An' your boyfriend and me been ridin' shotgun for about the same time. He's a good man."

Lila nodded.

"Fact is," Clay said, "as you know, Sunny and me are out of jobs now that Butterfield decided he's losin' money on account of that war back east."

"Yep." Sunny nodded. "So, we're gonna head west, out toward Tucson, maybe even California."

The waitress set two hot plates of tamales and enchiladas complete with frijoles in front of the men.

Lila dropped her fork to her plate. "West? That's plain suicide!"

"Yeah, I know." Clay pointed his forkful of enchilada toward Sunny. "But since I've driven that road for three years, both Sunny and me know it real good and know places to hide if need be. Trace knows 'em, too."

He slid the fork into his mouth while the conversation hung in the air.

Lila's half-eaten tortilla and eggs stared up at her. She disregarded the food; her stomach just wasn't ready for it. She looked at the men sitting with her.

"I've been doing some figuring," she said. "James' stage is the only one not accounted for. That's right, isn't it?"

Clay and Sunny nodded.

Lila clutched her napkin. "They're out there all alone."

"Lila, we're gonna look for James and Trace," Sunny said. "We'll bring 'em back. Since the sheriff ain't doin' nothin' about gettin' them, we will."

"I can't ask you to risk—"

"You're not asking us," Clay said. "We're telling you what we're gonna do."

Could she shake her head any harder? The men's faces blurred. "I can't lose you, too. First James and Trace, then Teresa said she's going to stay with her aunt in Santa Fe for a while, and...now you. I couldn't bear it."

Sunny played with his tortilla. "I'm sorry. We'll be careful. But, Lila, our minds are made up."

Lila leaned over the table and held Clay's forearm. "Sheriff Fuente said Fort Bliss would send out soldiers to look for them. Let them do it."

Sunny and Clay exchanged quick glances. Clay breathed deep and rested his hand over Lila's. "Guess Fuente's not man enough to tell you," Clay said, "but I will."

Lila searched Clay's eyes for understanding. She swung her gaze to Sunny then back to Clay.

"Lila, the soldiers at Fort Bliss have been sent to east Texas 'cause of that war. And Fort Fillmore's got just a skeleton unit, too. There ain't nobody *left* to go looking for Trace and James."

A tickle formed in Lila's throat. She swallowed it. Clay looked down and patted her hand.

"Sorry for having to tell you. But, you had to know that Fuente's leading you down the wrong path, getting your hopes up like that."

Sunny's voice took on a hard edge. "He knew weeks ago that the military was busy some place else." He gripped his coffee cup, his knuckles turning red then white.

Lila gazed at the table, her plate of unfinished breakfast sitting in front of her like a reminder of life left unfinished. Images of James and Trace in happier times raced through her mind. She saw Trace pulling the huge mule team up in front of the stage office, James jumping off the high seat with that heart-stopping smile on his face. She felt his arms around her as Trace tapped him on the head so that he could get a chance to hug her. It was a ritual every time they drove into town.

Lila closed her eyes, knowing that Clay and Sunny were watching. She didn't care if she was being rude. She couldn't be good company at this moment.

"I'm sorry, gentlemen. This is just such a difficult time for me." She caught herself. "An' I know it's hard for you, too."

Sunny's face. That caterpillar mustache draping over his upper lip accentuated his smile. His light brown eyes sparkled and the skin crinkled on either side of his eyes with the grin. Lila hadn't noticed it before, but somehow she found comfort there. How had he really earned his nickname? It couldn't be what James claimed—his aggravating grumpiness in the mornings. She found it hard to believe.

Sunny pushed back from the table and adjusted his hat on his head. "We'll find 'em, Lila. One way or another." He stood. "We'll find 'em."

# CHAPTER FOURTEEN

Even a sliver of shade was welcomed relief from the sun. The endless walking was taking its toll on Trace's strength and stamina. He leaned against a rough boulder, then slid to the sandy floor.

James leaned against the same boulder and examined the bottom of his boot. "Only a few more miles left on 'em. Never knew feet could hurt so bad. Can't even wiggle my toes." He pried off his hat and fanned his face. "How far you reckon we've walked?"

The sky held no answer for Trace. How long had it been now? A week? A month? One day melted into another. One mile melting into another. "Thirty, forty miles I'm guessing."

"Think we're any closer to home?"

"Sure hope so," Trace said. "Hate to think I've spent all these days and nights in the desert for nothing."

Leaning back against the boulder, James shut his eyes. "If Henry was right about the day, I'm figuring that yesterday was Saturday." He slid down to the ground, then looked over at Trace. "I got married yesterday."

The pebble he'd picked up sailed across the sand. James bit his lower lip.

"It'll be all right," Trace said. Or would it?

James sniffed. "And she doesn't even know if I'm alive."

Trace regarded his younger brother's red, sunburned face. His heart hurt for him. All Trace could do was offer the canteen. "Want a drink?"

James nodded and took a swig of water.

"Better make it last," Trace said. "It's all we got."

Trace's side throbbed, so he massaged his wound, and blood turned his fingers red. He glanced at James. There was no way he'd let on how dizzy he felt or how much he wanted to lie down and sleep—forever.

James returned the canteen, and Trace took one sip before he crumpled over onto his side. James gripped Trace's arm. "What's wrong?"

"I'm all right. Just need rest."

James bunched his coat under Trace's head, and Trace didn't stop him. He knew James would be cold, but right now he needed it. Just for a few minutes, just a little while.

"Lie right here," James said. "It'll be all right. You'll be fine."

"I'll shut my eyes a minute, then we gotta go."

Trace closed his eyes. He hated to admit it, but no matter how hard he and James tried, no matter how fast they ran, those Indians would find, capture, torture, and kill them. If he and his brother were lucky, it would be over in a matter of minutes. If they weren't...

* * *

Firm hands on his shoulders shook Trace awake. "Sorry, brother, but it's been half an hour. We gotta get going."

Exhausted, Trace attempted to stifle his groan. It erupted anyway. James offered him the canteen.

"Trace, from now on I'm gonna try real hard to keep my head together. I'll do the worrying for both of us. I'll be the big brother for a while."

"Hope you like it. Might make it permanent." Trace sloshed the canteen. "'Bout half gone."

James stared into the endless desert. "How much further you reckon to Apache Springs?" he asked.

"At least another day. Ten miles, maybe more. Help me up. They can't be far behind."

Silhouetted against the turquoise sky, black shapes caught the wind currents. A light breeze whispered through the mesquite bushes, shaking the thin branches. The cactus-dotted valley stretched into infinity and disappeared into pale gray earth. Somewhere in the purple distance, a coyote sang.

Coyote or Indian?

Trace pointed toward rising hills.

"I think there's an outcropping one, two miles south of the road," he said. "If we're anywhere close to that, we can hide. Good place for defense if they follow us."

Yards stretched into a mile as the Colton brothers trudged

through the Sonoran sand. They skirted prickly pear cactus and short scrub oak bushes.

Finally, Trace stopped and shielded his eyes from the late afternoon sun. "If I'm not mistaken, the road's not far from here. I recognize those rocks, that formation on the side, those piñon trees. Look there, James." He pointed east. "That's part of the road. See?"

"Thank God." James gripped his knees, bent over catching a breath.

"I think over there's a place to hole up," Trace said. "We'll be all right now."

"Really think we'll make it?"

"Like a Sunday stroll 'round the plaza." Trace pushed down panic. He had to be strong. He nodded, flashing a grin toward his out-of-breath younger brother.

"Soon as we get back to Mesilla," James said, "the second thing I'm gonna do is buy a new pair of boots." James held out one leg and wiggled his foot.

"What's the first? As if I didn't know."

"Grab Lila, hold on, and never let go. Never let her out of my arms again." James considered a moment. "Except when she's having kids."

"How many you planning on?"

"A yard full." James' cheeks reddened.

"Know what I'm gonna do?" Trace said. "Find Teresa, ask her to marry me, then sleep for at least a week. Maybe two."

"Married, huh?" James shook his head. "Teresa would make an excellent wife, but I'm not so sure about you, big brother."

"Meaning what?"

Trace glanced over his shoulder at James. He allowed a sliver of hope for their future. After all, James was also getting better. He hadn't seen imaginary Indians yet today.

"I can just see you now," James said. "Washing diapers and dishes at the same time!" A grin appeared. His voice rose a couple octaves to falsetto. "Yes, dear. No, dear. Certainly, Teresa dear."

"Think that's funny, do you? I'm man enough to take orders from a woman. Long as it's not very often. How about you? I'll bet Lila's already got your list of chores ready. All you gotta do is get your rear end home."

"I'm trying, brother. I'm trying."

The Colton brothers trudged on in silence. Trace planned

71

his future as if Mesilla was around the next rock with no hostile, angry Apaches close behind. The yards became a mile.

As they topped a low rise, Trace let out a long breath. "Stage road to Mesilla, James. Just right there." He pointed to the brown trail snaking across the Sonoran Desert.

"Path to heaven." James squinted. "Never thought I'd say that about a patch of dirt."

"We've already come quite a ways. Apache Springs's getting closer."

"Damn, that road looks good." James pointed. "If I had the energy, I'd run right down there and just trot on home." He unplugged the canteen and brought it to his lips.

"Better save that," Trace said.

"But the spring's not too far."

"We're not there yet." Trace ran a trembling hand across his mouth, then clutched his side. It throbbed worse than earlier. Did he dare hope? Could they make it safely back to Apache Springs and then on to Mesilla?

"Yeah, you're right." James replaced the cork and peered into the waning light. "Wanna head for those rocks up ahead?"

Trace nodded and bent over, shaky hands on shaky knees.

James grabbed his arm and held on tightly as he spoke. "You're awful pale." He surveyed the area—mesquite bushes, an arroyo to their left, boulders on their right. "You're gonna make it, Trace. There's a place to rest in the shade over there."

"No, not there. I'm all right. Let's go."

Long shadows of cactus, rocks, and mesquite played on the sand. A flock of doves scattered from bushes. James froze, shielded his eyes against the sun.

There. Behind that stand of junipers, something moved. He let out a stream of oaths.

"Jesus! Indians!"

Trace turned around following his brother's gaze. "I don't see anything."

"They're just behind us. I saw 'em, I swear. They're real this time."

"You sure? Hate to run for no reason."

"Run! Head for those rocks!" James yanked on Trace's sleeve. Bushes off to his left moved.

Trace held his side. "Don't stop no matter what!"

# CHAPTER FIFTEEN

The view from the hill gave Cochise quite the advantage. From here he watched his warriors crouching behind clumps of mesquite, jojoba, and boulders. The palo verde trees, grouped together like they were, provided not only protection but also a perfect hiding place for his smaller braves until the two White Eyes were in their most vulnerable position. Then, when Cochise gave the order, One Wing and the other warriors would attack.

He'd asked his war leader to take the White Eyes alive—and keep them breathing until they were no longer needed. Until they either died at their own hands or Coyuntura was free. However long it would take, Cochise would imprison these men, as his brother was. He hoped to see his brother before the days grew longer and turned warm. But no matter, the captives would provide something to trade for his brother.

To his left, the two White Eyes darted in and out behind rocks. One appeared to be injured, holding his side and not running as well as the other. Cochise looked closer now that they had reached a saguaro at the foot of the boulders. Those two men were built the same. Tall, wide shoulders, brown hair. They moved alike. Could they be brothers? What a wonderful gift. White Eye brothers.

A few of his warriors veered to the left behind the men, closing in like pumas. Cochise nodded.

*Those Americans don't know what's about to happen. True, they run, and run fast, but not fast enough.*

He signaled for the other warriors to head right. They cut off the men's escape route before the fugitives could reach the protection of the boulders at the base of the spiraling peaks.

The Apaches who brandished rifles loaded them; the ones with arrows readied their bows.

The two white men darted into shadows, zigzagged around bushes, and clambered over rocks. Just like frightened rabbits before the hawk swoops down and plucks them from life. Both ran with fortitude and bravery. They would not be captured without a fight, Cochise realized. Seizing these men would be a true honor for him.

He nodded to his warriors. It was time.

The mesquite, cactus, and piñons exploded. Painted ponies, red and yellow handprints marking their rumps, appeared out of nowhere. Chiricahuas streaked with blue and red war paint whooped and hollered.

Cochise kept his eye on the White Men.

One man dodged bushes, cactus, and arrows as he raced for the boulders. The other followed right behind. The first man had pulled a gun out of his coat. Cochise snorted. Did he really think that would save him? White Eyes. Always believing they're better than the Apache, that their weapons were stronger, more powerful. Another snort.

As the limping man slowed, his brother grabbed his coat sleeve and pulled him forward. Curses about rocks and thorns made their way to Cochise's ears.

The brother released the other one's coat and darted into the rocks, a maze of boulders that possibly afforded protection. The limping man scrambled over a large rock, coming face to face with his brother. They said something Cochise couldn't quite make out, but he figured it was calls of desperation and plans for their survival.

A v-shaped wedge of boulders off to the men's right held promise. The jagged crags could be a place to take refuge while they defended their lives. As short as that would be.

They disappeared into the rocks. Even better, Cochise thought. He knew One Wing enjoyed a good game of coyote and rabbit. Their capture would have been much too easy, with no honor, if they'd stayed in the desert to fight. After all, they could only run so long, then what honor is there when they collapse and beg for death?

One Wing galloped down a ravine as he pursued the enemy.

The brothers reached the narrow opening between two smooth boulders one right after another. They patted their coat pockets, more than likely looking for ammunition.

As if Cochise had given the signal himself, his warriors melted back into the desert. A ploy One Wing used to disarm and disorient his prey. It was a tactic used effectively. Still from his hilltop, Cochise spotted his warriors spread out, ready for the final attack.

One Wing had an easy shot with his rifle, the one he'd taken from those soldiers a few days before. Those army men had put up a good fight, but the Apache proved stronger.

Cochise turned his gaze on his war leader. One Wing's rifle aimed directly at the man on the right.

*Bang!*

The rifle smoked and the man grabbed his cheek. Even from where Cochise sat, he could see a red streak on the man's face. One Wing was a good shot.

With the first shot, the rest of the Apaches attacked at once. They scrambled over boulders and rocks, around bushes, through crevices.

The men fought like wildcats. Apaches swarmed them, pounding their faces, punching their stomachs, pinning arms behind them.

Both men slammed to the ground. They spun, knocking into Apaches like fish caught in a net.

The taller man crumpled to the sand. Before the other one could rush to his fallen brother, an Apache's moccasin connected with his head. He crashed to the ground, dust spurting up around his body.

Both men lay still.

# CHAPTER SIXTEEN

Sunny squirmed in his saddle. His rear end was numb, his days being spent on a stagecoach seat, not in a saddle. After riding past nothing more than scrub mesquite, saguaro cactus, coyotes and quail, he almost looked forward to spotting an Indian. Something to break the tedium. An excuse to get out of the saddle and stretch would be welcome about now. He rode in silence, he and Clay, searching mile after mile, exploring both sides of the now-deserted road. Praying for any sign of their friends.

"I've been studyin' on those people we talked to back at Steins," Sunny said. Maybe some conversation would help pass the time. "Think we're doin' right by headin' into trouble? I mean, all they talked about was them Indians."

"I've been thinking on it, too." Clay slowed his horse to a walk. "But we haven't seen hide nor hair of Apaches. All we've heard is story. Talk. Maybe the trouble's over."

"If the trouble's over, then why hasn't a stage or wagon come through in two weeks? Why haven't we seen James and Trace?"

An uncomfortable tightness controlled Sunny's throat. Clay took a long time answering.

"Don't know. Don't even like to think about it." His eyes met Sunny's. "Think they're in real trouble?"

Sunny knew the answer. It had become clear only a day or two into the expedition. No one was getting past those warring Apaches. No one was getting out alive.

Mile after mile they rode until the desert turned gold, the sun ready for its final plunge. They found a couple of boulders, sagebrush growing up tight against it, to use as a campsite. After tying their horses to a spindly branch and unsaddling the sweaty animals, the men rummaged through saddlebags. Jerky would have to do one more night.

"I'm sick of cold camps night after night, Clay." Sunny pulled his jacket around his shoulders and gazed into the graying sky. "What say we get a small fire goin' and make some coffee?"

Clay blew on his hands. "Coffee'd taste good, that's a fact. It's downright chilly." He shook his head. "But you know we don't dare light one. Them Apache see like cats at night."

Sunny popped the last bite of beef jerky into his mouth. "What I'd give for something hot right about now."

"We'll get coffee at Apache Springs tomorrow. Culver always has his famous brew sitting on the stove, you know that. He won't mind sharing." Clay leaned back against a rock and sipped out of his canteen. He picked up a pebble and tossed it at nothing.

Not ready to settle down for the night, Sunny wandered away from Clay, into the desert. He needed to be alone for just a few minutes, just needed time to think.

He climbed a low rise that afforded a view of the valley, the San Pedro mountains bluing in the distance. His gaze traveled across the desert, over the swells and cactus, past stands of saguaros.

Then he spotted it. A smoke cloud several miles southwest. Was it smoke or dust? Had to be smoke. No wind had turned up any earth today.

"Clay?" Sunny turned and trotted back toward his partner. "Clay."

Clay met him halfway. "What's wrong? You all right?"

"Look." Sunny pointed southwest. The brown plume spiraled up, then caught on a light breeze. "Indians?"

"I'd bet a year's salary on it."

"Think it's Apache Springs?"

Clay shook his head. "No. The way station's about ten miles from here and a little to the north." Lines of concern raced across his forehead. "Looks like it was a big spread judging by the amount of smoke."

"Damn, Clay."

"Yeah."

* * *

The image of the spiraling smoke still in the front of his thoughts, Sunny breathed out a sigh of relief when he spotted the Apache Springs way station the next day. It sat nestled at the bottom of two hills, with a wide meadow behind it, and a narrower one in front. Sunny nudged his horse toward the house. He was tired of sitting in a saddle, and the coffee aroma swirling under his nose tantalized his senses.

He reined up with Clay at his side. The only sounds he heard were their horses' whooshing breaths and the wind rustling the creosote bushes. Overhead, a few crows circled, their caws jarring. Sunny sensed something not right, out of place. He massaged the walnut handle of his new Colt .36.

After trotting down into the station's yard, Clay called out, "Mister Culver? Charles Culver? It's us, Clay and Sunny from Butterfield."

Sunny listened for any noise from the adobe building, anything to indicate the manager was nearby. He yelled louder than Clay. "You in there, Mister Culver? You all right?"

Silence.

"I'll go check the stable." Sunny said. He lifted his weight from the saddle just as the door opened. A rifle barrel glinted in the afternoon sun. Then a voice, hard, edged with caution and determination, cut the desert air like a Bowie knife.

"Get down off them horses."

Sunny eased to the ground, arms extending from his sides as his foot touched dirt.

"Mister Culver, it's just us. Sunny and Clay from the stage company—came through here 'bout a month ago. We're not gonna hurt you. Just hopin' for some coffee."

Clay stood against his horse, lead reins in hand, the other arm in the air. Culver squinted into the afternoon sun.

"Step closer. I'll see if I believe you."

Sunny and Clay edged closer to the door.

Culver cocked his head, then lowered the rifle. "Hey Clay, Sunny! Didn't recognize you right off. What the hell you standing out here for? Come in and get some coffee."

He stepped out and shook hands with both men. Sunny tossed a sideways grin at Clay as they tied their horses to the hitching rail at the side of the two-room way station. Over coffee the men swapped stories, exchanging as much information as they could.

Culver spoke into his coffee cup. "Yeah, those Apache been hittin' too close to home, if you ask me. They got the Rivera place just two weeks ago, then the Williams ranch. Guess I'm a little jittery." He bowed his head. "Even killed the two *niños*. Just don't know why anybody'd kill kids."

78

Sunny forced coffee down his throat. It tasted like iron. Culver's green eyes gazed off in the distance while Clay spun his cup on the table. Silence filled the room.

Clay's eyebrows knitted. He leaned forward. "And you haven't had a stage through here in a couple of weeks?" he asked.

"No. Nobody. You were the last."

"Haven't seen Trace or James? You remember them. The Colton boys? They left Tucson behind us."

"I know who you're talkin' about." Culver shook his head, his curly gray-streaked hair springing back every time he raked his hand through it. "They're fine boys."

Sunny pushed his tired body to his feet, then jerked a thumb over his shoulder. "I'll go tend the stock."

The wind swirled small dust clouds around his boots as he led the horses toward the barn. Hawks screeched, looking for a midday snack.

Hooves rumbled. Hundreds of hooves. Sunny froze.

They were upon him before he could bolt back into the stage station. Blue-suited cavalry soldiers trotted into the yard. Sunny stood rooted, mouth open, hand clutching the barn door.

One of the soldiers in front raised his hand, calling a halt to the procession. Two columns of men reined their mounts to a quick stop while in the middle, six Indian ponies topped with solemn Apaches slowed, then stopped as the soldiers pulled back on the reins.

A man with more gold stripes than the others called to Sunny. "This Apache Springs way station? You Charles Culver?"

At first Sunny shook his head, then changed its direction and nodded.

"Yes or no, boy?"

Sunny found his voice. "Well, sir, this is Apache Springs, but I'm not Mister Culver. He's inside."

"Good." The commander looked around.

Sunny extended his hand. "Tom Williamston, sir, out of Mesilla." He and the soldier shook hands. "Most people call me Sunny. Kind of a nickname."

"George Bascom." He met Sunny's gaze. "*Everyone* calls me Lieutenant."

Taken aback, Sunny, however, kept his composure. "Good to meet you...Lieutenant."

Sunny stared at the endless line of horses and men. He'd never seen that many soldiers in one place and certainly not with Indian captives. He wasn't afraid of these men. In fact, he was downright glad to see them.

Then the realization hit—he was in the middle of Apache wars. This was no joke. He and Clay had ridden right into the jaws of death.

Sunny took in Bascom's cold, steel blue eyes, the square jaw and thin lips. That face hadn't seen a moment of fun since the day it was born.

Bascom handed the reins to a soldier still mounted and barked an order to the next-in-command. The men sat still, six of them pointing guns at the Apaches' heads.

Then Bascom marched toward the station. Charles Culver appeared in the doorway, rifle in hand as Bascom walked up to the narrow porch.

They shook hands.

"Lieutenant George Bascom, sir."

"Charles Culver. I manage this place. Come on in." Rifle by his side, he jerked his head toward the small building.

Bascom turned again to his second-in-command. "Corporal Connor. Stand down. I'll be a few minutes."

"Sir."

Sunny followed Clay, Culver, and Bascom into the tiny station, where Bascom took Sunny's seat while Culver brought in a chair from his bedroom. The four men settled around the table and sipped coffee as Bascom spoke.

"Gentlemen, I'm looking for a place to rest the mounts and my men until tomorrow. I'd like to bivouac in this field next to you. We'll be gone at first light."

His gaze fixed on Sunny. A bayonet jabbed through Sunny's heart would've felt the same. Sunny met the stare over his coffee cup. What was it about this man that set him on edge? Something.

"Of course you're welcome to stay here, Lieutenant," Culver said. Then he leaned forward and lowered his voice. "But, I'm concerned about your captive Indians. Their presence will bring the other Apaches."

"I'll have lookouts on the perimeter. We'll be ready for them if they come. You'll be safe enough."

Culver took another sip of coffee, stood, then poured fresh brew all around.

"As long as I've been here," he said, "Cochise and I have been at peace with each other, Lieutenant. We have an agreement. I don't bother him and he don't bother me. We trade. He brings me firewood. I give him supplies. Now that you have his people, he'll make war on me." Culver shifted his gaze to Sunny and Clay, then back to Bascom. "Why are you holding those Apaches?"

"Last October, some of Cochise's men kidnapped a young boy from the Ward family ranch. We aim to bring the child back."

Culver scratched his head and rubbed his stubbled face. "Lieutenant," he said. "First of all, Felix Ward is half Apache. Pinal Apache. They simply took him back. And it wasn't Cochise's tribe that took Felix. It was the other band that stole him, not the Chiricahua, Cochise's people."

Clay's coffee cup hit the table. "You mean to tell us," he said, "these soldiers got the wrong Apaches?" He glanced over at Sunny, whose cup also hit the table.

Culver stood to his full five and a half foot height and leaned across the wooden table. "Lieutenant, if you don't set those Apache free, you're gonna open an all-out war. There's already been too many innocent people slaughtered. Hell, you're liable to get us all killed."

Bascom stood. "Mister Culver, if Cochise doesn't release young Felix Ward, we'll kill those six prisoners."

"But he don't have the kid. Not his tribe. You've got the wrong people."

"Oh, we have the right people, sir. They're Indians. That makes them the right people."

Bascom snorted. "What's even better is that three of these prisoners are related to that so-called chief. One's his own brother. Think he'll take notice then?"

Sunny couldn't take his eyes off this army officer. Who did he think he was? Bringing violence and war to an area full of hopeful settlers?

Bascom met the stare of each man, then touched his hat. "Gentlemen."

He turned and marched out the front door. It slammed harder than needed.

Half a minute ticked while Sunny digested what the army leader had said. He smoothed his mustache, then pulled off his

81

hat. "Jesus." He looked over at Clay.

Culver continued to stare at the back of the closed door. "Hope to High Hannah Cochise ain't on the warpath," he said. "Lord help us all if he is."

Clay stood and swigged the last bit of his coffee. "I gotta go talk to that lieutenant. See if I can make sense of what he's doing. There's gotta be more to it than what he just said." He stepped out of the stage station and into the warm afternoon sun.

Killing people. What a waste. Why couldn't everyone just live in harmony with each other? As he walked toward the edge of the barn where the commander stood, the realization hit him. Those six captives were more than likely the reason his friends were missing, possibly dead by now. It made perfect sense. Cochise would raid ranches and farms, waylay stages until his relatives were returned.

Clay removed his creased gray hat, wiped his forehead, then smoothed his mop of red hair. He eased close to Lieutenant Bascom and waited for him to speak.

"What?" Bascom spun to his right and snapped the question.

"Sir, I was just wondering. You been in this area for a while?"

Lieutenant Bascom nodded.

"Well, sir. Me and my partner have a couple friends who're missing. They're stage drivers, just like us. They were last seen in this area a few weeks ago. Just wondered if you've heard about them."

"No."

"But I haven't given you their names."

Bascom's eyes narrowed. "Not important. Haven't heard about or seen any stage drivers."

"Any stagecoaches? You know...attacked?"

"No."

Determined to receive better answers, Clay explained further. "We're pretty sure they started out of Tucson, but we know for a fact they didn't get here." He searched Bascom's eyes. "Haven't heard anything? Maybe some of your men know. Maybe those Apache can help us."

"I said no. Sorry." Bascom shook his head, yelled an order to a soldier near him, then turned back to Clay. "No need to talk to my men...and those Indians don't speak English."

Clay peered into the sky, working up the courage to continue. "Well, what are you gonna do with these Apaches? Especially now that you know they ain't the ones who kidnapped that boy."

Bascom glared at Clay. "An Indian is an Indian. They're all alike. Doesn't make any difference which tribe they belong to. They're all related. All guilty. Kill these six, that'll be six less to worry about."

Out of the corner of his eye, Clay noticed Sunny standing close. Words refused to form. Bascom hollered more orders to his men.

Sunny found his voice first. "Where are you takin' those prisoners?"

"Fort Bliss, Texas, by way of Mesilla."

Bascom returned a salute from a soldier. Clay knew he shouldn't ask, but his curiosity took control. "Why all the way to Fort Bliss?"

"My orders are to haul these savages down to the closest Army post to stand trial for kidnapping. They'll probably never make it that far. Gentlemen, I've got business to tend to."

He stepped around Sunny and barked an order. A soldier snapped to attention, then scurried toward the back of the barn.

Clay and Sunny stood side by side as soldiers unpacked gear, unsaddled horses, and set up camp.

Clay rubbed his forehead. "Damn, Sunny. What the hell'd we get ourselves into?"

# CHAPTER SEVENTEEN

Sunny sat bolt upright. What had ripped him out of solid sleep? Horses' hooves, men's murmurs, a distant bugle call. He rubbed his eyes open, then ran his hand over his face. Gray light filtered the room. He pulled on his shirt and boots, smoothed his hair, and stood. By the time Sunny found his way to the front door, Clay was also on his feet.

They stepped into the false dawn and stood next to Charles Culver on the station's porch. The soldiers were preparing for the next long leg of their journey. Sunny didn't envy them that dry ride back to Mesilla. He felt Clay at his elbow and heard a stifled yawn.

"Just ain't right," Sunny said. "Just damn ain't right."

He sprinted to Lieutenant Bascom's horse and grabbed the reins.

"Before you go, sir," he said, "let me talk to them Indians. Please. Might be our only chance. Let me find out if they know anything about our friends."

Lieutenant Bascom stared down at Sunny. "I told you. No one's seen anything—*Sonny*." He leaned closer and sneered. "You're keeping me from leaving."

"Damn right! You're sure as hell not goin' anywhere until I find out about Trace and James." Sunny glanced down the columns of soldiers. "Somebody's got to know something."

His unbuttoned shirt flapped in the early morning breeze. A hand rested on Sunny's shoulder. Clay's voice was in his ear.

"Calm down. Let 'em go. If they knew anything, they would've told us."

"Dammit, Clay! Not *this* son of a bitch. He knows plenty. He's hidin' something. Guaranteed. Now I'm gonna talk to them Indians."

He threw the reins back at the lieutenant and stepped toward the Indian captives.

Suddenly, Bascom kicked out with his leather boot, catching Sunny in the chest. His powerful thrust flung Sunny backward onto the hard ground.

"Corporal," Bascom barked at the man on his right.

Corporal Connor jumped off his horse, ran to Sunny, and knelt next to him. His cocked service revolver pressed against Sunny's temple.

"Ever try that again, boy," Bascom said, "and I'll have you shot—right where you lie." He turned to Clay and Culver. "That goes for you, too."

"Stay still, Sunny. That corporal'll shoot you in a heartbeat," Clay whispered out of the corner of his mouth. "He'll pull that trigger and you're a dead man."

Clay was right. Sunny's eyes riveted on the lieutenant. Few people he disliked, but this man he despised. With the revolver barrel pressed into his temple, he heard his heart pounding. Bascom was just like the gun—cold, hard, and deadly. A pain in the middle of his chest caught Sunny's attention. It burned like a knife wound. Sunny lay frozen, eyes fixed on Bascom.

"Corporal," Lieutenant Bascom said. "Release him. Mount up."

"Sir."

Corporal Connor eased the hammer down, holstered his revolver, and mounted. Bascom held his hand up.

"Forward, ho!"

The slow parade of men and prisoners rode east out of the station yard. When the captive Indians passed, one of them looked at Sunny, raised his bound hands, and held up two fingers.

Sunny knew the answers he and Clay sought were disappearing in the dust. He pushed himself upright. Frustration dried his mouth. Was sitting in the dirt his only option?

With the last soldier out of sight, Clay stepped over to Sunny. "You all right?"

Sunny nodded. "You see that, Clay? That Apache who raised his hands?"

"Sure did. Wonder what he meant?"

"Dammit, Clay. They know somethin'."

Swirls of dust trailed behind the cavalry. Clay pulled Sunny to his feet.

"I'm goin' after 'em," Sunny said. "I'll make 'em talk."

Sunny buttoned the bottom of his shirt, then frowned at the

blood dripping down his chest. He swiped at a glob running into his navel. "A boot print in my chest? Son of a bitch!"

Sunny stormed across the yard to the corral. When he reached the railing, someone's hand gripped his arm. He spun around. "Let me go."

Charles Culver didn't let go.

"Not in that mood. You're liable to go do something you'll regret. Let's get some breakfast, then think about what we should do. We'll make better decisions on full stomachs." A grin formed on his face. "Morning's never been good for you."

He ambled off toward the station.

Sunny's anger wouldn't subside. He yanked open the corral gate, but Clay stepped between Sunny and the horses.

"What're you doing?" Clay demanded.

"You know what the hell I'm doin'. Move."

Sunny pushed his friend back a couple of steps. He hated himself for these rash moments, but he just couldn't help it. That damn Bascom. Clay jumped in front of him again.

"Dammit, Sunny. You're gonna get yourself killed. All shot up when you didn't have to. I'm gonna find the Coltons and then what do I tell them? You died 'cause some ol' army jackass kicked you?"

He stared at Sunny and lowered his voice. "Hell, with you dead, I wouldn't have nobody to go to California with."

Sunny inspected his deep scrape and cuts. Again, Clay was right. Wouldn't do to get killed right now. He wrestled his rage down to mad and wiped more blood from his chest.

"Dammit. Those Apaches know somethin' about Trace and James."

He took Clay's offered neckerchief.

"Might. But ol' Bascom's not gonna let us near his prisoners." Clay shook his head and draped his arm around Sunny's shoulders. "Culver's right. You're a son of a gun before breakfast."

Over stew, beans, and coffee, the three men discussed the last twelve hours in detail. What did the Apache's signal mean? Why the complete lack of understanding on Bascom's part? Or was it refusal to understand?

Clay laid his fork on the side of the plate and wiped his mouth with an old napkin. "Good grub, Mister Culver. Thanks."

Sunny swiped the last of the beans with his tortilla. The wound tugged on his chest as he sat. More than the soreness, the idea that he was kicked, insulted by an army officer made him mad. No, more than mad. Furious.

"What're you thinking, Sunny?" Clay's voice interrupted his thoughts. "You're awful quiet."

"Sonuvabitch Bascom." Sunny rubbed his chest.

"Just leave it be," Culver said as he stood and collected the dirty dishes. "He's not worth gettin' shot over."

After the third cup of coffee, Clay stretched his arms up then behind him. "Guess it's time to head on west. Those Coltons gotta be somewhere." He stood and rubbed his stomach. "Thanks again, Mister Culver."

"Any time, Clay." Culver turned to Sunny. "You goin', too?"

Was he? If he rode hard in the other direction he could catch up to Bascom by noon.

"Sunny?"

He studied his partner. One of Clay's eyes had narrowed. Always a sign he was worried. Sunny smoothed his mustache. "Guess I'm going." He shrugged at Culver. "Can't let Clay be the only one out there playin' with the Apaches."

# CHAPTER EIGHTEEN

Trace's eyes fluttered open. Pain. Searing jabs. Flashes of agony. Tears pressed against his eyes. He grabbed at his head. Something held his hands tight. He jerked again. A turn of his head produced an explosion of pain.

After several attempts to focus, and only with strained effort, Trace pulled his world together. Two moccasined feet attached to two leathered legs stood next to his head. His gaze followed the legs upward to a bronze face. Narrowed coal eyes accentuated with a matching frown stared back.

His life was over. It was just a matter of time now and Trace would be no more. He spiraled into a welcome blackness. His mind took him home, somewhere safe.

\* \* \*

When he opened his eyes again, the pain wasn't as intense, as blinding. It still thumped and pounded, but his head no longer felt as if it'd been crushed in a stampede. This pain topped the time he and Sunny had taken Tubac by storm. The night the cantina ran out of whiskey.

He ran an inventory of his body. Head still attached, scalp still in its original location. His hands were tied to something, but they were still part of his body. Legs were tied to something also, but at least they moved. The roaring ache in his side reminded him of the shooting, but even that pain was manageable.

*Still in one piece, hurting, but thankfully alive.*

Trace eased his head to his left and recoiled. No more than five feet away lay James, stretched out, arms tethered to stakes in the ground. Dried blood matted his hair and caked across his mouth, covering one entire side of his face. Very little of this person resembled Trace's younger brother.

"James?"

Trace found the word hard to form. His throat had been dry for hours. He strained at the leather straps binding his hands and yelled louder.

James moaned, rocking his head side to side. He lifted his bound arms inches off the ground and yanked at the ropes. Then he pulled, twisted, and wrenched his body, desperate for freedom.

"James." Trace willed his voice to be calm and reassuring. "You're all right. But we're tied tight."

James's eyes flickered open and shut. His groan assaulted Trace's ears.

Trace wrenched his attention away from his brother, praying he was all right, and spotted an Apache heading for them. He remembered stories he'd heard about the Indians—what they do to captives.

The Apache squatted by Trace's face, then spoke in halting English. "I am One Wing. You are my prisoner."

His captor's shoulder-length black hair was kept down with a woven red headband, a square face set off with dull, black eyes, wide nose. The lips snarled as he spoke. A zigzag scar running down his left cheek brought attention to the hardness of his eyes.

"This is the camp of Cochise," One Wing said.

Every muscle in Trace's body caught fire. He squirmed and tugged at the bindings.

One Wing disappeared, then reappeared with a gourd dipper of water. Trace drank until it was empty. The Apache regarded James. "Much anger, much strength. Your brother?"

Trace nodded. "Yes."

"Same mother?"

"Yes."

One Wing snorted. "As I thought. You both will serve me well."

Trace cocked his head toward James. "Is he all right?"

"For now." One Wing eyed Trace, then stood. He turned around and kicked James in the ribs; the force sent James straining against the ropes.

Moans and ragged breaths. James muttered unintelligible words.

Trace tugged at the horsehair rope around his wrists. Blood trickled down his arm.

Like a wolf that had just taken down a full-grown puma, One Wing strutted over to Trace's side and knelt next to him. "What do you call yourself?"

"Trace Colton. Out of Mesilla." Trace stared into One Wing's cold eyes. "Why'd you kick him?"

"And him?" One Wing shrugged a shoulder toward James. "James...Colton."

"Trace Colton, you do what I say, or he will hurt much worse."

What was he supposed to do? If he didn't do what they asked, those Indians would kill them.

*Probably will anyway.*

James rocked his head side to side, and pain-filled sobs escaped his lips. Trace's stomach boiled. Afraid he'd lose whatever he'd eaten, he forced conviction into his words.

"Don't hurt him again, One Wing. We mean you no harm. I'll do whatever you want. Just don't hurt him. He's already been through enough."

He glanced over at James. His eyes were open. Trace caught his brother's blurry gaze and nodded.

"It's all right, James. Don't try to talk." He hoped he cloaked his rising panic, his own fears.

One Wing knelt by James and allowed him a sip of water from the gourd dipper. The Indian leaned back and sneered.

"You fought well. But not well enough," One Wing said.

He poured the rest of the water onto James' face, then turned his back on the men, and marched away.

James thrashed against the ropes like a newly branded calf. He gasped for air and blinked around drops of water. "What... Trace? Where..."

"Calm down," Trace said. "I know how you feel about ropes, being tied up and all, but fighting just makes them tighter."

Trace gazed up into the evening sky. The faint stars would be bright soon. But without cloud cover, it would get cold tonight.

"They're not real." James dropped his arms inches to the sand. "The Indians. Ain't real."

"James?"

"They're not real." James' words softened. "I'm dreaming again."

"James, we're in Cochise's camp." For the first time in

90

days, Trace wished these *were* James' hallucinations. "Very real Indians."

"You sure?"

"Yes."

"Oh, God!" James tugged like a mad man. "No!"

"We'll be all right," Trace said.

Who was he kidding? Within a few days, both he and his brother would be dead. Tortured and killed. But hope pushed into his brain. Again words erupted without thinking.

"Butterfield'll come looking."

"They're real." James' high whisper cut through the air. "Not gonna make it." His chest heaved with each pant. Trace sensed his brother's borderline hysteria.

"Yes, you will. You can do it, James. Think about Lila. Think about your lives together."

James yanked. The ropes held tight.

"James...breathe. Take a breath." Trace stared at his brother. "Look at me. Look...at...me."

Frantic gasps. Violent shaking. James was out of control. No amount of logic would help right now. Anguish pushed tears to the brim of Trace's eyes.

*How can I help you? How can I keep us alive?*

# CHAPTER NINETEEN

Sheriff Alberto Fuente jumped to his feet when the door opened and in stepped Lila Belle Simmons. Just her nearness lit up an otherwise cold, impersonal sheriff's office. Perpetual springtime and scents of lilac wafted around her. His pulse raced a little faster.

"Thanks for coming, Lila."

Fuente pulled out the chair in front of his desk. Her slim figure perched on the edge reminded him of pictures of queens and angels he'd seen in books. Where was her crown, her halo? However, her eyes—hard, cold, questioning—looked out of place. Mad. She must be mad about something.

Maybe some small talk would quiet his nerves. He couldn't recall being this tongue-tied since...since he'd first met his wife. No small or large topic sprung to mind as a good icebreaker. All right. Start off with business, since that's what she came for. He pulled his chair around and hoped his poker face was in place today. He kept his voice neutral.

"Lila, it's been a couple weeks since James and Trace were supposed to be back."

"You don't have to tell me, Sheriff. I can tell you how many hours and minutes." She sat forward, leaning closer into him. "Did you send word to the army, like you promised?"

"Of course I did." What had gotten into her? Fuente touched her hand. "Told you I would."

"You're not just saying that?" Lila's eyes softened, her lips began an upward spike. "Just to make me feel better? Just to get me to quit coming in here?"

He shook his head. Where had she gotten the idea? No, he liked her coming in. He wanted it. Looked forward to it.

"Then what did they say, Sheriff? They've had time to get out in that desert and come back." Her voice quivered. "Did they find

James?"

"No." He rushed his words. "I mean, no they haven't had a chance to report in yet." He grasped her hands. Soft, warm skin against his rough hand. His mouth dried. "Soon as I hear, I'll let you know. Trust me." He let his gaze linger over her face, then allowed it to travel to her chest. She filled out that green dress nicely. His thoughts turned to what lay under those clothes. Soft skin, rounded... He forced himself to return to reality.

"...lie to me, would you, Sheriff?"

Whatever she'd been saying didn't matter. Fuente knew to push down his desires or he'd be in real trouble. First things first. "Never. But I've got a little bit of news, thought you'd want to hear."

"Of course I do, Sheriff. I can take bad news."

"Actually, it's not bad. It's not necessarily good, either." Fuente raised one shoulder. "It's just news."

"Sheriff, I'm on the edge of my seat."

Lila eased her hands from his grasp, and Fuente struggled to keep his mind on the news at hand.

"This morning a cavalry scout came in from the Apache Springs way station. Seems a Lieutenant Bascom is bringing six Apache captives through here down to Fort Bliss to stand trial for kidnapping."

Lila drew in her breath. "James? Kidnapped?"

Fuente shook his head and rushed an explanation. "No, not James. They stole some kid who's half Apache, half white. But that's not the important part. Seems this scout saw Clay and Sunny there. He reports they've made it that far and are in good shape."

She let out a long sigh. "I'm happy to hear that, Sheriff. Did he know anything about the Coltons?"

"I asked, but he hadn't heard, although Sunny was pretty insistent that those Indians knew something." Fuente's eyebrows shot up toward his hairline. "Apparently Sunny got a little too close to the lieutenant and ended up on the ground with a boot embedded in his chest."

"Poor Sunny." Lila shook her head and looked down at her hands.

Fuente stifled a chuckle. "Had to have been early morning. Sounds like Sunny before breakfast."

"I don't think that's funny at all, Sheriff Fuente. Sunny could've been seriously injured."

Her southern drawl combined with her indignation brought a grin to one side of Fuente's mouth.

So pretty when she's mad.

"Probably just his pride took a beating, Lila. He's a strong boy. It'd take a lot to really hurt him." Fuente's grin faded. "Don't have anything else to tell you. The rest of the cavalry's supposed to arrive day after tomorrow. I'm sure you'll know when they get here."

Lila stood and extended her hand. "Thank you for lettin' me know. I'm happy Clay and Sunny made it that far. Maybe the other Army men will know more."

No other reason to keep her here. Fuente released her hand. Lila stepped through the office door, pulled it closed, and was gone.

He ran his hand through his gray hair.

"Lila, my dear, sweet Lila. What're you gonna do when I tell you James won't be coming home?" He pushed out a long stream of air. "What that scout told me is gonna break your heart."

# CHAPTER TWENTY

Early morning sun streaks turned the thin, high clouds to brilliant orange. James squinted into the rising sun. A small pebble dug into his back. He tried his hands. Still tied to stakes.

*For a dream, this sure feels real.*

He twisted to stretch out kinks, then turned his head to his right. There was Trace, also pegged.

*Helluva dream.*

He turned back around. A face glared inches from his. One Wing.

But now One Wing held a hunting knife with a tiny nick chipped out of the metal. The blade hovered over James' face.

James wrenched his head away and pulled against the ropes.

*He's not really there. Just my imagination. A really, really bad dream.*

A strong, leathered hand grabbed his chin and shoved his head back. James' world filled with that knife swinging back and forth, inching closer to his neck, to his face. The blade blurred into streaks of silver, and the tip pressed against his left cheek.

One Wing's hand clamped around James' jaw. James squeezed his eyes shut as the blade slid down his face.

Would Lila want to marry a man with scars?

By the time the knife finished its trek, James felt no stinging, no burning of flesh split open. Just the pressure of the blade.

A jab under his chin. James jerked.

"You will not move, James Colton, or I will kill you here, right now. Understand?"

James blinked.

"Good."

After what seemed a lifetime, James felt the blade's pressure let up. He swallowed hard. One Wing untied James' wrists, then dangled the ropes from his long fingers.

James sat up, massaging his aching ribs. Every other part of his body ached, too. He stopped rubbing his wrists and arms—massaging didn't help the bruises.

Would One Wing untie his ankles, too, and release him? Allow him and Trace to continue on their journey home?

Before James could make a second thought, One Wing grabbed his hands and tied them behind his back. The tugging aggravated all his sore places. James twisted his arms so that the circulation in his hands wasn't completely cut off. His fingers tingled, and he wondered how soon he'd lose all feeling.

James glanced over his shoulder. Trace's face was pale, too pale for this sun. "You all right?" James asked.

Trace nodded.

The Apache untied the ropes around James' ankles, then yanked him to his feet. His legs grew numb and his knees buckled before he could make them stand, but One Wing lifted his dead weight without effort.

*This man should be respected. No doubt he could snap necks like twigs.*

James twisted his back, hoping to get his muscles working again. One Wing's hand pressed his shoulder.

"Move."

The knife tip poked his back; it dug in deeper each time he slowed. He stumbled toward the center of camp, away from his brother, away from any security he'd had. James glanced back.

Trace nodded courage.

Deerskin wickiups, a large central cooking fire, meat drying on green wood racks heralded the center of camp. Smoke spiraled into the sky, some of it drifting into his eyes. His nose threatened a sneeze. Children stood, eyes wide. Women, bundles of wood in hand, glared. A commanding tug on his shoulder brought him to an abrupt stop. One Wing kicked the back of his legs, dropping James to his knees.

Apache murmurs and taunts rang in his ears. A violent jerk of his hair snapped his head back, and James gazed up into One Wing's coal-black eyes. The metal blade swung toward his face.

Pulled back hard against One Wing's legs, he felt those muscles tense. He closed his eyes and waited for the razor edge to slice through his skin, across his exposed neck—to end his life.

*God, if I gotta die, make this quick.*

The knife swiped at James' forehead hairline. A slight stinging. Bursts of Apache cheers and taunts. James trembled. One Wing held up a swath of James' hair. More Indian chants.

*I'm not dead.*

James gulped air over his surprise and relief. He'd known terror before, but even that gallows' rope around his neck last year paled in comparison. James looked into the faces of what seemed like hundreds of Apaches, all laughing and pointing at him.

Was this Indian going to play with him, like a cat with a mouse, until he dies of exhaustion? Or would death come quickly? James took a deep breath and faced what he knew—this cat liked to torture, play with his prey before killing it.

One Wing gripped James' arm, then yanked him to his feet. The world turned white and sparkled as he swayed. James struggled to stay upright.

*These Indians won't see how weak I am—how vulnerable. They've got to believe I'm strong.*

He stood straighter and lifted his chin.

One Wing grunted at two of the village girls who produced shy smiles before they scurried away. He grabbed James' neck and tugged him through camp, past countless wickiups, several small cooking fires, and half a dozen snarling, yipping dogs. Countless children skipped beside him. James planted one foot in front of the other.

Everything melted together in a montage of fear. The tribe's older children hit his arms and kicked his legs. A few dared to feel his skin, then turned to their friends and grinned.

One Wing growled and jerked James to a sudden stop, and James felt One Wing's hot breath in his face.

"You," One Wing said. "Your people thought they would take this land. This is ours, our home. We will never give our home to the White Eyes. This will always be ours. Many more people will die before all Americans and Mexicans know this."

One Wing spit. Globs of moisture rolled down James' cheek and dripped off his chin.

"I'm just a stage driver. Don't want your—"

James flew backwards, backhanded by One Wing. He crashed into a saguaro cactus, its hundreds of tiny needles ripping at his

97

clothes. A larger one impaled itself in his thigh as he slid to the ground.

One Wing knelt by James, untied his hands, then retied them behind the spiny cactus.

As much as the thorns hurt and the ropes cut into his skin, James knew not to struggle. He'd probably die if he fought back. He and Trace would wait, plot, and plan an escape. They'd get out alive.

One Wing leaned into his face. "Your death will be slow, painful. I'll use you to show the rest of the Americans and Mexicans what will happen if they don't leave our land now."

"We weren't trying to take your land." James straightened his shoulders and met One Wing's stare. "Just passing through. From Tucson to Mesilla. Cochise made a deal with the way station managers. Everyone would live in peace."

"No Americans *just pass through.* Cochise allowed this, but look what happened. The enemy—people like you—overran our land. My people, the Apache, have been wounded, imprisoned, slaughtered."

One Wing grabbed the front of James' torn shirt and pulled him within inches of his face. "We will get back what is rightfully ours—our land, our people." His eyes ran up and down James. "*You* will get them back."

"Me? But—" James reeled at a savage slap across his cheek. Tears blurred his vision. One Wing stood, turned around, then marched away.

*I won't let you see me hurt. We'll get out of here. Alive. That's a promise.*

# CHAPTER TWENTY-ONE

"What the hell?" Sunny frowned, squinting against the sun. "Look, Clay. Who'd do this?"

Sunny turned in a circle in the middle of what he figured had once been a house. Then he kicked at a piece of burned timber, ash swirling around his boots.

"Must've been the main house," Sunny said, "judgin' by the way these boards fell."

Clay knelt several feet away by a wooden cross broken in two and tossed near a grave. The fresh, light brown earth contrasted against the blackened buildings.

"Here's another one, Sunny. Hell, it's pure sacrilege. Who'd do this to crosses?"

Sunny spun at the sound of his partner's voice. "Lucifer himself."

"Yeah." Clay stood, running his hand across his mouth. "Five graves. Makes me sick. Think it was those Apaches that done this?"

"Most likely."

Sunny surveyed the charred ranch yard. His ear strained for any sound, any indication of people nearby, but he heard only his footsteps on the sand. Clay picked up the crude cross.

"Do Apaches bury people they've murdered?"

"Not that I've heard."

"Then who the hell buried them?"

Sunny tried to visualize someone besides Indians burying these victims. "Suppose Trace, James—?"

"We're miles off the main road. Why in the world would they be here? No reason to bring that stagecoach clear out this far." Clay shook his head. "No, it'd have to be somebody with a horse or mule. Prospector, maybe."

He ambled through more blackened ranch. Sunny shrugged at

his friend's back and wandered in the opposite direction. Several minutes of searching brought no new information. Who were these ranchers, these people who'd lost their lives defending a dry piece of dirt?

"Sunny, over here."

Sunny jogged over to Clay, who was squatting next to the remnants of a dead campfire. Clay held an empty can close to his nose. "Green beans," he said.

"I don't like green beans."

"Notice anything strange 'bout this can?"

Sunny shook his head.

"It ain't burned. Someone left this after the Apache came through. Probably the same person who buried the ranchers."

"Can't be the Colton boys. They didn't have supplies. Leastways, not any food." A strange empty feeling stuck in Sunny's chest. "Damn."

Clay dropped the can back into the ashes. "What?"

"They couldn't have survived, could they?" Sunny asked. "They were sittin' ducks. No food, no protection 'cept their guns. No one could've helped them." He lowered his head, balled his fists, then studied the sky. "They're dead, ain't they?"

Clay stood and stared into the desert. His voice turned soft. "Probably."

"Damn, Clay."

"Yeah."

# CHAPTER TWENTY-TWO

Giggles and voices startled James awake. Blurry images. Two young Indian girls. Indians, not Trace. Where was he? A wider sweep of the area revealed no brother. Was he all right? Or was he dying—or dead—at the Indians' hands? James fought down panic.

The girls squatted next to him. One held a dipper of water and a rag, the other a bowl of food. The aroma—rabbit stew? Venison? His mouth watered and his stomach rumbled.

One of the girls, a pretty black-eyed youngster with long, raven hair, held the wet rag to his skin. The coolness eased his throbbing cheek. When she dabbed at his face, the rag came away bloody.

The other girl, a year or so older, knelt by James and spooned stew into his mouth. After three spoonfuls, she stood and turned to the growing crowd of children. A grin filled her face and her eyes shone while she held up the wooden spoon. Then with great flourish, she knelt back down.

The meat in the stew was the best he'd tasted in weeks. It filled his stomach and soothed his nerves. James' world wasn't so bleak any more.

The smaller girl pressed the gourd dipper to his mouth, allowing him one more sip. Water dripped down his chin, but most found its way down his throat. She stood and backed away, staring at him like a hard-won prize, a trophy. Twenty or more children, all ages and heights, circled around. They stared. Silent.

James stared back and wondered what the children were thinking. Would they help keep him alive, or torture him and his brother? He'd heard stories. Frightening stories. His thoughts turned over what One Wing had said. How were the Indians going to use him to get whatever it was they wanted?

There was a flurry of excitement, loud Indian chanting, and then Trace's voice rose above the noise. He stumbled into view, with One Wing close behind him. Trace's hands were tied, and he too was missing a chunk of hair. James didn't hide the grin traveling up one side of his swollen cheek. Trace was still alive.

One Wing pushed Trace hard. He plunged to his knees, hit the ground, then twisted onto his back in front of James. His chest heaved.

"We didn't do anything," Trace said. "Don't want your land. Leave us alone. Let us—"

A swift kick to his head sent him rolling, and James couldn't control his outrage.

"How are we supposed to serve you?" he demanded. "By keeping us tied for days, watching us slowly die? How's that supposed to help you? How's that gonna help your tribe?"

He knew not to anger these Indians, but he couldn't help it. One Wing marched over to James and knelt. Then he grabbed the front of his shirt and pulled. The rope strained. One Wing slammed James back against the cactus. He yanked James forward and slammed him back again. Twice more.

Thundering sharp pain. Black dots. James shook his head.

"Do not speak to me with anger!" One Wing said. His words hissed. "You will respect your captors."

He jabbed James' stomach, then punched his sore cheek.

James tried to catch his breath. He knew he should stop, but words tumbled out anyway.

"Go ahead and kill us. We'll never help people like you. People who kill innocent women and children. Who have no regard for—"

One Wing kicked James in the stomach, then yanked James' head back and held his knife to James' throat. "I will break you, James Colton. Break your spirit like the wild horses we capture. I will enjoy your agony. Use you. Then kill you."

James knew he had just sealed his fate and probably his brother's too. His breaths erupted in short bursts as the metal edge sliced across his throat.

One Wing's grip on his hair, his head pulled back, made swallowing impossible. Warm liquid dripped down his neck. Was that Trace nearby?

"...he's young, speaks too quickly, One Wing. Don't take his life, spare him, please. Kill me if you must, but let him live." Trace lowered his voice. "We will do what you ask."

One Wing yanked once more, then withdrew the knife and

released James. He wiped the knife on his breeches.

Silence.

He turned to Trace, hoisted him to his feet, then slammed him back against the saguaro. After he'd tied Trace's arms, he stood back to regard the brothers.

"Cochise should be pleased," he said. One Wing slipped the knife back into its scabbard, wheeled around, and strode away.

James bit his lower lip.

*Almost got us killed! Just keep your mouth shut. Do whatever it takes to stay alive.*

James couldn't find the words to apologize to Trace. "Sorry" didn't seem suitable, and "thanks for saving my life" wasn't enough.

Trace leaned against the cactus and jerked with each breath he took. He rolled his head toward James. "Glad he didn't press that knife any harder. Are you all—"

A shadow fell over them.

"I am Cochise."

Cochise squatted next to the brothers and pointed at their faces. "I see fear, terror. I also see an enemy who is defeated. An enemy who has to run to save his life, an enemy too weak to stand up for his people."

"We're not your enemy, Cochise." Trace shook his head. "My brother and I...we drive for Butterfield stage. Remember you had an agreement with the company? You'd let us bring our stagecoaches through your land and we'd bring supplies for you. For your women and children."

"I remember." Cochise looked over and regarded James. "I also remember the White man's promise my people would not be harmed."

One Wing squatted next to Cochise, a respectful distance between them.

"My brother," Cochise continued, "my brother's wife, and son, along with three other Apaches have been taken prisoner by the White Man's army."

Trace shook his head. "I'm sorry, Cochise." He glanced from face to face. "You're planning to trade us for your brother?"

"When it is time." Cochise stood and stared down at Trace, then shifted his gaze to James.

Chilling sweat drenched James' face, and his throat burned.

103

The Indians, his brother, the wickiups, in fact the entire village, danced in front of his eyes. His breaths grew shallow.

Trace strained against his ropes. "James? Stay with me now. We'll be all right. You'll see."

James coughed. Panic rattled in his chest.

"Cochise, my brother is not well," Trace said. "He needs water, maybe medicine. Please help him. I'll do whatever you ask. Anything to keep my little brother alive."

"You will do what I ask, even if I do not help your brother."

"Please."

Cochise took a long time answering.

"I need one of you alive." He swung his gaze from brother to brother. "Young James lives one more day."

# CHAPTER TWENTY-THREE

Shortly before sunset, fifty-four cavalry troopers leading six Apaches paraded into Mesilla's plaza. Sheriff Fuente met them at the old cottonwood tree growing next to the *acequia madre*, the main ditch running behind the Mercantile. He greeted the lieutenant with a handshake and surveyed the bedraggled men. Several sported bandages tinged with blood; most looked as if they'd fought the entire Apache nation.

"Commander," Fuente nodded. "Welcome to Mesilla, New Mexico Territory. If there's anything—"

"Yes, there is something I need." Bascom glanced behind Fuente toward the jail. "Some place secure for these six prisoners. Some place safe. Guess your jail will have to do."

Before Fuente could offer or refuse, Bascom ordered the six Apaches, shackled together, to be marched across the plaza to the jail. Fuente ran to keep up with the soldiers escorting the prisoners.

Once the Indians were locked in adjoining cells, Bascom posted two guards inside the jail and two outside. Fuente and Bascom stood in the middle of the office.

"The Army appreciates your cooperation, Sheriff. We'll be gone soon. In the meantime, I insist that no one comes in here. Not even you." Bascom dismissed him with a salute and turned toward the sheriff's desk.

"Excuse me, Lieutenant. This is my desk, and I'll need to stay here to conduct my business." Fuente placed a hand on Bascom's shoulder.

"Remove your hand, sir." Bascom's eyes flared. "No one touches me."

"I can see that," Fuente mumbled as he stepped back. "But, that's still my desk and this is still my office. I'll be glad to move a few papers so you'll have a place to put yours. I'll even give you that chair, but I *will* have my office."

"Perhaps we got off on the wrong foot, sir," Bascom said. "I apologize, but I get a bit single-minded when it comes to Apaches."

"Apology accepted, Lieutenant."

A solid knock at the door caught the men's attention. Bascom jerked the door open. "What's the problem, Private?"

Lila pushed her way through the door, arm grasped by a soldier. Her cascading hair, usually held back by a ribbon, fell over one eye. She brushed it away. "I just wanted a chance to talk to the Indian prisoners, sir. I'm not gonna help them escape or anything of such a nature."

Fuente took Lila by the arm, escorted her into the room, and closed the door behind her.

*She's even prettier when flustered.*

After brief introductions, Bascom shook his head. "Miss Simmons, I'm afraid you're going to have to leave this office until after we're gone in a few days."

Bascom opened the door. Lila pushed it shut with her foot.

"Lieutenant, I'd like a chance to talk to those Indians. I want to see if they know somethin' about my fiancé, James Colton."

"Small world, Miss Simmons," Bascom said. "Mister Arrington and Mister Williamston made the same request."

"I heard about what you did to Sunny," Lila said. "How can you—"

"I'll tell you exactly what I told those boys. These Indians don't speak English, and even if they did, you can't believe what they say. They'll lie, say anything just to keep from hanging."

Hanging? Fuente regarded the lieutenant. Not only was this man hard, he was deadly.

"Mister Bascom?" Lila's hand caressed her neck. "You're gonna hang those men just for bein' Indians?"

"No. I'm going to hang them for being lying, kidnapping Indians. Little Felix Ward isn't in his home any more because of them. He's somewhere in the desert, his pa worried sick."

Lila regarded Fuente, then eyed Bascom. "Can I at least try?"

"I'm sorry, Miss Simmons. No." Bascom opened the door again. "You'll have to leave now."

Fuente held Lila's elbow and nudged her toward the outside. "I'll see what I can find out," he said. "In the meantime, just keep on hoping and praying." He nodded a goodbye.

Fuente turned back to Bascom as he shut the door. "You'll be here longer than overnight, Lieutenant? I thought you were in a hurry to get down to Fort Bliss."

"Hurry? Yes, I'm in a hurry. I want to see those savages hanged, pay for what they did." Bascom's fists balled. "They don't deserve to live any longer than absolutely necessary."

"So you're already judge and jury? What happened to a fair trial?"

A snort from Bascom. "Oh, it'll be fair. Then they'll hang."

"Listen, Lieutenant, before you hang those Indians, I need information about those stage drivers." Fuente jerked his pointed finger toward the cells. "They know. I'm sure of it."

"And I'm sure of this." Bascom pointed over his shoulder. "Get in my way and I'll toss you in there with those savages."

"Get in *your* way?" Fuente slapped his hand on his desk. "This is my desk. My office. My jail. Stay out of *my* way!" He moved closer to Bascom. "And since this is *my* jail, I'll interrogate those prisoners. Miss Simmons and I have a right to know."

"You have no rights, Fuente." Bascom's glare locked on Fuente's eyes. "If I find any of you people snooping around, you won't get a trial—fair or otherwise. Is that clear?"

Fuente clenched his fists. "What makes you such a sonuvabitch?"

# CHAPTER TWENTY-FOUR

James tugged the leather straps securing his hands to a pole. Tight, as usual. The rawhide bindings around both wrists allowed him to roll onto his side or, if he maneuvered right, onto his back. It wasn't comfortable, but at least he could move. Unlike the first few days.

Those days, possibly as many as five or six, blurred. Details evaded recollection. He and Trace had spent hours tied hand and foot like captured wild animals, allowed freedom only to relieve themselves—twice a day. They were fed by the children, then kicked and tormented by everyone else.

After James took sick, he remembered women soothing his cuts and welts with some sort of sage-smelling paste. Those memories pushed aside his images of terror. The quiet chatter over his head had brought the first grin to his face. Their touch was gentle, more so than he'd expected. One woman, in particular, took extra time helping him. She was younger than the rest, which surprised him.

At some point, they'd cut off his boots and replaced them with new moccasins, those *teguas*. He liked the way they rose almost to his knee, and the soft, supple leather protected his legs from brushy thorns. His feet didn't bleed any more like they had when his boot soles had worn through.

More images took form. He and his brother working. Toting stacks of dried deer hides, carting buckets of water for the women, carrying bundles of firewood—all under the vigilant eyes of several Apache guards. He couldn't even breathe without his guard readying his hunting knife. James knew that one wrong move would send that knife into his chest quicker than a heartbeat. And maybe they'd kill Trace, too.

A rock poked his shoulder, but he scooted around until it no longer dug into his sore muscles. From this position on his back, he stared up at the night sky. Stars were out in full force tonight.

Sky clear and cold. The camp was quiet except for an occasional coyote song or the scurry of some creature.

A light breeze stirred the branches of the trees in this little valley. The tribe had already moved at least twice since he and Trace had joined them. The chill gave James goosebumps that rose higher when he recalled the look in One Wing's eyes whenever he tortured James.

*Only need one brother alive.*

Cochise's words rang in his ears. James vowed it would be Trace who survived. Even after a few days, it'd become clear that One Wing would torment James until he died. There was no doubt. James tugged again. The bindings still held firm.

He peered through the darkness at his brother on his right. "Gotta talk to you, Trace. You awake?"

"Shhh." Trace twisted against the rawhide straps. "Those Indians hear real good. You all right?"

"Just cold." James rolled onto his side. "I've been thinking."

"Shh. Go to sleep. You'll warm up."

James slid up closer to the post that tethered his hands, easing the pressure on his wrists. They had bled so many times that he knew he'd have thick rope scars for the rest of his life—however long that may be.

"Can't live like this," James said. "Never been so scared in my whole life. Every time I breathe, One Wing's hurting me again." He swallowed hard. "He's gonna kill me, one way or the other."

"No, he's not. Once Cochise's brother is returned, they'll let us go."

"No, they won't."

"Shh. They will."

There was something wrong in Trace's voice. James knew his brother didn't believe any of it. Trace was just trying to be brave for both of them. The plan James had been formulating for days would save Trace. A deep breath and James explained.

"Way I figure it, they don't need two of us. With me gone, they'll *have* to keep you alive to trade for Cochise's brother."

"Gone? What're you talking about?"

James closed his eyes and whispered. "I'm gonna escape, bring back help."

"Good Lord Almighty, James. That's plain crazy—suicide. I won't let you do it."

"Got no choice. I'm a dead man. One Wing's not gonna rest 'til he kills me. You and I both know that."

James twisted his wrists harder than before, the thong reopening cuts and deep gashes. He winced at the stinging, then he swore he'd escape and save his brother. At the very least he wouldn't be taken alive. "Might as well die tryin' to get us outta here."

Trace fidgeted with his bindings, too. "You can't."

"Look at this from One Wing's thinking," James said. "He wants to be a big man, an important man, and what better way than to torture me a long time? He'll prove his strength and I'll just keep dying by inches. So, the longer I live, the longer he's gonna keep it up."

A quick look left and right, then Trace eased closer to his brother until his binding strained at the pole.

"Think, James," he whispered. "Think before you do this. You won't win. They'll kill you. At least staying put, doing what they want, you have a chance."

"Staying here, I'm a dead man. One Wing's almost killed me a couple times already. If they capture me, maybe it'll be quick." James took a deep breath. "Made up my mind."

"We don't have to keep either of you alive, James Colton."

James flinched. One Wing.

"You want to escape?" One Wing knelt between the brothers, but he stared at James. "All right. When the sun stands high I will give you the chance. See how fast you run."

\* \* \*

By the time the sun threw no shadows, James and Trace had carted more firewood, skinned two rabbits and endured more angry fists and knife jabs. Had One Wing been a dream last night? James fought to remember if it'd been real. Trace hadn't said anything, but he was keeping a close watch on him. And One Wing strutted across camp like he always did. A dream? No. James still was planning to escape.

James knelt on the ground trying to pull rabbit fur from its meat. A hand clutched his shoulder. James recognized One Wing's grip, its claws more like eagle talons than fingers. They dug into his muscles.

James froze.

"It's time," One Wing said.

*Definitely not a dream.*

James dropped his rabbit as his captor yanked him to his feet, then pulled him toward a meadow near camp. More than twenty Chiricahua warriors stood there in two columns, facing each other, each wielding a stick, knife, or clenched fist.

One Wing stopped James near the opening of the gantlet.

"If you make it to the other end on your feet, you may walk away from camp a free man."

"My brother free, too?"

One Wing shook his head.

James licked his chapped lips. One warrior at the head of the line produced a leather thong spiked with metal studs, and he smiled with cruel anticipation. James eyed two youngsters near the middle. One twisted his mouth into a snarl and ran his hand down a knife blade. The other's eyes grew wide with excitement as he gripped a thin cane.

A shudder. James questioned his chances. Would he even make it to the other end alive?

As he stood at the mouth of the human tunnel, close enough to touch the nearest Indian, James hesitated, heart thundering in his chest. Apache commands and an English oath jerked James' attention to his right. The towering Apache guard shoved Trace, who crashed into the dirt and rolled into a mesquite bush. James caught the panicked look as his brother found his knees. Their brown eyes met.

"Don't do it, James. You don't have to."

James jumped at the knifepoint jammed in his back and the voice hissing in his ear.

"Wrong. You *will* do this."

Over gulps of air, James brought his tied hands up in front of his face. They trembled just as hard as his entire body.

"Now." One Wing prodded James with his knife.

*I have nothing to lose.*

Courage gathered, James tucked his chin into his chest and sprinted between the first pair of Apaches.

A fist to his shoulder knocked him left. Another fist plowed into his ribs. He shielded his face with his hands and pulled past two more warriors. Apache taunts. Jeers. The voices melted into a cacophony of chaos.

The spiked leather thong raked his arm and back. James picked up speed. Fists pounded his body, knives sliced at his arms and back. Something speared his legs.

A stick whacked his right leg, the impact sending him to his knees. Images grew, then shrunk. Faces blurred. James had to get up or be beaten to death.

He struggled to his feet, but blows, swift and severe, slowed him. His back and ribs burned. Sticks whipped the back of his legs. James used all his energy to plant one foot in front of the other.

A fist in his ribs shot pain through his entire body. He collapsed. Could he just lie here and die? Yells, shouts, Apache curses. More knives, fists.

*Have to survive. Marry Lila.*

James brought his knees under him and rolled over. He pushed up, then crawled forward. Where was the opening? He turned right then left. A circle of light caught his eye—the good eye—the only one not swollen shut. He turned around and willed hands and knees to move forward.

"Wrong way, brother! You're going the wrong way!"

James nodded. Using strength dredged up from instinctive survival, he struggled to his feet, turned around, and then plowed ahead. A few more yards to freedom.

A rib-shattering kidney punch brought tears to his eyes and sent him to the ground again. Moccasined feet slammed into his ribs and back. Arms outstretched, his fingers dug into the sand. He clawed inches forward. A couple feet more.

A knife sliced his upper arm. James screamed at the agony, the fiery gash deep in his flesh. He curled into a ball on the rocky sand and prayed the warriors would let him go. Then he realized the foolishness of that prayer.

James rolled onto his knees and willed one to move in front of the other. A few more inches and he'd make it. Freedom screamed. The light beckoned.

A deerskin boot to his head took him down—down to a dark place without pain or fear.

# CHAPTER TWENTY-FIVE

Lila pulled a new boot off the shelf and stared at it. James had said he needed to buy a new pair next time he was in town. These were his size. Maybe she'd buy them and keep them until he got home. She shook her head. Here she was again overwhelmed with thoughts of her man. Now that information might be close, she often found herself standing in the middle of the store, just staring into space. More than once customers nudged her out of the way.

Mid-afternoon, three cavalry soldiers entered the store. They were still a little dusty from their long ride, but they had managed to shave and wash their faces. Months of tracking and fighting Indians etched their scrubbed cheeks. They spent several minutes looking at the goods, picking up items then putting them down.

"What can I help you with, gentlemen?" Lila asked.

The tallest of the three privates, with a thin mustache setting off his hazel eyes, smiled at Lila. "We're enjoyin' being in civilization again, ma'am. Hope you don't mind us just lookin'."

Lila flashed a half smile. "Course not. Take your time. If you need me, I'll be around."

They picked up axes and boots, examined food and ranching supplies. The latest rifle produced an extended and elaborate discussion.

Arms full of new blankets, Lila walked past the men. Key words caught her attention. She stopped.

"Woulda liked this rifle on that lonely road out from Tucson. Nothing on it but coyotes and that old stagecoach." The private replaced the new rifle.

Lila caught her breath. Had she heard right? She stepped closer to the soldiers. "Excuse me, gentlemen. Did I hear you say somethin' about a stagecoach near Tucson?"

"Yes ma'am." The one who'd been speaking touched the brim

of his hat. "I'm Private Jamison, ma'am. Jack Jamison."

He wasn't much taller than Lila, but certainly had a good forty pounds on her. A full mustache edged around his cheeks and met long sideburns. The dark brown hair framed his wide face.

"Tell me about it, please," Lila said. "You see, I've lost someone out in that desert. He drives a stage. I'm wonderin' if it's his."

The third soldier cocked his head to one side. His tanned face accentuated kindness in his brown eyes. "Wish we could tell you something you want to hear, ma'am. The stage was several miles east of Tucson. Nobody around it." He shrugged. "It did have the name 'Butterfield' on the side, though. Does that help?"

He looked at the other men for confirmation.

Tears pushed against Lila's eyes. What she'd feared all along was presented to her right here, right in her face. Words tumbled out.

"Did you find any...people?"

The three soldiers looked at each other. One removed his hat, scratched his head. Jamison ran his hand across his mouth. The tallest spoke again.

"I'm Private Bill Patton, ma'am." His eyes flitted around the store, then rested on hers. "Yes, ma'am, we did find a...body. Only one, though. But a ways down the road. Had been a nice looking, older fellow. Dressed in a black suit, red tie. Buried him near there."

Lila knew she had to find out, even if the answer wasn't what she'd been praying for. "You didn't see anyone who looked like the driver or shotgun guard?"

"No, ma'am. No one of that description," Jamison said. "This fella looked like he was a passenger, being how nicely dressed he was and all."

More words refused to form for Lila. Images, questions, pain. They collided in her head. The inside of the store spun. She swayed and dropped the blankets she carried. Jamison steadied her, his arms strong, comforting around her. He set her on the pile of blankets, then knelt beside her.

"We're sorry, ma'am. Didn't mean to upset you," he said.

Hazel-eyed Bill Patton touched her arm and turned to his friend. "Best get the doctor, Rivers. She's lookin' right peaked."

Lila held up a hand. "No. Wait. Just a few more questions. Please."

The men glanced at each other, then Bill Patton knelt next to her, across from Jamison.

"Just a couple. Looks like you need some rest."

"What else did you find? That can't be everything." Lila's shaking hands clutched her throat.

Private Rivers continued the story. "Like Bill here said, that's really about all we found. A few miles from the body, we saw where the stagecoach had been attacked, ma'am. Plenty of signs in the sand where people had been, but no more bodies."

Bill glanced up at his friend. "Lots of dried blood on the stagecoach seat."

Adding onto the story, Jamison spoke. "We wanted to go into the desert and look for more bodies—maybe even survivors. A few of us saw tracks, but Lieutenant Bascom wouldn't hear of it. Said they weren't important enough."

Tears streamed down Lila's cheeks. Her trembling hands covered her face. "James. It was James and Trace out there."

More sobs.

"Excuse us, gentlemen."

Lila blinked through tears at Mrs. Grey, the Mercantile's owner. Her hair, always pulled back in a bun, tightened the skin over her sunken cheeks. Thin lips did nothing to add a hint of beauty to his woman.

"This has been a terrible few weeks for her, but now she knows what the rest of us knew all along." Mrs. Grey helped Lila to her feet.

"Teresa should know, Missus Grey. 'Bout Trace." Lila swiped at the tears cascading down her burning cheeks.

"She'll be back from Santa Fe in a few months. You should've gone with her." Mrs. Grey regarded the men. "Tried to get her to go. But, no, she had to stay and wait for somebody who wasn't coming back." The woman guided Lila away. "Let's get you some tea."

\* \* \*

The three soldiers stood on the plankboard sidewalk in front of the Mercantile and gazed across the plaza at the jail. Private Bill Patton pointed at the two guards standing in front, rifles ready to shoot any intruder.

"Suppose those Indians *do* know something about that lady's friends?" Bill asked.

"They might," Rivers said. "But, Bill, how're we gonna find out? Bascom won't let any of us get near."

Jamison pointed his chin toward the jail. "Besides, it sounds awful risky. You know Bascom'll have you swinging with those Indians if he catches you."

"Don't worry. I'll be careful. Don't plan to be swingin' from anything but a señorita's bed." Bill looked back at the Mercantile and wagged his head. "Just can't get that woman's face out of my mind. I sure feel bad for her."

Private Rivers hitched up his trousers and tucked in his shirt. "Right now I'm feelin' kinda sorry for me. My stomach's rumbling. Like I haven't eaten in a year."

"Hell, you're always hungry." Jamison elbowed him.

Rivers ambled down the boardwalk. "I hear there's a good restaurant down this way. How 'bout if I buy supper? Maybe food will help you think straight, Bill."

* * *

A full stomach combined with a long stroll around the plaza cemented Bill's idea. After leaving the company of Jamison and Rivers, he reported for duty as outside night guard of the Apache prisoners. Bill, a little older, a little more experienced, convinced the young soldier who was assigned to inside guard duty that *outside* duty was much better than watching savages sleep all night.

"And," Bill elbowed the private, "I hear the saloons shut down 'round midnight. All the bar girls come paradin' out shortly afterwards. Come right down through the plaza here." He winked. "You might even get lucky."

The private shifted his rifle to the other shoulder. "Suits me fine. Rather take my chances with pretty girls than ugly Indians."

It had been so easy that Bill almost laughed. He didn't laugh, however, at the thought of what Lieutenant Bascom would do if he found out why Bill and the other guard really traded duty stations. Bill watched the youngster close the door.

As he stood in front of the jail cells, each containing three

Apaches, Bill thought about what to say and how to say it. Did they speak English? Bascom had insisted they didn't. Would they even be willing to talk? On the other hand, what did they have to lose?

He gathered his courage and stood in front of one cell. A wide-shouldered Indian stared back; the other two appeared to be asleep. Bill noted the Apache's shoulder-length, raven-black hair and black eyes, his smooth tanned skin. Muscles in those shoulders danced with every movement.

"You speak English?" Bill asked.

The Apache nodded.

"Good. I have a few questions for you. But, I'll have to be quick."

The Apache perched on his cot like a mountain lion selecting an antelope to take down.

"My name's Bill...Bill Patton." He glanced side to side, hoping, praying no one would come in right now. "Know anything about two men who were driving that stagecoach outside of Tucson?"

He waited for acknowledgment of his question, confirmation of what he thought he already knew. A blank stare.

"The one that was attacked, with the passenger killed?" Bill continued. "I met a young lady. Her husband-to-be was the stage driver. She's worried sick about him. Can you help?"

The Indian rose from his bunk. His black eyes fixed on Bill.

"Speak," he said.

Bill's stomach twisted like it was on fire. "Do you know what happened to the driver and shotgun guard on that stage? Were they killed? What happened to the bodies?"

"Before I answer your questions, we make bargain." The Indian's rich baritone voice, honey-smooth in tone, resonated against the stone walls.

"What kind of bargain?"

"I am Coyuntura, brother of Cochise. My son," he pointed to the adjoining cell, "is Lone Fox."

Bill froze. Good God! The brother of the ruthless, feared Cochise. And Cochise's nephew. No doubt everyone's lives were in jeopardy. It was surprising there had been only one attempt so far to free these captives. Bill was sure there would be more.

"Does Cochise know you're being held?" His words spurted between breaths.

117

"Yes."

"Jesus." Bill stepped back until he ran into the wall. "Does Lieutenant Bascom know who you are?"

"Yes."

"Jesus."

Bill took several deep breaths before continuing with his questions. "What kind of bargain do you have in mind?"

"Freedom. You free us and I tell you about the two men."

Bill paused.

How much trouble did he want to cause? He remembered Lila's grief-stricken face, those beautiful blue eyes brimming with tears. What good would it do now just to find out where her man died? Was it worth his court martial?

Coyuntura steadied his gaze and leaned closer to Bill. "I know about men, but you must release us. All of us."

"I can't."

"My brother's son sent word of a stagecoach attack. It is most likely the one you question." Coyuntura's eyes traveled up and down Bill.

"Sent word? How'd you find out? Weren't you already captured?"

A nod. "Do you think all we do is sleep at night? White Eye soldiers sleep. We do not." Coyuntura glanced at the other Indians. "We use the dark."

While Bill mulled over the new information, Coyuntura remained motionless, studying him.

At long last, Bill shook his head. "I just can't. You're prisoners. Cochise's family. I'll be hanged with you if I do. Sorry, I can't."

"Too bad. She should know what happened to her man."

Coyuntura turned his back on Bill and lay down.

# CHAPTER TWENTY-SIX

James gripped the rock he used for skinning the deer a little tighter each time One Wing strutted across the camp. The carriage of that Apache's body, those shoulders pulled back farther than usual, the tilt of the head, the longer strides today, perplexed James. What was he up to? Whatever it was, James was sure he wouldn't like it. Wasn't sure he could even survive it.

Today had been the first day since running the gantlet that he'd been able to stand without Trace or an Apache guard helping. Trace told him that after he passed out at the end of that ordeal, several Apaches had wanted to kill him right then. The beating continued for a while before Cochise stepped in—stopped with just a wave of his hand. Trace figured James owed Cochise his life.

The eye swollen from the attack had shrunk, and James could see most things again. Several of the welts and cuts were healing too, thanks again to the women who were allowed to spread that agave poultice on him. His cracked ribs still ached, but his head wound from the stage attack had healed.

A sharp whack on his back accompanied by an Apache growl prodded him to continue scrapping the hide. He didn't mind this work. He could sit and think. Think how he and Trace would escape. He'd get back to Mesilla, some how, some day, and marry Lila. He set his jaw.

He kept half of his attention on the deer hide and the other half on the Indians. They had a habit of sneaking up and attacking when he least expected it. Now he was on guard all the time. They beat Trace, too, but James knew he was their main target.

The rock slipped from his hand—grease from the fat deer made holding it difficult. He reached over to pick it up and reeled from One Wing's backhand. James somersaulted then sprawled on the sand. Another sucker punch. The Apache war leader kicked him onto his back and knelt on him, knee pressed into James' chest.

One Wing's cruel lips snarled. "You do not work fast enough, James Colton. I should kill you right now." His words hissed like cold water on hot rocks. He slid the knee off James' chest, then sat on James like he was riding a horse.

James took the full weight of the Indian. Breaths came in rasping bursts. "It slipped."

Another backhand. This time stronger. James' cheek burned like a thousand fires.

"Do not speak to me, old woman." One Wing grabbed James' face and puckered his cheeks together. "When I want you to speak, I will tell you." He squeezed harder. "Understand?"

Tears blurred the Apache's image. James couldn't nod, couldn't speak. He blinked. Something wet ran into his ear.

One Wing released his grip and leaned back, his weight pressing James' hips into small rocks. James stared into the Apache's face and noticed something in the long black hair cascading around his shoulders. Something other than the eagle feather he kept entwined in a hank of hair braided along the right side of his head.

The object flashed gold against the sunlight. The Apache swung his head, and James recognized it. Lila's wedding ring.

James twisted under One Wing's weight.

*Lila's ring. Attached to an Indian's hair.*

He envisioned reaching up and yanking One Wing's hair out of his head. Globs of black hair would dangle from his fists as One Wing cried in pain. Then James would caress Lila's ring, place it next to his heart. He'd keep it safe until he could slip it on her pretty finger.

James knew not to speak, but his mouth wouldn't obey. "Give it back."

One Wing snorted and raised a fist.

"Mine." James spoke through clenched teeth, but winced at what he knew would happen.

"You were not strong enough to keep it, James Colton. It is mine now." One Wing made a show of opening his fist, then stroking his hair. He fingered the wedding ring. "Shines."

"Give it back." James fidgeted.

A sneer snaked farther up One Wing's face and his black eyes glowed. James wished he could take back his demand. His face still stung, but not as much as his heart hurt right now.

*No matter what One Wing does to me, I'll get that ring back.*

One Wing raised his body off of James and stood. He yanked James to his feet.

"I keep this," One Wing said. "Maybe I go take the woman, too."

* * *

Second Lieutenant George Bascom called his company to attention as the sun peeked over the majestic Organ Mountains. Shades of crimson, gold, and purple bathed Mesilla's plaza, reflecting off the white plaster of the Corn Exchange Hotel. Bascom's men—all trained, veteran soldiers—waited by their mounts, ready to continue their trek into the state of Texas, onto the post of Fort Bliss.

"Corporal," Bascom barked over his shoulder. "Mount up."

Fuente stood near the corporal and surveyed the group of men under Bascom's command. The men were saddle-weary, despite a day or two of recuperation, and they were still recovering from the Apache attack a few miles south of Steins. They were ready to reach Fort Bliss and enjoy several days of rest. Three months in the Apache-held Sonoran Desert was too long for any of them. Bascom especially, Fuente decided, could use a rest.

"Company," Connor said. "Mount up."

Sheriff Fuente moved closer to Bascom, who stood clutching his horse's reins. He noticed Bascom's white knuckles, the tight lips and tense body of a man too tired, too high-strung to lead exhausted men on a sixty-mile journey. But, Fuente knew Bascom would do it. He'd push his men until they were all killed by Apaches or dropped dead of fatigue.

Fuente shook hands with the lieutenant. "It's been interesting having you here, Bascom. Can't say it's been pleasant, but it's sure been interesting."

Bascom's attention was not on Fuente. "Yeah."

Fuente eyed the man. What was on his mind? Those Apache prisoners? His men too injured to continue with the company? Well, whatever it was, it wasn't his concern. He was glad, more than glad—relieved—to see Bascom and his troops leave. He ran his hand over his mouth to hide his growing smile.

Before Bascom could step into his stirrups, a soldier galloped into the plaza and reined up in front of the company. He swung

121

out of the saddle while his horse was still in motion. The soldier saluted Bascom and stood at attention.

"Lieutenant Bascom?"

"Private?" Bascom returned the salute.

"Lieutenant, I have an urgent message for you from Captain Griggs at Fort Bliss." The soldier fished in his uniform jacket and extracted a folded letter. "I've spent days tracking you, sir. Glad you've made it this far. Would hate to have to go into Apache country to find you."

The soldier babbled on about Indians, coyotes, and sleep deprivation when his gaze fell on the six Apache captives. He froze.

Fuente chuckled at the soldier's obvious breech of etiquette and the panic on his face. While Bascom read the note, the sheriff stepped over to the young man.

"Where're you from, soldier?" Fuente hoped his question would bring the young man back to reality.

"Fort Bliss, sir." He shook his head, turned, and caught Fuente's stare. "Them Apache?" he whispered.

"Sure are. Captured by Bascom and his men near Tucson." Fuente studied the contempt on the female captive's face.

The soldier leaned closer to Fuente. "Fearsome mean lookin', ain't they?"

Fuente gazed at the faces of the six prisoners. He saw people yanked out of their homeland, destined to stand trial with a partial jury, then carted off to certain death.

"Corporal." Bascom waved two fingers at his second-in-command.

Connor slid from his horse and rushed over. "Sir?"

"Corporal, we have a situation."

"Sir?"

"It appears that the entire company at Fort Bliss has been called east to assist with some damn skirmish between a couple of states. Only a skeleton crew's still there. We're to bivouac here until further orders."

Bascom motioned to Fuente. "A moment of your time, sir."

*Now what the hell? Can't he just leave?*

Fuente ambled over.

"There's been a change of plans, Sheriff. It seems Fort Bliss' entire company has been sent east. We'll be staying here for a while."

Fuente rubbed his stubbled face. "There's gonna be some mighty happy folks and some mighty unhappy to hear that, Bascom. I'll be truthful and tell you I fit in that second category."

"Whatever your personal opinion, Sheriff Fuente, I'm confident you'll give us your total professional cooperation." Bascom spoke to Connor. "Have the men dismount."

As the soldiers climbed off their horses, Fuente and Bascom discussed the best place to set up camp. The sheriff recommended an area on the northern outskirts of town that lay adjacent to the Rio Grande. Plenty of water and feed for the horses.

Bascom pursed his lips, then nodded. "All right, Fuente." He turned his back to the sheriff, stopped, and spun back. "Thank you."

Fuente raised one eyebrow.

"Corporal," Bascom said, "take the prisoners back to the jail, post extra guards inside and out." He held out a hand, palm up. "If that's all right with you, Sheriff."

Fuente produced the keys and led the prisoner procession across the plaza.

# CHAPTER TWENTY-SEVEN

A firm hand clamped over Sunny's mouth, jerking him awake. He clawed at the strong grip, then recognized the worried face inches from his. He relaxed and searched Clay's wide eyes. A quick nod and Sunny breathed out as the hand left his face.

Clay pointed toward a stand of alligator junipers twenty yards to his right, the sun not quite high enough to give the bushes their normal color. Sunny eased onto his side, the wool blanket bunching in front of him, then grasped the cold metal of his Hawken rifle. He pushed his body to his knees.

Shoulder to shoulder, the two men peered into the cool desert morning—searching, searching. Sunny waited for a glimpse or noise from whatever had startled his friend.

Clay rose to a half crouch and cocked his head toward the juniper. He held up two fingers. Sunny peered into the bushes. Brush rustled and feet scraped against the sand behind him. Sunny turned just in time to catch an Apache hurtling toward him.

The hard-muscled body caught Sunny square in the back. Finger still on the rifle's trigger, he reflexively pulled. *Bang!* The shot echoed off nearby boulders.

Sunny and the Apache flew face forward, hitting the ground and rolling. Even as he rolled, Sunny cursed the rifle's firing and prayed the bullet hadn't hit Clay. The Apache and Sunny scrambled to their feet.

Sunny locked his stare on the Indian, but his concern was with his partner. "Clay?" He didn't dare take his eyes off this attacker.

"Here. All right?" Clay's words were strong.

"Yeah," Sunny said. With both of them still on their feet, each with an Indian, maybe this attack would be over soon.

Then the Apache pounced on Sunny, and locked in an embrace,

the men somersaulted across the sand. The Indian raised up to a crouch, knife poised overhead. He slashed the weapon toward Sunny. The blade swung closer and closer.

Sunny scrambled backwards, like a crab, then twisted up to his feet. The Apache lunged. Sunny took the impact of the muscled Indian square in his chest. Grunts and hot breath in his ear. The blade swished past Sunny's eye. He grabbed the hand gripping the knife and held on.

Grunts, breaths, and oaths from Clay reminded Sunny that his partner was not too far away. Still alive. Still fighting his own fight.

The men spun and twirled as if in dance. Chest against chest. Both of equal strength. The Apache lowered one shoulder, and Sunny's hold loosened. In that split second, the Indian attacked.

Sudden fire raged down Sunny's left shoulder blade, embedding itself in his back.

Sunny pushed away. "Damn!"

Pain streaked down into his leg. He wanted to grab his back and stop the pain, but if he lost focus, the Indians would claim another victory over the White Eyes.

The Apache circled him, crouching, waiting for the chance to thrust that knife into Sunny's chest.

Sunny circled opposite and spotted his Hawken lying several feet to his right. He sprinted toward his weapon, but as he bent over for the gun, a hand clamped around his ankle and pulled. Sunny rammed face-first into the ground.

Undaunted, he clawed his way toward the weapon. Sunny gripped the warm metal of the rifle barrel. In one fluid motion, he rolled onto his side, sat up, and swung his rifle like a club. A stomach-wrenching *thwack* echoed against the boulders. Blood splattered over both men. The Apache released his hold.

Sunny pulled in deep drafts of air and waited for his world to quit spinning. He reached over his shoulder, wincing as he strained, and grabbed at the pain. He clutched only wet material.

"You all right?" Clay's voice jerked Sunny's head up.

Sunny held his hand in front of his face. Sticky blood smeared across his palm.

Clay leaned close, chest heaving from his own fight, and frowned. "You hurt?"

"Maybe."

One of Clay's eyes narrowed. "Let's see what happened. Unbutton your shirt."

He moved behind Sunny and peeled the shirt and undershirt down to Sunny's elbows. Clay whistled through his teeth.

"What?" Sunny craned his neck twisting, trying to see what his friend saw.

"Ain't too bad. Just a scratch." Clay stood. "I'll get the canteen, clean it up, and you'll be good as new. You just sit here. Just *sit*. Don't move. I'll be right back."

Clay's footsteps faded. Sunny reached again for the pain in his shoulder.

*How can a scratch hurt so bad? Those Indians—Just two?*

His eyes swept the open expanse of desert. There should be more. Lots more. Sunny shrugged his shirts up around his shoulders and then scrambled to his feet, his legs wobbly. He staggered over to Clay, who was pouring water onto a neckerchief.

"We better go," Sunny said. "Their friends'll be looking for them...and us."

"I know." Clay wrung the cloth. "But gotta fix you up first. Stop that bleeding."

He pointed to a flat rock. "Sit."

Sunny did as told. He listened to Clay dig around in the saddlebag and wondered what he was doing. His stomach turned sour, and his back still burned like the rising crimson sun. The damp cloth cooled his skin.

"How bad is it, Clay?"

"I'll be honest, Pard. It's a little more than a scratch."

Sunny swung his full attention to his friend. Clay spoke in Sunny's ear.

"That Apache just about got you good. Cut's 'bout five inches long, almost an inch deep. If it'd been a little lower, I'd be writin' home to your ma."

Clay's hand pushed against Sunny's back. He squirmed.

"Hold still now. Gotta sew you up."

"Damn, Clay."

"Yeah."

# CHAPTER TWENTY-EIGHT

"How much longer you think we're gonna hold still and wait, Bill?" Rivers asked.

Private Bill Patton shook his head and poked another stick into the fire. The heat warmed his hands, but nothing quieted his guilt. His two friends shifted in the dark. The horses in the makeshift corral munched on oats and barley. A twig in the fire snapped.

"Don't know, Tom. Don't know what else to do."

"Those Indians could help that poor woman. I saw her in town today. She sure is sad. Heart's broken."

Private Tom Rivers sipped his coffee. Bill looked at his friends, their eyes reflecting the flames.

"Don't tell me that," Bill said. "I feel bad enough I didn't find out about her man. But I got to thinking about what you two said. If Bascom or Connor caught me, I'd hang with them Indians. We all know that."

Bill kept his voice low. Other soldiers in camp might overhear, go tattling to Bascom. Or maybe not. Bascom was pretty much hated by everyone.

"Sure would," Jamison said. "That sonuvabitch Bascom'd hang you first. Sonuvabitch. Hell, he'd hang his own mother if she looked crosswise at him." Jamison snapped a stick in half.

Bill regarded his friend. Jamison had a right to be angry and bitter. Bascom had busted him from sargent major down to private in front of the entire company. Then Bascom had berated him for three-quarters of an hour. And for what? Jamison was guilty of helping a squaw and her child hide during an attack on their village. He'd saved their lives.

Silence surrounded the small campsite. The men adjusted their weight on the rocks, slurped more coffee, and buttoned their coats. Rivers tossed out the remainder of his coffee.

"How about if the three of us talk to them Indians? Maybe we can convince 'em to tell what they know even if they stay jailed."

"Now why in the world would they talk? Their freedom's the only way they'll tell us what we want to know."

Bill glanced around the camp again, half expecting Bascom or Connor to be standing over him. Rivers scratched his stubbled chin.

"I don't know. How 'bout it? Even talkin' to those Indians is better 'n sittin' around here doin' nothing. Never can tell what'll happen." Rivers looked from man to man. "I'm game if you two are."

"Hell yeah." Jamison grinned. "Ol' Bascom can't bust me any lower. Might even put a burr under his saddle."

"More than that, Jack." Bill swigged his coffee. "Maybe those Apaches will talk."

"How?"

"Look at it another way." Bill held his hands over the dwindling fire. "If they tell us where those two drivers are, dead or alive, and we can get the bodies back, maybe the Army won't hang 'em. You know, in thanks for cooperating."

"They'll be like heroes!" Rivers tossed a handful of dried leaves into the fire. "Then maybe the Army'll be so grateful they'll release them and Cochise'll release the kid."

Jamison held a stick up like a sword. "Hell, we'll all be heroes!"

"It could work," Bill said. He looked at his two friends. "Probably should go see Miss Simmons first."

\* \* \*

A couple days later, the three were dispatched into town for supplies. They spent an hour at the feed and grain store, then made a quick stop at the blacksmith's. The men at last found themselves inside the Mercantile.

Lila smiled. "Welcome, gentlemen."

"Miss Simmons." Jamison touched the brim of his hat. "Hope you're feelin' better."

Lila shook her head. "No sir, I'm not better, just not hysterical now." She looked from man to man and stammered. "I wanted to apologize to you for bein' so...so weepy the other day."

128

Bill took her arm. He hated to ask, so he formed the words as gently as he knew how.

"Have you heard anything?"

"No. Nothing." Lila twisted her hands. "Everyone's given up. It's just that—I guess I knew all along James wasn't comin' back. That he and his brother are…" She took a deep breath then wiped at a tear. "That they died doin' what they both loved."

"Yes, ma'am." Bill Patton squirmed in his boots. He hated watching women cry.

"I just wish I could have his body back for a decent burial. That way I could at least visit him."

Tom Rivers peered out from under his slouch hat. "You remind me of my sister when her husband got himself killed. She cried for months." Rivers caught himself and cleared his throat. "Ma'am, I promise we'll do everything in our power to see he gets back. It just ain't right leaving him out there and having you here."

"Miss Simmons," Bill said, "don't fret so. We got ourselves a plan."

A blond curl dangled around Lila's forehead and bounced when she shook her head. "No, I can't ask you to do anything. Please don't."

Bill patted her arm. "Our minds are clean made up, Miss Simmons. You'll be hearin' from us."

The men stepped onto the boardwalk and stopped. A cool breeze swirled around the few people hurrying past.

Bill Patton clenched and released his hands in his coat pocket, his rational thoughts colliding with feelings. If it hadn't been for those tears, the hopelessness, the heart-wrenching pain he saw on Lila's face, he might have been happy with just talking to those Indians. But now, he realized it had to be more. He had to make sure something was done.

"Lord, she's sad." Jamison pulled out a wad of tobacco and stuck it in his jaw. Bill slapped his hand against the adobe building.

"Dammit. The Army ain't got the brains to know a hero when it sees one." He glanced toward the jail. "We're just kiddin' ourselves. Even if them Indians told us those two drivers are safe and just where to find 'em, ol' Bascom'd probably shoot 'em then hang 'em anyway."

Jamison spit. "Sonuvabitch Bascom."

"What exactly are you talkin' about, Bill?" Rivers moved in closer.

"You been in the Army too long, Tom." Jamison thumped Rivers on the head. "You ain't thinkin' right. What Bill means is that we're gonna free us some Indians."

"Jesus. It's a big chance we're takin'."

Rivers fixed his stare on the sheriff's office across the plaza. He stood frozen as if planted there.

"I keep thinkin' 'bout my sister," he continued. "She knew when her husband died, but what if she had to spend the rest of her life not knowin' what happened? Not knowin' the next thirty, forty years? I'd think mighty kindly on someone who'd find out."

Bill nodded at both friends.

"Let's do it."

Jamison spit a brown stream onto the dirt street. "Just think. Indians escape and Bascom gets blamed." He spit again. "I'm gonna enjoy this."

# CHAPTER TWENTY-NINE

One day faded into another one as James and Trace struggled to stay alive. James tried to figure out how long they'd been held. Hard to say, but the days were getting warmer, and a little longer. Longer for them to have more light in which to work.

His one bright part of the day was mealtime. At least he could sit and eat, his work ended for the moment. He'd have to get up soon enough and endure more work, more jabs, more spiteful insults. But right now, he could eat, renew his strength. This morning's breakfast sat in his bowl like a friend greeting him. He would have smiled at it if his face hadn't hurt so badly.

And he would have smiled at the young woman who brought his bowl. Her shy smile and sideways glances warmed him. She was pretty—those high cheekbones and raven hair that shone in the morning sun lit up his day. Then he'd think about Lila. He'd wonder how she was doing and if she thought he was never coming back. James knew not to dwell on her too long. His heart could only take so much hurt.

Trace sat a few feet away, with an Apache guard at his shoulder. Trace shoveled in his breakfast stew as if it'd be yanked away any moment. And it might. James knew all too well.

As James scooped the last few bits of rabbit and onion stew into his mouth, he glanced up, his bowl poised halfway. Standing Pony, the brother of One Wing, towered over Trace. Then Standing Pony's meaty hands clamped around Trace's upper arm, and jerked him to his feet. Trace's bowl clattered to the ground, the remainder of its contents splattering onto the sand.

James stood, his own bowl forgotten. He flexed the three inches of horsehair rope binding his hands. Three inches allowed enough room for him to do plenty of chores around camp, but they also allowed enough room to cause some damage if need be. He'd never been given the chance, but he stayed always ready.

"Trace?"

"It's all right. Stay put, James." Trace glanced back over his shoulder while Standing Pony yanked him away.

"Where're you taking him?" James felt an Indian at his elbow, but focused on his brother. Standing Pony was leading him toward a saguaro. "Trace?"

One Wing joined the other two Indians, a wet rawhide band dangling from his fist.

Shudders raced over James' body. The tribe had made only one move since the rawhide had been wrapped around his head. He remembered it all too well. Too-recent images swam before him.

Sun growing hotter. Wet leather shrinking. Squeezing. Unimaginable pressure. Begging. Lightning flashes and raging fire. Muscles convulsing. Screams.

Vomiting for hours.

"Trace!" James bolted across camp. "Fight 'em. You'll die. Fight 'em." Apache feet thundered behind him. He didn't care. He had to save his brother from the agony.

James plowed into the back of Standing Pony, sending him sprawling. Then James launched himself on top of Standing Pony's back, yanked his black hair up, and with it, his head.

"Son of a bitch!" James swung his bound hands under Standing Pony's throat and tugged the horsehair rope up against soft flesh. He yanked. "Leave my brother alone! Leave him alone!" He yanked harder. "You'll never break us! Never!"

Gurgling, strangling noises. Shouts. His grip tightened. Hands pulled and grabbed at his shirt and body. He wrenched away.

"I'll take you down." James strained against the bucking Indian and thrust up the three inches of rope. He pulled the garrote with strength dredged up from base survival instincts.

"We're gonna live. Gonna live!"

Arms and hands smothered James' body. Someone pried his hands from around Standing Pony's throat. He thought he heard a finger bone crack.

More arms and hands pulled him to his feet. He was wedged between several enraged Apaches. James stared through the crowd at his brother.

"No!" James raged against the tightening grips clamped around his arms. He wrenched loose of one hold, stomped a

132

moccasined foot, then bent over and rammed his head into a stomach.

"You'll never break us!" James swung his clubbed hands into an Apache's face.

Arms encircled his rampaging body. His head was thrust up tight against an angry chest. A warm body pressed against his back. Labored breathing and hundreds of furious words rang in his ears.

One Wing hissed, then said, "Break you? We'll kill you."

James shook. "Cochise won't let you."

One Wing's seething face appeared inches from James. "He has gone to meet scouts with news of his brother. He will return too late."

"Stop it, James. Stop it. They'll kill you!"

James squirmed. He strained against strong arms. He kicked out, connecting with an Apache's groin. Someone grunted. Furious hands and arms pushed him to the ground. Rocks poked his back. He rolled side to side and then kicked up, connecting with a chin.

A foot plowed into his ribs. Breath knocked out, James gasped for air and stared up into One Wing's snarling face. The mouth opened and closed, words erupting from One Wing's lips. A few James understood as his world took form again.

"…you will pay with your life."

"Please, God, no. *Please*." Trace's appeals screamed above the noise.

Voices grew in fury. The volume increased until even his brother's yells were lost.

James' gaze swung to his brother, who was standing behind One Wing. Two Apaches gripped Trace's arms as if they feared he would fly away. A knife's tip pierced his neck.

After a deep breath, James rolled to his side, but strong hands pushed him back down. He looked up in time to watch Standing Pony straddle him and sit. Close to two hundred pounds of Apache mashed his body against the ground.

Someone grabbed his head, and before he understood what was happening, his ankles were weighted with someone's body. James wriggled and twisted, but his hands were pinned.

One Wing's face hovered over his. James stared at Lila's ring entwined in the Apache's hair. If he could just reach up—

One Wing gripped a fistful of sand and positioned it over

James' mouth. Grains sprinkled onto his face, into his eyes. He clamped his teeth together, clenched his jaw with all his strength, and pursed his lips.

He willed his head to shake from side to side, but managed to move only his eyes and grunt resistance. Two strong fingers pinched his nostrils together, and his lungs screamed for air. James opened his mouth.

In that instant, his mouth and throat filled with rocks and sand.

James stared into One Wig's eyes, squirmed, and tried not to swallow. A hand clamped over his mouth. Spitting and breathing was impossible. He swallowed. Strong fingers pried his mouth open and held it wide while the next handful of dirt poured in. James choked and tried to cough.

Another handful of sand struck his face.

Screams and screeches pounded against his ears. Nothing made sense. His heart thundered, arm muscles strained, his throat on fire.

Help me! Please, God help me!

He wheezed in fragments of air and choked on the dust coating his lungs. The same hand clamped down over his mouth and pinched his nose.

Sand and dirt in his eyes, James squeezed them shut. Tears streamed. Rocks slid down his throat, tearing the lining as he bucked, desperate to throw off the enemy.

An angry baritone voice exploded through the taunts and jeers. Staccato Apache words shot around his head. The crowd quieted.

After what seemed an eternity, the weight on James' ankles and body lifted, the clamp around his head and nose released. Strong hands rolled him onto his side, slapping him twice on the back.

James vomited. Coughed. Gasped. Spit.

"You will live for now, James Colton."

*Cochise?*

Another hand hit his back and pushed him onto his stomach. He vomited red sand.

"Foolish. You act before thinking."

James pulled his knees under him and propped his forehead against the ground. More sand and rocks erupted from his chest.

With each breath he sucked in, sand swirled into his lungs. He choked and coughed.

More Apache words shot back and forth. He spit.

A sudden sneeze blew small rocks through his nose. He screamed. Familiar hands patted his back; his brother must be somewhere close. He sneezed again. Red rocks and sand blew into the ground.

James lifted his head and opened his puffy eyes just enough to recognize Cochise's legs as they turned and walked away. He made out Trace's pants, Trace's body kneeling inches in front of him. James leaned over his brother's legs, allowing his full weight to sag across Trace's lap.

"You'll be all right, James. Everything'll be fine."

James didn't argue, but he knew his brother was lying.

# CHAPTER THIRTY

A few days passed while Private Bill Patton and his two friends designed intricate plans. A checklist grew hour by hour as they realized what a monumental task they had undertaken.

The three men had the chance to act during the evening. Assigned inside guard duty, Bill knew this was possibly his one opportunity to get to those prisoners, those Indians who could bring back the dead stage drivers, help Miss Simmons, and release that young boy. A lot to ask, he knew.

Bill changed duty with the daytime guard, then walked into the sheriff's office and located the other private standing in front of the occupied jail cells.

"Private Garcia," Bill said, "Corporal Connor sent word you're to stand watch outside instead of inside tonight."

"What?"

"Yeah, I don't understand it, either. You'd think with two guards inside and one outside, that'd be fine, but he wants both of you outside. One in, two out."

"I don't know—"

"Said there might be trouble brewin' down by the saloon later on this evening, so we need more people outside." Bill watched the soldier's face contort into a puzzled frown. He thumbed over his shoulder. "You and Private Watson are ordered to be outside. I'm in here. That's all I know."

"But why—"

"I do know one thing," Bill continued. He nudged the private toward the office and then toward the door. "If you don't get outside and he comes by, you'll be in mighty big trouble." He pointed toward the door again and nodded.

The young private frowned deeper, his head swinging from Bill to the door and back again.

"Big trouble." Bill raised both eyebrows and cocked his head toward the door.

"All right." The private took a hesitant step forward. "But call me if anything happens in here."

Bill nodded and waited for the private to close the outside door. Then, he pulled in a deep breath to quiet his pounding heart. It didn't help. He stepped into the back area where the Indians appeared to be asleep on their bunks.

At Coyuntura's cell, Bill waited for what seemed an hour. Was he doing the right thing? What if the plan backfired and the entire Apache nation descended on Mesilla and the Army?

Coyuntura silently rose from the cot and stood at the cell bars. His shadow from the moonlight fell over Bill.

Bill craned his neck up to stare into the Apache's face. He kept his voice low. "Been thinkin' on what you said, Coyuntura." A brief glance left to right. "My friends and I are willing to help you escape in exchange for the information you have about those two men."

"Men?"

"The stage driver and guard, killed by your brother's tribe." Bill's tense voice soaked into the adobe walls. "We're ready to get you and your people out of here if you'll cooperate. We gotta act fast."

"How do I know this is no trick?"

"I give you my word as a soldier of the US Army."

Coyuntura spit on Bill's boot. "Soldiers."

Bill shook his head. "Yeah, well, tell us exactly where they are, how we can bring the bodies back, and you're free."

Coyuntura stared at Bill. "What makes you think when the key unlocks this door, I won't kill you and the others?"

"You're a man of honor, like your brother."

Coyuntura regarded him. "Unlock the doors, release the others, and I will tell you what you want to know."

He spoke in rapid-fire Apache. The others nodded.

"Good." Bill found the keys in the front office. He fumbled the key twice before inserting it into the lock.

"Before I open this door, you need to know what to do." He looked at the three prisoners in the other cell. "Stand in the outer office here, stay away from the windows, and wait for me to open the door. There are horses tied around behind the courthouse."

137

The Apaches nodded. Bill turned the lock, and its click bounced off all the walls. Bill feared the sentries outside would burst in and spoil the escape plan. He hurried. The first three Apaches stepped into freedom.

Key in the other door's lock, Bill hesitated. Would this Indian keep his word or kill him? Could he trust this Apache, this brother of Cochise? What choice did he now have?

Through the open door, he watched the freed Apaches hunker down in the front office. Bill turned his attention to the man in front of him.

"Now. Where are these Colton brothers' bodies? Did they die right away?" Bill's heart thumped and pounded until he thought he'd pass out.

"Men did not die. They're not dead—yet."

Bill knew he hadn't heard correctly. It had to be the beating of his heart that muffled the words. "What?"

Coyuntura arched one eyebrow. "They were captured at Apache Springs, near the stage coach station there, taken to my brother's camp, held prisoner."

Bill grimaced.

*Good God. Apache captives!*

"Where's your brother's camp at? How can I get them back?"

"My brother will use them until all white and Mexican people are gone from our land. Then, he will kill them."

"Jesus!" Bill's palms turned clammy. "Tell him to let them go. Them and that boy. We released you in good faith. Tell him we want peace with the Apache."

Coyuntura snorted, then said, "Peace comes at a high price." He jerked on the iron bars. "We did not take boy, but I'll tell him. Now, I have told you what you desired. You keep your promise, Bill Patton."

"I still don't know how to get them home. You haven't told me where your brother's camp is."

Coyuntura sneered. "You asked where they died and where their bodies are. I told you. Unlock the door."

Bill shook his head and backed away. "I didn't know they were still alive. And I still don't know where Cochise's camp is."

"His camp moves often. But, even if you find him, you will not make it into his camp. There are guards everywhere. They will kill you."

Bill jumped as the wooden door squeaked open. An Apache glared at him. Bill turned the key in the lock.

Coyuntura pushed the door wide open and waited for the other two prisoners to step out before he stood towering over Bill.

Bill looked up at Coyuntura and cleared his throat. "Wait in the front office 'til I give the signal. Then grab those horses and go. But first, I need you to do something for me. Something to keep me out of jail."

Coyuntura jerked his head up and down.

"I'll need you to tie me up, knock me out, and lock me in that jail cell. It's the only way I can think of to keep *out* of jail." Bill shook his head. "Hope it works."

Without waiting for confirmation, Bill stood on a cot in the cell, waved his yellow bandana from the window, then stepped down.

"Now, if all goes well, my friends are gonna have a big fight."

A few minutes later, shouts and high-pitched laughter erupted down the street, and the soldiers outside discussed whether to leave their posts and break it up or stand guard and ignore it.

Bill opened the door a crack. "Hey, Private, what's going on?"

"Looks like a little too much tequila."

"You gonna break it up?"

"Nah. Looks like it ain't all that bad." The private glanced around Bill. "You better get back inside. No tellin' what them Apache might do."

"Yeah, you're right." Bill started to close the door, then opened it again. "I'd sure hate to see Lieutenant Bascom waked up tonight. Bet he's gonna be really angry at this ruckus. No tellin' what he'd do to us when he finds out we could've stopped it."

Private Garcia looked at the other guard for help. Then they both shrugged. "Guess Bill's right. We better get this broke up quick. Looks like it's a couple of our soldiers, anyway. You all right to stay here, Bill?"

"Fine." Bill held up a hand. "Them Indians are sleeping like babies."

Bill watched Rivers and Jamison at the far end of the plaza rolling around in the dirt. "Just be quick about it," he added.

He shut the door as the guards rushed toward the saloon.

By the time they reached the fight, seven men were exchanging blows, shoving and pushing each other. Rivers and Jamison managed to slip away into the dark corners of the street. Fifteen minutes later, the quarreling men had been sent home, the saloon chairs righted, and most of the broken glass swept up.

The soldiers hurried back to their posts in front of the jail, secure in the knowledge their Apache prisoners were locked behind bars.

# CHAPTER THIRTY-ONE

Sunny shielded his eyes against the midmorning sun glaring off sand dunes and coating mesquite and alligator junipers.

He and Clay topped a mesa and reined up. From this vantage point, a hundred square miles of rough, cactus-laden hills stretched forever. A few hills, Sunny figured, could even be called mountains, as high as they were. A brown ribbon snaked through the desert.

Clay squinted into the distance, then pointed. "There it is. Stage road to Tucson."

"Right now it's the road to nowhere, since nobody's gettin' through. How many times you reckon we've driven over that?" Sunny asked.

Dust, pushed by a cool wind, curled around Sunny. He untied his bandana and blew his nose into the gritty cloth. Clay shrugged and gulped water from the canteen.

"'Course we haven't been watchin' the road all the time," Clay said, "but we should've seen dirt clouds." Both eyebrows knitted. "Kinda spooky ain't it?"

"Sure don't feel natural. I remember it was busy all the time—wagons and riders and such."

"Yeah, lots of traffic." Clay plugged the canteen. "We've spent three days now searching the north part of the road. What d'ya say we try the south part? There's gotta be a hint around here somewhere. Those Colton's couldn't have just vanished."

Sunny gyrated, his left shoulder pumping up and down like a piston in a steam engine. He pulled off his coat. The knife wound burned and itched.

Clay eyed Sunny. "You hearing music I don't?"

"Damn Indians!" Sunny said. "This itchin's driving me crazy."

Clay gigged his horse over to Sunny. "Stop squirming. You'll rip those stitches out." He offered his canteen. "Have some. Want me to put new bandages on there?"

Sunny straightened up and accepted the canteen. Cool water flowed down his throat. He shook his head and gave the canteen back. "No. Maybe later tonight."

"All right then. Let's go find them Coltons." Clay nodded and tugged his hat lower on his forehead.

"Clay?"

"Yeah?"

"Thanks."

Clay wrapped the canteen's straps around the pommel, tossed a quick grin at Sunny, then spurred his horse.

\* \* \*

A pale blue sky peeked around orange clouds edged with crimson. Sunny leaned closer into the crackling fire. Its heat felt good this morning. Although the days were growing warmer, winter was still in the morning air, and he was glad for his thick sheepskin coat. Smoke from the fire spiraled straight up, but there was no wind. Sunny pulled in mesquite fumes. He smiled.

A string of quail darted from bush to bush, the biggest in front followed in sequence by smaller ones. Sunny listened to his world. Clay slurping coffee, quail scurrying, and the fire's chatter. Maybe today they would find their friends. Maybe today would be the day.

Clay froze, coffee cup halfway to his mouth. "You hear that?"

"What?"

"That." Clay put his cup on the ground and eased to his feet. He fingered the revolver on his hip. "Sounds like animals. Maybe a horse or mule."

Sunny listened hard. Clay always had a knack for hearing things that nobody else could.

"How many? More 'n one?" Sunny asked. His cup grated against the sand.

Clay cocked his head toward the sound, and Sunny heard it, too. Hooves, creosote bushes rustling, footsteps.

Nerves tight, he thumbed the leather safety loop off his revolver and eased the weapon out of his holster. Whatever it was, it seemed to be headed right for them.

Sunny spun the cylinder on his new Colt .36. He knew the

chambers were full, but he always liked to be sure. He peered into the desert. Nothing. Just the same noises, only louder.

The horse snorted. Both men crouched low. Noise now came from two sides, and Clay pointed to a boulder nearby.

Sunny nodded. He took two steps, then stopped. A grunt on his left startled him. Bushes moved. He hit the desert floor and cocked his revolver.

The footsteps stopped.

A voice from the north side of their camp.

"*Quién es?*"

Sunny glanced at Clay, who put a finger up to his lips. The voice didn't sound Apache, but Sunny knew some Indians spoke Spanish. He frowned.

Clay eased closer to the boulder while Sunny crawled over to a mesquite bush. It was hard to hide now. A rustling of the bushes brought Sunny to his feet, revolver pointed.

"Come out with your hands up! Right now or I'll shoot you where you stand."

If it was an Apache, he'd shoot now and ask questions later.

"Now, I said!" Sunny stepped toward the sound.

Hands held high above his head, a man moved into full view, an old pistol gripped in his hand. Sunny rushed the man, grabbed the gun, then tossed it to Clay. His own weapon remained pointed at the stranger's head.

The man trembled. Sunny moved in closer.

*Mexican.*

Dark hair stuck out from under his hat, dark eyes matched the dark mustache draping over his upper lip. The clothes were homespun, several years ago. Sunny gripped the man by the shirt collar and jammed the gun barrel into the man's temple.

"*Quién es?*" Sunny demanded.

The man's wide eyes darted from Sunny to Clay then back. His mouth opened and closed. No words, Spanish or English, emerged. Sunny shook him.

"I asked who you are!" He shook him again.

"Cisco Medina, *señor.*"

"Why're you sneaking up on us?"

"*Señor*, my family and I are fleeing the *Indios.*" Cisco shrugged. "We did not know you were here. I thought you were my *niñas* playing a game. We should have known, but we are too tired from

143

walking all night."

A horse whinnied. Clay spun.

"Come on out! We know you're there."

No answer. Clay yelled again. "Now! Come on out!"

Cisco spoke up. "Perla. *Venga aqui.*"

Bushes parted. A weary-looking woman, much smaller than Cisco, emerged. On her back wiggled a small bundle. She reached behind her and grabbed at the precious cargo. Seeing Cisco at gunpoint, she froze.

"Where's the horse?" Sunny asked. "Don't tell me you ain't got one, 'cause I heard it."

The Mexican, arms still raised, pointed behind the woman.

"Hey, Sunny?" Clay lowered his weapon. "I think we got us a family here. How 'bout putting your gun down? You're scaring the lady."

"Can't be too careful. What if they aim to kill us?"

Clay holstered his revolver and smiled.

"With a baby?"

"It's a trap, Clay. Bet there's Indians just on the other side, waitin' for us to put our shooters away."

"All right. Keep your gun ready, but how about taking it out of that man's face?"

Sunny released his hold, eased down the hammer, and nodded at Cisco's arms. They dropped to his sides. The woman hurried to Cisco and stood next to him. He slid a comforting arm around her shoulders, gazed down at her, then nodded.

"*Señors*, this is *mi esposa*, Perla."

The woman nodded, but moved even closer to Cisco.

"And this is my *niño*, José." Cisco pointed to the bundle on Perla's back.

Although he'd had breakfast, Sunny allowed his early morning irritation to surface. Maybe these were innocent Mexicans and maybe they weren't.

"The horse?" he asked.

"The horse is with my two *hijitas* and my *papá*." Cisco crossed himself and gazed at the sky. "The rest of my family was killed by the Apache. We escaped with very little."

Sunny lowered his gun, but kept it in hand. "Bring 'em out and let's have a look."

Cisco called.

An old horse parted the bushes with an old man draped over its neck. He sat up straight when he spotted Cisco with Clay and Sunny. He jerked back on the reins, stopping a few feet from the small group.

Sunny saw movement near the horse, and he craned his neck for a better view. Two little dark-haired girls hid behind the horse's legs and clutched the tail. The smallest peeked around the leg.

Sunny nodded at the children. He couldn't hide the smile climbing up one side of his face. Those big brown eyes...their innocence.

The old Mexican's hands reached upward. He trembled. "Please don't shoot us, *señors*."

"We won't," Clay said, signaling to the old man. "Hands down. *Esta bien, señor. Esta bien.*"

Cisco tied the horse to a nearby tree branch, and the elderly man slid off into Cisco's waiting arms. Once the man stood straight, Cisco knelt and hugged his two little girls.

A smile took over Clay's face. He knelt on one knee in front of the taller of the two girls.

"My name's Clay Arrington. What's yours?"

Nothing but a shy grin in return. Clay looked up at Sunny. "Probably only speaks Spanish. How do you say—"

"*Tu nombre, niña?*" Sunny gazed into the child's dusty little face.

Still silence.

"I remember now." Clay tried again. "*Mi nombre* Clay." He waited. "*Tu nombre?*"

"Maria."

The voice was tiny, but the grin was wide, displaying a mouth with a gap where two front teeth usually stood.

"*Tu hermana?*" Clay smiled at the other little girl clinging to her father.

"*Sí, señor.*"

"*Tu nombre?*"

"Cecilia."

Her grin was as wide as Maria's. Clay smiled then tipped his hat at both children. Giggles erupted from the girls. The oldest hid her mouth, but both stared at Clay's bright red hair.

Clay looked at Cisco. "Beautiful children. This your father?"

The old man extended his hand. "Marquez Medina, *señor. Gracias.*"

Sunny glanced around the area. No more sounds, no horses or raiding Apaches.

"I'm Sunny Williamston out of Mesilla." He slipped the gun into its holster. "*Con mucho gusto.*"

The aroma of breakfast stew carried on the wind. He sniffed. This family was probably hungry. Sunny squatted by the fire and stirred the stew. "Let's get these people something to eat, Clay."

"Please do not bother to feed us, *señor.*" Perla shook her head. "We have already caused you too much worry."

"No trouble, ma'am. It'll take just a minute." Sunny held up the stew-coated spoon. "You must be starved after walkin' all night."

"More tired than hungry." Perla looked at her children, who were eyeing the pot of stew. "But the children are hungry. They have not eaten much since leaving our *casa* four days ago."

"Please sit." Sunny motioned toward the fire. "*Sentense.*"

"*Gracias.*" Cisco nodded. "Four days ago the Apache raided our rancho. Our cattle, horses run off...my mother and our other son...*el muerto.*" He crossed himself as a tear formed in his eyes, which gazed heavenward.

While Sunny and Clay prepared more food, Perla nursed the baby and the girls gathered a few sticks of firewood as their grandfather watched them.

Within ten minutes, the stew was replenished, plates filled and emptied.

Stomachs no longer rumbling, Perla lay with the baby and the girls on Sunny and Clay's bedrolls, a blanket spread over them. She sang as their eyes shut.

The men sat around the campfire and swapped information. Sunny was impressed with Cisco's English. It was almost as good as his.

"Did you happen to see a stagecoach anywhere along your journey, Cisco?" Sunny's voice dropped low.

Cisco and Marquez exchanged glances. What did that look on their faces mean? It wasn't promising.

"We're looking for two friends of ours who drive...who *drove* for Butterfield Stage Lines. It's been a couple of weeks, so any information you've got would sure be appreciated."

Cisco's eyes flitted to his father, then down to his hands. His shoulders seemed to sag just a bit more. "*Señors*, you won't like what we can tell you."

"We need to know, Mister Medina," Sunny said.

Lines appeared across Cisco's forehead. "After running from our burning rancho," he said, "we crossed the road late in the evening. We walked right past an overturned stagecoach. No one was around it, and we saw no bodies close by, but dried blood was on the driver's seat. We could see it clear."

Sunny clenched his fists and looked away. Poor Colton boys. Never had a chance.

What a helluva way to die. At the hands of the Apache. No defense, no final good-byes.

James and Trace were dead.

"True, no bodies were near the stage," Marquez said. "Your friends could've escaped."

Sunny knew better.

He ambled from the small group and stopped several yards farther away, then leaned against a boulder. Something burned in his throat.

*Why did James and Trace have to die?*

He picked up a rock, aimed for the nearest pinon tree, then threw as hard as he could. It hit a lower branch, breaking it. He picked up a bigger rock, launched it at the same tree. More rocks. Bigger rocks. He threw harder.

*James and Trace dead. Especially the kind of death the Apache inflict.*

The stories he'd heard. The cut on his back tugged.

Clay handed Sunny a rock, then chucked one across the desert.

Several minutes later, Clay stopped throwing rocks. "Maybe we should rethink going to Tucson just now. Might be walking into our own death trap."

A final rock then Sunny nodded. "Maybe we oughta go back to Apache Springs with the Medinas. Give 'em just that much more protection. "

He fisted his hands, then released them. He looked over at Clay, who seemed to have aged ten years. Sunny placed a hand on his friend's shoulder, as much for his sake as Clay's.

Clay stared up into the sky. "Dammit, Sunny."

"Yeah."

# CHAPTER THIRTY-TWO

Clay spotted the children and Perla awake and busy fixing dinner as he and Sunny rode back into camp. Their four-hour search around the area had whetted his appetite, and right about now old socks would have tasted good. His stomach rumbled with the smell of rabbit roasting over the small fire, the fat crackling as Maria turned the spit. Perla grinned and nodded. She offered them a fresh cup of coffee.

"*Gracias, señora*," Sunny said. In two gulps he finished the cup. He held it out for a refill, and a crooked grin planted itself on one side of his face. "Sorry, Clay. Hers is much better than yours." He sipped again.

Cisco, who had been asleep nearby, roused and whipped the gun out from under the folded clothes he used as a pillow. He aimed it at Clay. Marquez propped himself up and pointed his old pistol at Sunny.

Sunny and Clay crouched. Clay held up a hand. "Whoa, Cisco, it's just us. We're not gonna hurt you."

Cisco rubbed his eyes, then peered closer. Two more blinks and he stood. He holstered the gun. As he helped his father to his feet, he said, "You're lucky I recognized you so soon, *señors*. I almost shot you."

"Didn't mean to startle you, Cisco." Clay glanced at Sunny. "Guess we're not used to having other people around. Sorry."

He offered his cup of coffee to Cisco. Sunny held out his coffee cup to Marquez. The older Medina holstered his revolver and accepted the offered coffee.

"Mister Medina," Clay said, pointing over his shoulder. "Sunny and me spent the better part of the afternoon scoutin' around here. There's no sign of Indians, but we thought we'd ride with you over to the Apache Springs way station. The manager's a friend of ours, and he'll be glad to help you for a few days."

148

Sunny chimed in. "The girls can ride with me. Missus Medina and the baby can take your horse. If your father gets too tired, he can ride behind Clay. His horse is big and strong, can carry double with no problem."

"No, *señors. Gracias*," Cisco said. "We cannot ask you to go back the way you already came. We have caused you too much trouble already. As soon as we eat, we'll be leaving. Another day or two we'll be safely past Apache Springs."

Clay shook his head, then watched the two little girls playing with a rock and a stick. Their long, black hair shone in the waning light.

"Well, do what you want, Mister Medina. But Sunny and me are heading back that way, anyway. Mind if we ride along with you then? I'd surely appreciate someone else's stories. I've heard Sunny's at least a hundred times."

"A hundred and one, partner." Sunny thumped Clay's chest with his cup.

Perla entwined her arm around her husband's waist. She gazed up at Clay. "We'd be honored to have you accompany us, *señors*." She released her husband. "Supper is ready."

During the meal, the party decided not to set out until morning. Everyone was exhausted, and another night of sleep wouldn't hurt. Clay volunteered to stand watch half the night and Sunny took the second half.

The campfire was extinguished well before dark, and the six Medinas settled down to a quiet night under the stars. Clay rechecked his revolver, picked up his canteen, and sauntered out of camp to stand watch. Sunny walked with him.

A few boulders formed a ring a couple hundred feet from the campsite. Clay leaned against one of the boulders and surveyed the valley. Nothing moved. No winking signs of fires in the distance, no clouds of dust indicating riders. Nothing. Sunny rested one shoulder against the boulder. Silence filled the darkening sky.

After several starts and stops, Sunny broke the silence. "Clay?"

"Yeah?"

"Suppose they died quick?"

Clay glanced at his friend and then into the night. "I've been praying all day they did."

"Yeah. Me, too."

149

* * *

The party trudged over steep hills north and eastward, fought their way through cactus and mesquite bushes, and took turns encouraging each other. At long last, they stood within shouting distance of the Apache Springs way station. Clay thought about the hostile greeting they'd received the last time he and Sunny approached the station. Keeping the Medinas at a safe distance, he and Sunny rode up near the door.

Clay leaned forward over his saddle. "Mister Culver? It's us again, Clay and Sunny."

No response.

"Mister Culver? Open that door. It's just us, we ain't gonna hurt you. Brought you some more friends."

Silence. Clay's smile faded.

"Probably out back tendin' stock," Sunny said. "I'll go see."

Sunny dismounted, then handed his reins to Clay. He disappeared around the side of the square, rock-walled stage station.

Minutes passed while Clay sat, waiting. He turned once to look at the Medinas, then shrugged.

A yell. Sunny's voice from far behind the station. A second yell. This time Clay recognized his name.

Clay slid off his horse, and his gun cleared leather.

"You all stay here." He held up a hand at the Medinas. "I'll be back."

He sprinted around the corner of the station.

"Sunny?"

As Clay raced toward the barn, he envisioned his best friend captured and tortured by the Apache. Sunny's muffled voice called again.

Clay jerked the barn door open, aimed his revolver waist high, and glanced inside. Empty. He charged back into bright daylight, running past the barn and into the blacksmith's shop. No sound of people scuffling. Nothing.

"Sunny?" Clay called.

Silence.

Clay stepped outside and squinted against the sun. Another yell. Sunny's voice? Sounded too high to be his. Whoever it was had come from the field just north of him. He steeled himself for what he prayed he wouldn't find and bolted through the grama grass, around a small hill, and into the field.

He spotted Sunny several yards ahead of him, kneeling in the high grass. Clay swept his eyes right and left, searching for the attacking Apaches. Nothing. He slid to a quick stop and knelt by Sunny, now on one knee. His friend's ashen face turned to him, and his hands shook. Clay followed Sunny's gaze.

Three feet in front of them lay Charles Culver, two arrows standing at attention in his back, the top of his bloody head missing its hair.

# CHAPTER THIRTY-THREE

One Wing snorted and kicked at James. James grunted, rolling with the moccasin's jab to his leg. A stiff morning breeze cooled the warm air that had attached itself to these sun-filled days. One Wing nodded. Soon, it would be time. Time to break these men forever.

The Apache war leader stood between the two men, these two brothers. Both had endured more than he thought they would. The days had been many since their capture, and yet, they did not give up. He wasn't finished with them, though. Not for a few suns more. But, soon enough.

He looked down at them and allowed his contempt, his utter hatred for the white man to take over. It felt good. Both men glared up at him, but he knew this was one of their last days. He'd tolerate it.

"White Eyes. You think you're so mighty? Look at you now!"

James yanked against the tether wrapped around his wrists. The wooden stake held firm. He squirmed harder. "Sonuva—"

"Give up." One Wing narrowed his eyes and glared. He pointed his chin at the ropes. "You try and try, but you have not broken free. You never will."

"We won't give up. Never." James strained against the bindings. "Not until you bury us."

One Wing's foot plowed into James' ribs. He smiled at the gurgles and groans that this prisoner made. The noises were most entertaining. Each day they grew softer, but just as desperate. "I'll never bury you, James Colton."

Trace strained against his bindings. "We won't give up."

He admired the attitude. They would've made good Apaches. One Wing pulled a knife from his leggings, then knelt by James. His eyes held the prisoner's gaze.

"After I drag your pathetic body into the desert, I'll let the

wolves tear you apart. Let them haul you off for their cubs to chew."
He held the knife up. Sun glinted off the steely blade. "Wolves are
too good for you. I'll leave your body to the buzzards."

The White Eyes squirmed. They weren't so tough any more.

One Wing cut James' bindings, then Trace's. They both just
lay there while he stood. A sneer curled up one side of his mouth.
It felt good. He had won. These brothers reminded him of dogs
waiting for their master's orders. Especially the older one. They
were his captives, his human animals to do whatever he wished.

"Up. Get up. Eat." One Wing watched these two men try to
stand. Try to be men. Try to stay alive. Each day it took longer
and longer for them to obey his commands, their bodies and spirits
more and more broken.

Once they had been like wild horses—unruly, headstrong,
almost impossible to break. The younger one had caused much
trouble and endured his best torture. One Wing admitted that this
James was strong willed and survived when no other prisoner had
before. However, even he was bending and would soon break. One
more thing to do before he and Cochise would use them to get
Coyuntura and all of their land returned. One more thing.

He allowed the brothers to sit shoulder to shoulder around
the campfire this morning. Their guards sat on either side, and
everyone held a bowl of breakfast stew. One Wing watched Quick-
to-Run, one of the girls who was coming of age to be a wife, brush
past James. She tossed a shy smile at him, then hurried toward
her parents' wickiup on the outskirts of camp.

While that was amusing, even better was the white man's
eyes watching her. Perhaps he had forgotten his own woman in
Mesilla. One Wing spotted lust on his face. Perhaps he desired to
be with Quick-to-Run. Perhaps she could add to his disgrace.

Before he could plot any further, five warriors rushed into
camp. They were greeted with the customary blessings and good
will. Cochise stepped from his wickiup and spoke with the men.

"Tell me your stories." Cochise nodded to an Apache, lance in
hand, a scalp dangling from the tip.

The warrior thrust out his chest. "The old man at the spring
house. It is his."

One Wing didn't bother to hide a smile. The manager of the
Apache Springs way station was dead! Victory, indeed. Now,
Cochise's men wouldn't have to bring firewood to the White Eyes

ever again.

James shook his head. "He was a real nice man. Didn't deserve to die."

At One Wing's shoulder stood Two Bears, a brutal warrior by any Apache standards. He'd taken his turns torturing the Colton brothers, and One Wing had to admit that he'd learned some new techniques watching him.

Two Bears hovered over James. "All white men deserve to die." Their eyes met. "You are next."

\* \* \*

After breakfast, One Wing joined the warriors as they paraded through the village. Victory would be swift and joyous. His fellow Apaches had worked themselves up into a frenzy with dancing and drumming. Now it was time to finish the Coltons. Today, they would give in. Today they would at long last become useful. Yes, today they would be broken.

He led James and Trace through the crowd to the remuda. Usually, the warriors ran wherever they raided, but today's raid was far away from their camp, so the horses stolen from other tribes and soldiers would be used. Most of the horses were pintos, their brown and white coats shining in the morning sun. They all sported red handprints, Cochise's sign, done earlier by the boys not yet old enough to raid.

Now at the remuda, One Wing held out a rawhide strip and wrapped the leather twice around James' wrists.

"You cannot be trusted," One Wing said. He brought the loop up between James' hands and knotted the binding.

Trace moved in closer to James.

"Soon," One Wing continued as he gave a final tug, "we will raid a large hacienda far from here. You will ride with us." He enjoyed the confused look on both men's faces. "You will see firsthand what my people can do. Then you will gladly help get the land and Cochise's brother returned."

James frowned. "You mean, we're supposed to help you kill settlers? Run them off their land?"

One Wing nodded.

"Won't kill innocent people." James glared at One Wing.

One Wing cocked his head. "Wouldn't you kill to keep what's

yours?"

"I would." Trace nodded, then looked at James. "I'd kill for my brothers, to keep them alive. But not for land. There's been enough bloodshed already."

One Wing laughed and said, "We've only begun." He pointed to the nearest horse, its rope reins tied to a bush. "You, Trace Colton. Get on."

Trace shrugged at his brother, then grabbed the horse's mane and swung up.

Nodding, One Wing turned his attention to the rebel James. He grabbed his shoulder and shoved him forward. James struggled against the grip.

"I won't kill! Won't." James planted his feet in the sand. "Let me go!"

This White Eyes was strong, One Wing realized again. But not strong enough. He kicked the back of James' knees and enjoyed watching him plow into the sand. One Wing moved in front of his prisoner. "You're weak. Nothing but an old woman."

James mumbled something One Wing couldn't quite understand. No matter. By this time tomorrow, James would be dead.

He yanked James up to his feet, bringing him inches from his face. "You ride with us. You kill with us. Or you die."

James pulled his shoulders back and thrust out his chest. But, he said nothing.

The Colton brothers joined the Apache raiding party.

* * *

"Care to join me for some dinner, Miss Simmons?" Sheriff Alberto Fuente leaned into Lila's ear.

She spun around and clutched her throat. "Sheriff. You scared the livin' daylights outta me."

A tight smile replaced the panic on her face. Her eyes, dulled with grief, sparked for a moment.

"Sorry 'bout that," he said. "I thought you heard me come in." He touched her arm. So far, he'd only talked to her here in the Mercantile or in his office. He hoped that after today he could take her other places.

Lila glanced around the store and brushed a loose strand of

hair from her forehead. "Guess I was off thinkin' again."

Fuente also glanced around the store. One customer lingered in the back area. Fuente held both of Lila's arms and gazed into her eyes. "It's hard to let go, I know. When my wife died, I did just what you're doing." He paused, allowing memories to take control for a moment.

Lila nodded. "It is hard."

Fuente eased his arm around her shoulders and dropped his voice to his most comforting tone. "James would want you to get on with life as quickly as possible. He'd want you to be happy. To live for him."

Lila nodded. "That's just what Missus Grey says."

"She's a smart woman." Fuente gave Lila his best smile. "Ask her for an hour off, and I'll take you to El Pinto. They make great enchiladas. Besides, you gotta eat, keep your strength up."

"You're right. I'll be back directly."

At the restaurant, an hour passed in conversation. Lila pushed her food around her plate while Fuente finished off tortillas, beans and enchiladas, then ordered dessert.

Over more coffee, Fuente realized he'd been doing most of the talking. He reached across the table for her hand. "You know, Miss Simmons, I met you over a year ago, but I don't really know much about you. Care to share?"

"Not much to tell, Sheriff."

"Call me Alberto. I'd be honored if you would."

Lila nodded. "I was born in South Carolina. My pa died before I could really remember him. Ma's family, thankfully, took us in."

"Family's a good thing. Something we take for granted." Fuente sighed. "You're lucky."

Lila shook her head. "It was fine for a while. But about three years ago, the fever struck. Everyone died but Ma and me. We headed out west to escape the fever and the memories."

Fuente reached for her soft hand. Her pretty blue eyes had seen their fair share of grief. He wanted to draw her close to him, hold her against his chest—never let go. He forced himself to release her hand. He clutched his coffee cup instead.

Lila swiped at a tear perched in the corner of her eye. "I'm sorry, Alberto. Didn't mean to turn this lovely meal into something morbid. I apologize."

"Never apologize to me, Miss Simmons. *Any* conversation

with you is always welcome." His pounding heart launched itself into his throat. So close, yet still so far away.

"Thank you for the compliment, Alberto, but I'm afraid I've got to get back to the store. Missus Grey will wonder if I ran off with the sheriff."

*If only you would.*

Lila flashed a dazzling display of teeth.

Fuente's knees weakened as he rose and held Lila's chair for her.

*Calm down. James isn't buried quite yet.*

Fuente stopped at the door to the Mercantile and gripped the handle. "Thank you again for accompanying me. We'll have to do it again some time, Miss Simmons."

Lila's southern accent wafting around Fuente's ears rang with the sweetness of church bells. "I'd be delighted, Alberto."

She produced that damn alluring smile.

"And...call me Lila."

# PART THREE

# CHAPTER THIRTY-FOUR

Sun battered the desert. Hooves thundered. Sagebrush and cactus flew past. Mile after mile, hour after hour, James rode. His legs quivered with fatigue; his shoulders screamed at the kinked muscles. The raiding party galloped past a ranch burned to the ground. Puffs of brown smoke still rose on the wind. Their route around a small mountain range took them through a narrow valley and across an endless meadow.

As they galloped, James regarded his brother by his side. What was he thinking?

They topped a steep rise and pulled to an abrupt stop. One Wing's eyes were narrow and hard, blood lusting. James looked down the line of warriors. Their faces mirrored the same lust, the same anger, the same passion for death and destruction.

Surrounded by several outlying buildings, a large ranch house was silhouetted against the turquoise sky. A mule team plowed the earth, a man urging them forward. Children laughed, chickens clucked, and a dog barked. Somewhere, possibly out back, a woman called for the children.

Without a word of warning, Cochise raised his lance and let out a cry that raised the hair on the back of James' neck.

The other warriors followed his lead, hollering, screeching, and urging their mounts down onto the unsuspecting settlers.

The rancher and children stopped and looked up. One Wing slapped the rump of James' horse. James yanked back on the reins, but his pinto paid no attention to his command and raced forward, appearing to enjoy this raid as much as the Apaches. James and Trace charged alongside the others, their horses galloping into the ranch yard, scattering people and livestock.

The woman appeared in the front yard. James screamed, "Grab the kids. Run!"

His warnings died under the war cries. He spurred his horse

toward the left side of the yard, then rode hard to catch up with the hysterical woman, to shield her from the warriors. He leaned over his pinto's neck. She froze, staring.

"White man?" Her eyes grew wider.

Tied hands extended, James leaned down. "Get on. I'll help you!"

Before she could respond, two Apaches swooped past James. One leaned over and grabbed the woman around the waist, hoisting her onto his horse.

James kicked his pinto and galloped behind the terrified woman. Stretching out his bound hands, he tried to knock her out of the warrior's grasp. From out of nowhere, Cochise rode alongside James and grabbed the reins. He jerked both horses to a stop.

James squeezed his eyes shut as the woman's screams faded.

"Do not interfere, James Colton. You are here to watch and learn. Nothing more. Soon it will be up to you and your brother to make sure no one else dies like this. You can prevent this."

Cochise flipped the reins back to his captive and spurred his horse toward the rear of the main building.

James studied the receding image of the powerful Apache chief. Then he turned his attention to Trace, less than five yards away. Those wide shoulders were pushed back, his chin jutting out. James knew the shape of a frustrated brother. He rode up next to Trace.

"Let's escape. They won't notice."

Trace grabbed James' reins. "Told you once before. No. We wouldn't get ten feet."

James glanced over his shoulder and caught One Wing's stare. He turned back to his brother. "Damn. At least gotta help these people."

"I agree." Trace's worried eyes turned on James. "You got a plan?"

James shook his head. "No. But I just can't sit here." He spurred his pinto and aimed for the back of the house where he thought the children had been.

From somewhere close behind him, he heard Trace's horse.

At the back of the mud plastered adobe house, both men reined up as three Apaches dogged two running men. Finally, their lances embedded into the ranchers' chests.

Many of the warriors waited, watching their victory. Several were on their feet shouting, dancing, enjoying the moment. One Wing grabbed James' arm, yanking him off his horse and forcing James to stand at the Apache's side. One Wing spread his arms, showing off their handiwork.

"Look. Look what my people can do."

Two more ranch hands were dragged to the backyard, deposited like discards against the two recently killed. Their limp bodies rolled into each other. Sobs and cries for mercy from the few people still alive. James felt their terror. He knew.

James looked back at his brother. Trace's shoulders sagged, his entire body slouched, and his head wagged side to side. Trace's black and white pinto stood in the middle of the noise and violence as if he did it every day, waiting for the man on top to choose the next victim.

The backyard of this house, which until moments ago rang with children full of life, now tolled with death. The stench overwhelmed James. He gagged. Blood flowed around his feet as One Wing pulled him closer to the dead.

Bodies convulsed in death throes. Moans. Chanting Apaches. Stench of death. Burning animals. Fiery heat.

Crimson blood.

Blue sky.

White clouds.

The devil himself played this hand.

The grip on James' arm tightened as One Wing pulled him over bodies and around to the far side of the massacre. That woman. The woman James tried to rescue lay sprawled face down at his feet. One of her legs quivered.

One Wing pulled his hunting knife from his tegua and slapped it into James' tied hands.

"You, James Colton." One Wing's deep voice resonated against James' ear. "Scalp this white woman."

James looked down at the knife in his hand. "What?"

His heart thundered. The cold knife grew red hot in his hand.

One Wing pushed James to his knees. James looked at the woman, then turned to his brother. What would Trace do? What should he do?

His brother's eyes grew hard; his mouth set a tight line. "She's already dead, James."

One Wing, kneeling next to James, gripped a fistful of the

163

woman's hair and pulled. Her head wobbled in his grasp.

"Take her scalp."

James inched the knife forward. Trace's words echoed in his head.

*She's already dead.*

The woman moaned.

"She's alive!" James jumped to his feet. The knife clattered to the ground.

A hand pushed the back of James' head down and forward until he knelt over the woman once more.

Someone grabbed his hand and folded his unwilling fingers around the knife's handle. Then One Wing wrapped the woman's hair around James' hand and the knife. James struggled against it.

"No. Please. She's not even dead!" James untangled his hand and dropped the knife. He scrambled to his feet.

One Wing tackled him, forcing him to his knees again. "Scalp her," he hissed.

"No, I won't!" James shook his head.

The knife handle once more jammed into his hand.

More feminine groans.

One Wing shook as James struggled against him. His words spurted between clenched teeth.

"You *will* obey."

Without warning, the whooping, chanting, and cheering stopped. The Apaches turned their full attention on the unfolding drama. Indian arms wrapped around him, James twisted like a rabbit in a snare.

"Never."

James prayed his voice was strong enough to cover his absolute terror.

"You will bend to my wishes." One Wing gripped James. "Cochise watches. You will break right now." He tightened his hold, squeezing. "I will be honored in song tonight. Then I also will have a tribe."

"Never."

James couldn't breathe, the embrace too strong. Another shallow breath, then One Wing relaxed, pulling him away from the woman.

One Wing grabbed James' tied hands. Their eyes met.

"It is time, James Colton."

One Wing had James right where he wanted him, and James knew it. There was nothing he could do but stand up as One Wing yanked. Then One Wing waved a knife in front of James' eyes. Parts not dulled by blood, glinted in the sun.

A quick downward stroke. James' hands snapped free.

Terror. Confusion. Anguish. He held his freed hands in front of his face, not understanding. One Wing's face hovered inches from James' ear.

"Now, you will use *both* hands to take the enemy's scalp." One Wing held up James' arms like a prizefighter and shouted to the gathered warriors. "He is no longer bound and will take the woman's scalp of his own free will."

James' breath spurted through his nose; his heart thundered in his ears like the drums he'd heard for weeks. One Wing's grip on his arm tightened, forcing him to kneel. The woman twitched. James shook his head.

"Now!" One Wing's words stung James. "Or I will peel the skin from your brother's entire body. Then I kill him."

*He's angry enough to do it this time.*

"I'll skin him like a rabbit," One Wing said, "then leave his carcass for the scorpions."

James gulped a lungful of air.

"Her...or your brother."

James stroked the woman's head, caressing a fistful of hair as he gripped the knife. The hair felt like Lila's—full and silky with a slight curl. It wasn't the same color, but it was soft, freshly washed.

The woman twitched again. Another moan? Pounding in his ears shut out noise. Her head flopped.

"Kill her?" James gripped the handle until his knuckles glowed white. He clenched his jaw. "Now I kill this woman?"

"Now." One Wing's words sizzled in James' ear.

James whirled and slashed at One Wing with the knife.

The Apache clutched his chest and left arm, as a line of red soaked through his shirt. James sprung up, thrusting the knife again and again at One Wing.

"No! I won't be like you!"

Like a wild man, James slashed at air, at Apaches, at memories.

Someone grabbed the back of his shirt and yanked. He stumbled backwards.

"No!" James scrambled to turn around and get to One Wing.

One step. Two. In a flash, his world caught fire. Bright lights. The back of his head ignited. Whooshing in his ears. Knees on the ground. Dirt in his mouth.

A groan. Then black.

# CHAPTER THIRTY-FIVE

"Imbecile! An incompetent imbecile! That's what you are, Fuente." Lieutenant Bascom's voice rang off the walls of the sheriff's office. "Totally, completely incompetent!"

"Now wait just a minute, Bascom," Fuente said. "My jail held those Indians. It was your people who let them escape."

"Let them?" Bascom came within inches of Fuente and stood nose to nose. "The hell *let them*."

"How else did they get out?"

"Your incompetence as a sheriff. Your pathetic jail, your inability to do your job! You ought to be fired." He turned his back and marched the entire length of the office. "Ought to get somebody in here who knows what he's doing."

Fuente exploded. "That's it! Out! Get out! I won't be talked to that way." He charged Bascom, spun him around, and then grabbed the front of his uniform.

"Take your filthy hands off me, Fuente, or I'll have *you* arrested." Red faced, Bascom spit the words.

Corporal Connor and a sergeant stepped forward. Fuente released Bascom, then stepped back. Connor's hand hovered over his gun, ready to kill. Fuente figured he'd do it, too.

"Look, Bascom," Fuente said. "Instead of blaming me and arguing, shouldn't you be spending your energy out looking for those Apaches? I hear they've got quite a head start."

"There's a full detail out now. We'll find those murdering savages." Bascom wheeled around. "Corporal Connor."

"Sir?"

"Bring me Private Patton and the other three guards on duty last night."

"Sir, Private Patton's still at the infirmary. Got beaten pretty badly I'm afraid."

"Can he talk?"

"I believe he has recently regained consciousness, sir. I'm not sure how much he'll remember right now, though." Connor's stone face revealed no hint of emotion.

Bascom eyed Fuente. "Put Patton on report, Corporal. He's to be confined to bed and then to jail as soon as he's fully awake."

"Yes, sir." Corporal Connor nodded. "Should I send in the other three guards now?"

"One at a time. Let's see how well their stories match."

Bascom sat behind Fuente's desk, then looked up at Mesilla's sheriff as if surprised to see Fuente still in the room.

"This is a military matter," Bascom said. "You're not needed here. Why don't you go do something? Something that doesn't require any thinking?"

Fuente leaped headfirst over his desk, plowing into Bascom. Both men crashed to the floor. Papers, wanted posters, and a coffee cup flew off the desk. Fuente landed two teeth-jarring punches before Corporal Connor and the sergeant pulled him off.

Hoisted to his feet by Connor, Fuente trembled, rage curling his fists. He fought against Connor's death-hold on his arms.

Bascom brushed aside offers of help and scrambled to his feet. His pointed finger jerked toward the cells behind the closed door.

"Lock him up."

"Sir."

Corporal Connor shoved Fuente past Bascom, through the inner door and into the closest cell. After slamming the metal door closed, Connor turned the key. He nodded at the click of the lock.

* * *

Two hours of interrogating the three guards brought Bascom no closer to solving the puzzle. The pivotal clue had to lie with Patton, and he was still in no condition to talk.

Bascom paced the office—window to desk, desk to wall, wall to window. Connor waited, watching and ready to obey orders. Bascom wandered the office, picked up a wanted poster, then tossed it back onto the stack of papers.

"Have Patton ready to talk tomorrow."

"I'll make sure, sir."

Bascom nodded. "Patton has two close friends, does he not?"

"Rivers and Jamison."

Bascom raised an eyebrow. "Get those men in here. Let's hear their story."

He sat behind the desk and shuffled papers while his officer slipped out the front door.

Within a half-hour, the two privates stood at attention in front of Bascom's desk. He paced behind it, arms crossed on his chest.

"Now let me get this straight." Bascom stopped mid-stride. "Neither of you were in town last night?"

"Correct, sir." Jamison nodded.

"And even though two of the guards here thought they recognized you, you swear you were back at camp? All night?"

"Yes, sir," Rivers said.

"You know you can be executed for lying, gentlemen?"

"Yes, sir."

"Who else saw you at camp?"

Jamison spoke first. "Probably no one, sir. We stayed in our tent playin' cards most of the night."

"Just the two of us, sir. No one else wanted to join us." Rivers looked straight ahead.

Bascom eyed the men. A deep breath. He played with a pencil on the desk. "All right. That's it for now. Dismissed."

The privates saluted their commanding officer and turned to go. Jamison pivoted back.

"Sir? How is Private Patton?"

"I understand he'll live," Bascom said. "Just proves what lying, cheating, murdering savages those Apaches are. This world'll be a better place when we exterminate all Indians."

* * *

Bascom looked up from the desk as the door opened and Lila Belle Simmons stepped in. Her beauty stole his breath. His face grew warm, and a stirring started its journey from his stomach downward. He fought the attraction, learning years ago to keep feelings buried. No one would hurt him ever again. Ever.

He stood as she shut the door.

"What can I do for you, Miss Simmons?" Bascom lowered the papers still in his hand. His mouth turned dry.

"I'd like to see Sheriff Fuente, sir. I understand he's bein' held against his will."

Lila's eyes glowed as her gaze met his. Was that anger? Concern? It certainly lit up her pretty face.

"Yes, he is. He assaulted a United States Army officer. That crime's punishable by death."

Bascom thought of the attention Washington would give him when they received word of this sheriff's arrest. Another thought struck him. Maybe it was attention he didn't welcome. There would be too many questions about the Indians' escape. Questions he couldn't answer. They might even question his ability to lead his troops.

"I'm sure the sheriff was only defendin' what he believes in, Lieutenant." Lila's southern charm and drawl warmed the room. "I was wonderin' if I could see him."

Bascom languished in her shining blue eyes. Lila moved closer.

"I'd just be a minute. I don't have any weapons or jail keys, Mister Bascom." She spread her arms out to her side. "You can search me if you'd like."

Bascom's cheeks burned. "Go ahead, Miss Simmons."

He stuttered and hated himself for it. Soft. Too damn soft. "Three minutes."

"Thank you, sir. I'll be quick."

Lila opened the door to the jail cells, stepped through, and disappeared.

* * *

Fuente wanted to run to her, grab her, and hold her forever. Instead, he forced himself to stroll over to the bars. He couldn't help but smile.

"Good to see you again, Lila. You're lookin' pretty as ever."

"Thank you, Sheriff. Sorry to see you in here. Came soon as I heard. How can I help?" She gazed into his eyes.

"You already have. Just by bein' here." Fuente breathed in lilac, soft words, and radiant eyes. His hand reached out and stroked her soft face.

Lila's cheeks turned a deep pink. Her smile melted into a frown. "I just can't help but think this is all my fault. When they said they had a plan, I didn't think it was talkin' to the Indians. And you wouldn't be behind bars, and that private wouldn't be almost dead."

Fuente leaned in closer. "What'd you tell them?"

Lila related the conversation with the three privates. Leaving nothing out, she spoke for a few minutes.

"Did Private...what's his name?" Fuente soaked in every word.

"Patton."

"Did Private Patton tell you anything? Did the Apaches talk?"

"That poor soldier's just now comin' to, but his memory's gone. Doctor Logan called it a...a concussion. Says Private Patton won't be able to tell us what happened."

Fuente shook his head. He was as puzzled as Bascom how those prisoners managed to escape. No signs of forced entry. The window bars were still intact, and the lock wasn't broken. It had to have been a key. But who? Those soldiers must've been involved. But why?

His thoughts refocused on the young lady in front of him. Fuente reached through the bars and took her hand. "Sorry to hear about that private. When he talks, let me know what he says."

"Of course, Sheriff."

"Alberto, Lila. Remember. Please call me Alberto."

Pink radiated over her face. "Missus Grey says you're a good man. Says..." The cheeks reddened.

"What does Missus Grey say?" Fuente hoped for the right words.

Lila gripped the bars. "Says I should find a place for...for James, but concentrate on the living." She ducked her head and peeked out from under a blond curl. "She says you'd make a fine husband."

Fuente placed his hand over hers and stroked the slim fingers. Just what he'd wanted to hear. Inch by inch his hands slid up her arms, pulling her toward him.

The kiss was soft, tender, passionate.

# CHAPTER THIRTY-SIX

Fiery jolts. Incessant throbbing. James' eyes fluttered open, then snapped shut. His stomach flip-flopped.

Breathing proved difficult. His ribs throbbed and ached at every movement, every breath, every beat of his heart. Dying couldn't possibly hurt this much.

*Must still be among the living.*

That dream. It seemed so real. More dream memories. The panic of those dying ranchers, their screams, the terror on their faces. The woman—her hair.

A hand on his shoulder. He curled into a ball, cowering, waiting for the fist to pound his face again. At the very least, a sharp kick to his stomach.

The hand shook him. He jerked away, tucking his chin into his chest.

"James?" A familiar voice whispered in his ear. "It's me."

James inched away from the hand and voice. Had to be a trick, something One Wing would do just so he could beat him again, torture him until he cried like a baby. He hated himself for being weak, sobbing and begging in front of One Wing. But there were times when he couldn't help it; the pain was just too much.

"I'm not gonna hurt you. It's Trace. Open your eyes."

One more ragged breath and James pried his one good eye open. The other, still too swollen, remained clamped shut. The early morning sun warmed his face. He squinted against it and took in the silhouette of his brother.

"Trace?"

James held his ribs and uncurled. A soft blanket under him cushioned his sore body. It took effort to roll onto his back, but then it struck him—he was free. His hands were not tied, his feet not tethered. No part of his body was bound to heavy wooden stakes or prickly cactus.

He sat up. "Trace?"

"Don't try to talk." Trace held a gourd dipper to James' bruised mouth.

Water slid down his parched throat, soothing most of the raw places. He leaned against Trace's chest. Arms around him. Strong, protective. He shut his eye and relaxed.

"Trace?" James' voice grated husky, raw.

"Yeah?"

"We still alive?"

"Yeah."

"Free?"

Trace paused. "No."

James hung his head and let out a long stream of air. "Had a terrible dream last night. We helped kill a woman. Had to scalp her." He rubbed his eyes, desperate to block out the images.

"Wasn't a dream."

James twisted around at Trace. Jabbing pain shot down his back.

"You don't remember?" Trace asked.

James rubbed his temples, then looked at his brother. Had Trace slept at all last night? Despite his tanned skin, he was pale.

"It's all a blur." He scooted around until he faced his brother. "God. I thought it was a dream."

The raid, the massacre, burning, killing, screaming... scalping.

"I killed that woman!" James' eyes locked on his brother's. "He made me kill her! That sonuvabitch made me kill her!"

"You didn't kill her. She died before..." Trace hesitated. "You didn't take her scalp, James."

"Did One Wing scalp her? But, how—"

"Shush, now."

Trace squeezed James' shoulder. Both men sat still. In the background, women chatted to each other while stirring pots of stew, children laughed at their chores, dogs growled over a tidbit of food.

James swiped at a hank of his shoulder-length hair plastered to his black and blue cheek. He turned his hands over. "No ropes?"

Why? Trace would have the answers—he always did.

173

"What's going on?" James asked.

Trace shrugged. "After we got back last night, One Wing just told me to sleep here."

"They've never let us get this close before."

James swiveled his entire body to survey the surrounding camp. Less than ten feet away sat Cochise's wickiup, another twenty feet, One Wing's.

"Certainly beats being tied to one of those cactus, doesn't it?" James asked.

Trace nodded. A group of Apaches hurried past, a few of them slowing to stare.

James met the gaze of one, Standing Pony. More painful memories. James rubbed his forehead. "I just remember her hair. Lila's hair."

"Dammit, James, forget the damn hair. It wasn't Lila." Trace shook James' shoulders. He paused, then lowered his arms and voice, pulled in air. "But something happened you need to remember."

James frowned. Trace's voice was edged with worry—or was it something else?

"What?"

Three blinks, Trace started then stopped. "During that raid, you..." Trace frowned and glanced away. "Well, you sliced One Wing pretty good. Chest and arm."

"Good God." James grabbed his brother's shirtsleeve. "How bad? Did I kill him?"

Trace shook his head.

"Wish to hell I did. Needs it."

"Listen to me," Trace said. "After that, you passed out. Cochise brought you back head-first down over his horse."

"Cochise?" James shuddered. "He let me live. Why?"

Trace shrugged.

"And brought me back? Himself?"

Trace nodded.

James studied the ground, then his hands. "Damn, don't remember any of that. So that's why every inch of my body's killing me. All those hours draped over a horse." He searched his brother's face for understanding.

"One Wing's gonna kill me for sure now," James said. "That old Indian's tried but—"

A shadow slid across Trace's body. A young Apache woman knelt beside the two men and offered them water from a small jug. They both accepted. She aimed a shy smile at James, then hurried away.

"Know her name?" Trace watched the slim figure disappear into a crowd.

"I think somebody called her Quick-to-Run or something like that. She's kinda pretty. She's the one who's been slipping us extra food and water." James cut his eyes sideways at his brother. "Suppose she likes you?"

Trace shook his head. "Nope. She likes *you*." He recoiled. One Wing hovered over them.

James gazed up into the anger on One Wing's scowling face. No, not anger.

Rage.

"Up!"

Determined to appear strong and unafraid in front of One Wing, James pushed to his knees. One Wing prodded until James staggered to his feet. Trace was right behind him.

Although One Wing's upper arm was bandaged, a tinge of pink bled through the material. A fresh shirt and bandage covered his chest. One Wing poked James.

James held his head up high. He balled a fist, ready for another fight.

Instead of attacking, One Wing cocked his head toward the center of camp. "Eat," he said.

The Colton brothers limped toward the fire. The aroma of venison stew combined with mesquite smoke wafted through the air. If it hadn't been so sore, James' stomach would have grumbled.

Before James reached the fire, One Wing grabbed the back of his shirt and spun him around.

"You brought shame, humiliation to me, James Colton. You disobeyed...*defied* me in front of Cochise."

One Wing shoved James so hard that he windmilled backwards several feet. James thudded into the dirt and slammed his head against the ground. He fought to roll over, get to his feet.

One Wing attacked before James could push himself up. Both men tumbled across the sand, cartwheeling over and over like two men in a prison yard brawl. James shoved One Wing off, landing a quick jab in his stomach before a vicious blow to his chest knocked the air out of his lungs.

Without warning, the attack stopped. James sucked in gallons of air. His heart pounded.

Cochise hovered over him.

One Wing spoke to his leader. Pointing, gesturing, obvious anger was all James understood.

Trace squatted by James. "All right?"

James struggled to sit up, wincing as air filled his aching chest. A nod. Blood trickled into his mouth. Staccato Apache words swirled around him.

"Again, One Wing couldn't kill me," James said. He spit red.

"Don't get so uppity, little brother. Talkin' like that'll get you killed for sure." Trace raised his eyebrows toward the Indians. "They're arguing about something. Gotta be you."

James listened to the argument. One Wing jabbed his extended arm toward him and then in the direction of the raided farm. Cochise shot back with quick motions of his hands alternating between the farm and James.

Cochise snapped a final word at One Wing, then marched away. One Wing watched the leader's back disappear into a small gathering of warriors.

One side of One Wing's mouth curved into a sneer as he jerked James to his feet. He cocked his head toward the tribal leader, then back at his captives. "You eat now. Then we counsel with Cochise."

One Wing narrowed his eyes; the stare was hard, cold. "Do or say one thing wrong, James Colton, I will cut out your heart and feed it to you before you hit the ground."

James swallowed hard.

# CHAPTER THIRTY-SEVEN

For seven long days, Bascom waited for word from Fort Stanton. Further orders since his prisoners had escaped. That's all he wanted. Now that he had his orders, Lieutenant Bascom gripped the paper.

He reread the message. Between the lines, they were threatening to take away his command. How dare they question his leadership, his ability to keep six hostiles in captivity until delivered to their final destination? How dare they!

He snorted. If the almighty General hadn't sent so many troops out of Fort Bliss, by now the Indians already would have been delivered to the officers there. But, no, the Army had to make life difficult. Had to throw as many obstacles into his life as possible.

His orders were clear. Find the missing Apaches. Recapture them. If he failed, the Army would rescind his commission. He would become a civilian. A disgraced civilian.

Someone would pay for this. He wasn't going to take the entire blame for the Apache fiasco. He crumbled the paper in his fist.

"Corporal Connor." Bascom barked at his second, who was busy filling out requisitions on a makeshift desk—two chairs placed seat to seat—next to Fuente's larger desk.

"Sir?"

"Get Private Bill Patton in here. Now."

"He's locked up in the cell right behind you, sir."

"I *know* that Corporal. Bring him here."

Connor jumped out of his seat, rushed to the cell, and brought out a limping Private Patton. Connor gripped Patton's arm as they stood next to each other in front of the commander's desk.

"Private Patton." Bascom's voice rang hard, cold.

"Sir."

"With that damn war coming closer and the need for

expediency, I'm waiving your right to a court martial. I hereby strip you of your rank of private and grant you a dishonorable discharge from the United States Army."

Bill's eyes widened, while his mouth opened and closed. Words refused to take proper shape.

"But sir...I explained...that Indian—"

"I remember our conversation, Private. Committing perjury can put you in prison for years if that's what you'd prefer."

Private Bill Patton looked at Bascom, then Connor, then back to Bascom. He hung his head.

"No, sir."

"Corporal Connor will put together the necessary papers for you to sign. After you do so, pack up your gear and get out of town."

Not waiting for any further rebuttal, discussion, or argument, Bascom saluted. "Dismissed."

Lieutenant George Bascom picked up a stack of papers and turned his attention to more important matters. From the corner of his eye, he watched Connor escort a limping Patton back to his jail cell, that mouth still flapping like a dying sucker.

Bascom shuffled papers, sorting, and resorting. He smacked the stack on the table, dropped the papers, and stared at Connor.

"Corporal?"

"Sir?"

"Prepare to move the troops out first thing in the morning."

"Yes, sir. Where're we going, sir?"

"This Coyuntura was small potatoes, Corporal. We're going after the big man himself—Cochise."

Bascom nodded and leaned back in his chair. His fingers tapped on the desk. "Washington'll sit up and take notice now," he said. "Yeah, they'll know who I am."

\* \* \*

Within minutes, Private Bill Patton became Mister Bill Patton. He stopped in front of the Mesilla Mercantile, then limped inside, searching for Lila. His gaze rested on the young woman at the other side of the store. He waved as best he could. His ribs were nowhere close to healed, but a healthy dose of laudanum allowed him to move at least.

Lila rushed over and helped him to a seat in the corner. "You shouldn't be out of bed so soon, Private Patton."

He shook his head and thought about what he had to tell her. "Not Private. Mister. Got thrown out a few minutes ago."

Lila knelt beside him. "I'm so sorry, so very sorry. It's all my fault. How can I help you?"

He shook his head. "Bascom says I gotta leave town."

"Can he do that?"

"He just did. If you see my two friends, tell 'em I had to leave. I'll write when I settle down somewhere."

"All right, Mister Patton, I will." Lila sighed. "I hate to ask, but did you talk to those Indians? Did they tell you anything about James and Trace?" She looked away, then wrenched her gaze back to Patton. "Where their bodies are?"

He grasped her trembling hands. "I'm sorry. I don't remember anything much about that night. Just that Coyuntura hits really hard."

Lila stared into the distance. A small breath passed over her lips. "Probably for the best anyway. I need to put James to rest for good, and I know there's no hope of recovering his body. It's been too long now." Her eyes met his. "Best leave him here in my heart."

Bill Patton rose to his feet.

"I'll be glad to speak to your friends, Mister Patton. They come in here every chance they get." Lila gave him a quick kiss on the cheek and smiled at his smile. "I truly appreciate your tryin'. Don't know how I'll ever thank you."

"Glad to do it. Sorry it didn't work out better." His grin melted. "Guess I better be movin' on."

"I guess we both need to, Mister Patton." Lila returned his nod. "We both need to."

# CHAPTER THIRTY-EIGHT

In his wickiup, Cochise sat on a tightly woven blanket, its gray, red, and white stripes wide. He studied the three men in front of him—One Wing and the Colton brothers—seated on smaller blankets, and he knew the time was right.

One Wing's anger was obvious. He had promised to keep James alive long enough to accomplish the Apaches' goals, but this proud warrior would make the young prisoner's life very difficult. Even more than he had already.

Cochise eyed James. There sat a man whose life would be traded for the entire future of the Apaches. Admiration and respect for James welled in his chest. Here was a White Eyes who dared defy One Wing, a ruthless killer. James defended his brother, never wavered in his beliefs, and as far as Cochise knew, never lied. His attitude was still quite spirited, although toned down in the past weeks. Admirable traits.

Too bad he would die.

He turned his focus to Trace, a man who would willingly sacrifice his own life for his brother's. Now he was broken, the fire dead inside this stage driver. His face painted the picture of a man trying to survive, but not expecting to. Yes, Trace would serve his purposes well.

Several minutes ticked by while Cochise chose his words.

"My people have been pushed farther into the desert. We have lost our homeland, but we will get it back. We will do whatever it takes for as long as it takes." He paused, watching the captives' faces.

James and Trace stole a glance at each other.

Cochise continued. "As you know, my brother, Coyuntura, his wife, son, and three other Apaches have been captured, taken prisoner by your army. My brother is to be executed. You, Trace Colton, will get him back before that happens."

Trace frowned, furrows creasing his forehead, mouth open. "What? How?"

"I have word they are in jail in Mesilla, held by a man named Bascom, a leader in your army." Cochise's voice resonated against the wickiup's skin. "You will travel there, free all of them, bring them here. Alive." His words left no room for discussion. "You will also order the army to ride away. Leave us alone."

Trace turned his hands palm up. "I'm just a stagecoach driver. No one listens to me, Cochise. My words will be hollow. How am I supposed to get your family released?" The words caught in his throat. "How am I supposed to get the army to leave?"

"You must find a way. Your brother's life depends on it."

One Wing spoke for the first time. "We waited until we were sure you would not try to escape. You proved it yesterday, Trace Colton. You proved you would follow commands."

"You can be trusted, unlike your brother." One Wing glared again at James, then returned his attention to Trace. "Yesterday you showed us you will stop at nothing to save him."

A smirk returned to his face. One Wing spoke to James. "Did you see the scalp hanging outside?"

James nodded.

"That scalp is the one your brother took yesterday, to save your life. It will be a reminder to you he is stronger, a better man than you. He does what is required."

Mouth open, James leaned away from Trace. "You? You scalped that woman?"

Trace stared at his hands, his shoulders slumped, sorrow lining his face.

Silence.

Cochise waited.

Both brothers frowned, cocked their heads, stared at the ground, but neither could speak to the other.

After another moment, Cochise said, "James Colton, you will stay here while your brother rides to Mesilla. If he does not return soon, you die."

One Wing removed something from beneath a blanket. "Every day you are gone, Trace Colton," One Wing said, "your brother will receive five strokes of this." He held up a black rod with three feet of braided leather thong. "Is this whip familiar?"

Trace sat bolt upright. "It's mine."

181

One Wing displayed the initials **TC** carved into the leather handle. "We took many things from your stagecoach. This is my favorite." A sneer crawled up his face. "I cut the whip in half and used the rest of the rawhide to bind you."

"Cochise, One Wing." Trace swung his gaze from man to man. "I will do whatever you ask. I'll ride faster than the wind. But, I beg you, don't whip my little brother. I promise he will obey you."

One Wing snorted and ran his hand across his bandaged chest. "I see how he obeys." His chin tilted up. "No, you will ride fast for your brother's life and he will obey me to save his worthless skin. Each time he does not follow my orders, I will add five more strokes."

"When I return with your brother and the army promises to ride away, Cochise, will you release James?" Trace raised both eyebrows.

Cochise's gaze melted into memories. "When I was young, I walked all over this country, east and west, and saw no other people than the Apaches." Cochise sighed. "Today, I see too many people taking our land." He stared at Trace. "We will spill much more blood if necessary. I do not care how you get my brother free. Your white man's army must know we will keep our land. We will fight until all this is ours once more."

"But—"

"Your brother will be released when Coyuntura is by my side and the army is gone. Only then." Cochise raised his hand in a signal to One Wing. "You have my word, Trace Colton."

James squared his shoulders. He picked his head up high. "Cochise, One Wing. I know why you ride against the settlers." James' voice echoed renewed strength. "I understand wanting your land and your brother returned to you. But killing is no answer." He looked at Trace.

"I'll get it done, James," Trace said.

No matter how brave his words were, Cochise knew this man was grief-stricken, probably thinking that his brother would die here in camp. He was right. As weak as James was, unless Trace rode hard and fast, his brother would end up a coyote's meal in a few days.

James stared at the black whip clutched in One Wing's hand. "Cochise, what if...I die before—"

"I send out a war party, hunt your brother, kill him."

James took a deep breath and met One Wing's stare. "So that I won't die by your whip, I'll obey you. Won't cause you any trouble."

"We will see," One Wing said.

Eyes trailing up to Trace's face, James said, "At least you'll be free to live for both of us. Grab Teresa and hold on. Don't come back. Whatever you do, don't come back."

"Shush, now." Trace held James' shoulder. "I'll get the army to leave, find his brother, and you'll be home in time for Sunday dinner."

Cochise pointed at Trace. "You will leave as soon as supplies and water are packed on your horse."

One Wing slipped a length of thick rope from under his shirt, then knelt in front of James. In less than half a minute, James was bound once more. He looked away and grimaced as the ropes cut into his skin. One Wing hoisted James up, tugging him toward the wickiup door.

Trace scrambled to his feet and grabbed at James' shirt.

"I'll be back—soon," Trace promised.

James buried his face in Trace's chest. "All the torture put together doesn't hurt as bad as this," he said.

"I know," Trace said.

One Wing wedged himself between the brothers and shoved James backward through the wickiup's opening.

James, eyes red and shirt spotted with tears, yelled at the brush-covered lean-to.

"Tell Lila I love her!"

* * *

Within a half-hour, Trace swung up on the same muscled black and white pinto he'd ridden the day before. The Indian blanket under him emitted a warmth, a vague sense of security he needed. Although there was no saddle, this horse was bit broken— no doubt stolen from some ranch. Rope reins hung on either side of the pinto's mottled neck.

Trace sat motionless astride that horse, ready to ride away. He could ride anywhere he wanted—his hands weren't bound, and no one held an arrow or rifle to his chest. For weeks all he'd dreamed about was riding away, escaping into freedom, but now,

183

without James, he wanted to stay. All desire to leave evaporated.

One big breath and he nudged the horse east, toward Mesilla, toward uncertainty. He prayed the army would listen to him, let Coyuntura return. Free James. He rode past the camp's outskirts.

A whack. Apache taunts. Soft moans. Trace reined up.

Another snap of the whip. He gripped the reins tighter.

A third snap stung Trace's ears. He gigged his pinto and raced out of camp.

# CHAPTER THIRTY-NINE

Behind the Apache Springs station and to the east rose steep hills covered with barrel cactus, mesquite, and cholla. Wind rattled the mesquite beans still clinging to the tiny branches, as if waiting for a herd of deer or wild cattle to come nibble them.

Trace wiped beads of sweat off his forehead, even though coolness hung in the air. The stage station welcomed him like a mother's arms.

*A few more yards and I'll be safe.*

He urged his pinto forward. He'd see old Charles Culver and everything would be fine. Wait. Culver was dead. He'd seen the scalp. At least the Indians said it was Culver's.

Was anyone there now? Surely Butterfield would've sent someone else as soon as they'd found out about Culver's death. How long had that been? No telling. Didn't matter now. Soon as he ate, he'd head toward Mesilla, toward freedom for his brother.

Smoke puffed from the chimney, and smells of cooking ham wafted from the house. His stomach rumbled. The less swollen part of Trace's face pushed to a smile. Someone was there and fixing breakfast. Everything would be all right. Normal.

At the front of the stage station, Trace dismounted and tossed the rope reins over the railing. With great care, he twisted and turned his aching body, cracked ribs shooting agony through his chest and down his leg. His head throbbed, and the rest of his body hurt, but the relief of just being here eased the pain.

His arrival may not have been noticed, and he knew he was taking a chance just walking in, but hunger and exhaustion ruled. He stepped onto the porch and gripped the doorknob.

The door jerked open. A pistol jammed in his face.

"Hold it, *Indio!*" The voice was deep, the accent thick. "Drop your gun."

"I'm not Indian. I don't have a gun." Trace froze, hands inching skyward.

"I don't believe you. You look...smell *Indio*. Besides, nobody rides without protection."

"My gun was taken by real Indians. I truly am unarmed. See for yourself."

Trace didn't move, didn't dare blink.

*Who's this man holding a gun on me?*

A short man stepped into the daylight. The gun barrel pressed against Trace's chest, the round iron denting his shirt. "Keep your hands where I can see them. Move and I'll shoot."

"No need for the gun. Just lookin' for some grub and the manager." Nerves on alert, Trace peered over the man's shoulder into the station.

The man shook his head.

"I'm...I'm..." Trace tried to explain, but nothing made sense. "Look. I'm tired...hungry...I have to ride—"

A woman appeared next to the man with the gun.

"Not before you eat," she said. "Cisco, allow him in."

A wooden spoon in her hand, she reminded Trace of his ma when she'd been cooking all day and Pa would come in from the field dirty, tired, and hungry. She had that same look on her face. A woman who knew men's appetites.

Trace nodded to the woman. Cisco shot a warning glare at Trace, then stepped back, allowing entrance to the stage station. Immediate relief and safety washed over Trace. His long weeks of captivity melted. He turned twice in the room before blackness took him down.

\* \* \*

"Well, I'll be damned! Good Lord Clay, that's not an Indian. It's Trace Colton!"

Trace jumped at the voice. Cochise? One Wing? As if on fire, his hands flew up to his face. He tucked his chin into his chest and scooted against the bed's leg.

A hand on his shoulder—not gripping, not clutching, not squeezing. A comforting hand. Trace opened his eyes. A wooden floor under him, not sand. Wooden bed legs near him. Not cactus. A room. He was inside.

"Back off, Clay, we scared him."

Trace recognized the name. His friend from Mesilla. He untucked his chin and rolled over. His gaze inched up toward faces coming into focus.

"Trace? It's me, Clay Arrington. From Butterfield." Clay cocked his head toward his partner. "Sunny's right here, too."

A timbered roof. Adobe walls. A washstand in the corner. Trace closed his eyes and massaged them.

Will this miracle disappear if I open them? Is it just a dream? Imagined like James' Indians?

Someone knelt beside him. Another hand on his shoulder. Trace dared to open his eyes. When he did, Clay produced a wide smile.

"Welcome back."

Sunny leaned on one knee and grinned. "You all right?"

Trace focused on Sunny, then Clay. "Don't know."

Clay gripped Trace's upper arm and tugged until he sat up. Trace winced at the pull of cuts, bruises, and healing bones. But, damn, it felt good to be with friends.

"What the hell are you doing here?" Trace's raw voice echoed off the walls.

"'Bout to ask you the same question, partner." Sunny held out a hand. "Can you stand?"

Trace nodded. Clay moved around and grabbed him under the arms, lifting him to his feet.

Trace squeezed his eyes and hoped he'd stifled that groan. Balanced on his feet again, he pulled in air and opened his eyes. Sunny inspected the wide, red rope marks around his wrists. Their eyes met, but Trace couldn't find words to explain. Instead, he hung his head.

Clay took a quick look, then steadied Trace. "Wanna wash up? Take some of that desert off your face. Some water'll make you feel better."

The knot over Trace's right eye throbbed. He massaged it, but discovered other places that hurt as bad. He limped toward the washstand. Clay and Sunny's reassuring grips quieted the guilt thundering in his heart, threatening to explode. Trace pushed James' image aside.

"I got clothes that'll fit you, I think." Clay dug through a saddlebag, held up a clean blue shirt, trousers. Trace looked down at his own tattered shirt. Dirt, mud, dried blood covered every inch.

After washing and a cursory shave, Trace turned to his

187

friends. "Good old soap and water. Wish James was here."

Sunny held the towel. "Didn't want to ask, but we're wonderin' where he's at."

Trace stared out the curtained window.

*Out there somewhere—dying.*

Silence filled the room. His thoughts were all jumbled, nothing made sense.

Cisco stuck his head in the door. "Supper's ready."

"Thanks." Clay held Trace's arm. "Why don't you change and then we'll eat."

Trace nodded and watched his trembling hands unfasten the only two buttons left on his shirt. Was that James' dried blood smeared down the right side? Memories flashed. His hands shook harder. Did he want his friends to see what those Apaches had done to him? Bruises, welts, and gashes covered every square inch of his body. He eased to the bed, grateful for the softness. He fumbled with the sleeves.

Clay frowned and moved closer. "Need some help?"

Trace hated to admit it, but his strength was gone and his sore ribs kept his movements small. Trace pushed aside his bravado, something he found easier to do every day.

"My ribs. A couple are broken." He bit his lower lip.

"I'll find something to wrap them with." Sunny spun around and disappeared into the other room.

Once his ribs were tied up, Trace, with Clay's help, finished removing his clothes. He watched his two friends' faces lose color and turn away.

When he'd finished dressing, he tried to stand, but his body refused to help. Clay guided him to his feet. "Let's eat and you can tell us over food."

"Can't stay but a minute," Trace said.

"All right. Long enough to get some of Missus Medina's fine cooking in your belly."

"Who?" Trace furrowed his forehead.

"Missus Medina. Her and her family are staying here until Cecilia feels better."

"Who?"

"Come on. You've already met them, but I don't think you were in any shape to remember."

Sunny led them into the other room. After introductions,

Trace turned to Clay.

"I'll ask again. What are you and Sunny doing here?"

Perla set a plate of roasted rabbit, beans, and tortillas in front of him. Clay chuckled.

"Looking for you."

The Medinas sat on the floor to eat, allowing the three friends to sit at the table and swap stories. Over mouthfuls of beans, Trace told as much as he could face right now. Most of it he left out, too painful to even think about, much less tell friends. Some day he might share the whole story. The terror, the constant fear. He'd tell them how sometimes the pain had been so intense, so unspeakable, he and James begged to die. Twice they even plotted to kill each other.

Clay pushed away his half-eaten meal. "How can anyone do that to people? Why?"

"Justice. To get back what's his." Trace swallowed the last bite of rabbit. "Cochise knows exactly what he wants and will stop at nothing to get it. A little pain on the part of the white man is nothing, Clay." He paused and eyed his two friends, lucky to have them. "By the way, how long have I been here?"

Clay glanced out the window. "We'd gone hunting right before you got here this morning. We were out all day, got back late afternoon, so you've been here, sleeping, most of the day."

Trace put his fork down, wiped his mouth on his sleeve, and then remembered to use his napkin. He stared into his plate.

"Three," Trace said.

"What?" Sunny held his coffee cup halfway to his mouth.

"It's been three days. James gets five lashes each day I'm gone. One Wing, Cochise's war leader, uses my own leather whip to do it."

Sunny rubbed his forehead, then glanced at Clay. Trace touched his aching forehead.

"Don't know how much more James'll be able to take," he said. "He was barely holding on when I left. One Wing hates him. If it wasn't for Cochise, James would've been dead a long time ago."

"So Cochise is human after all." Clay's eyebrows arched.

Trace nodded. "He's an honorable man, wants to do what's right for his people. Seems to admire James, says he's brave."

"Sounds to me like you both are."

Trace shook his head. "Just trying to stay alive. One Wing

beats James even more when he doesn't obey. But, you know my little brother. Hasn't changed. Still has a mind of his own. Even if it means losing extra hide." A whip snapped. Moans. Another snap. Trace balled his fists against memories.

"What can we do to help?" Clay leaned forward in his chair.

Trace stood and looked at his two friends. He wiped his mouth on his sleeve, but clutched his napkin.

"Three things. First, believe what I said because every word's true." He held the napkin to his bruised mouth and noticed his hands trembling. "Sometimes, I don't believe it myself."

"Second?" Sunny leaned closer.

"Loan me a gun."

Clay whipped his Colt out of its holster, checked for full chambers, then handed it to his friend. Sunny handed over a fistful of paper cartridges.

"Third?" Clay asked.

"Pray for James."

Silence thundered in the dining room.

Trace looked at his friends, then turned to Perla, who picked up a dish from the table. "Missus Medina," he said, "thank you for the grub. I can't remember ever having a finer meal."

Perla smiled. "We will all pray for you and your brother, Mister Colton. I know you will be successful." She put down the plate and gave him a hug.

"Gotta go." Trace shoved the gun in his saddlebag. "Got a long way to ride." He picked up the leather bag repacked now with extra jerky and a flask of whiskey Sunny had thrown in.

"It's late, Trace, and dark. Why not wait 'til tomorrow at sunrise?" Sunny's voice echoed deep concern.

"James. He's relying on me."

Clay held Trace's sleeve. "We promised Lila we'd find you and James. But, when we thought you were...well, dead, we told the Medina's we'd help them." He cocked his head toward Sunny. "We'll go with you right now if you need us."

A corner of Trace's split lips raised. He shook his head. "Appreciate the offer. But no, I'll be fine."

"What about the Apaches?" Sunny asked

"Somehow Cochise sends word out to all of his tribe, so they know to let me alone." Trace held Sunny's arm. "I'll be all right. Just gotta ride fast as the wind. Gotta get James out."

"All right. Just watch yourself." Clay nodded toward the Medina family. "Soon as Cecilia's better, we're heading east ourselves. We'll see you out that way."

Trace nodded and shook their hands.

Sunny and Clay stepped outside with Trace. The full moon and crisp night air flooded the surrounding rocks and hills with a luminescence like glowing pumas' eyes.

Trace mounted his horse and grabbed the rope reins. He looked down at his friends, leaned over, and patted Clay on the shoulder. That one eye narrowed. Clay was worried.

"See you soon," Trace said.

Before either could respond, Trace gigged the pinto into a full gallop.

* * *

Clay, with Sunny at his side, watched Trace disappear over a hill. When the final rumble of frantic hooves died out, he caught Sunny's worried stare and nodded toward the stage station.

The room was quiet as the two men sat back down at the table. Sunny gulped the remainder of his cold coffee, stood, then poured another round. He leaned against the doorframe and stared outside, his fingers tapping against the wood. He forced out a tight stream of air, then tossed the black liquid at the ground. Sunny spun around. He waved the empty cup at Clay.

"If that Bascom doesn't release Coyuntura, I'll personally kill him. If he can't do what's decent to save a life, then I'll shoot him right between the eyes. Leave him with a bootprint in his chest." He banged the tin coffee cup on the table. "Did you hear, really *hear* what Trace said? If Bascom hadn't taken Coyuntura, James would be a free man today."

"Or dead." Clay knew to keep his emotions under control, though his anger and concern mirrored his friend's. Sunny stared at Clay.

"Maybe, just maybe," Clay continued, "Coyuntura's arrest is the only thing keeping James alive right now. Trade brother for brother. It's the only bargaining chip Trace has. Without that, Cochise'll kill James in a heartbeat."

Sunny took a deep breath and looked away.

"I hate it when you're right."

# CHAPTER FORTY

Although cactus needles pricked his back, James sat relaxed against the tall saguaro's base. Tight horsehair rope bit under his arms and around his wrists, but he still enjoyed the respite from the constant drudgery—the toting, the skinning, and the heavy lifting. With the sun now at its zenith, the rays warmed his face, and he wondered how soon it would be before the heat became unbearable.

Living outside, never being allowed in a shelter, had taken its toll on his body. James was sure his own mother wouldn't recognize him if she came walking into camp. His skin was now darker than his old boots; he wore no hat. Any extra pounds he'd carried earlier were now muscle, his dark hair longer and tied back out of his face. In fact, he not only looked like the Apaches, but he thought like them, too. He knew how to fight, how to lay low and blend in with the scenery, how to take down a deer while running. He could erect a wickiup without thinking, eat a bowl of stew without a spoon, and understand most of the conversations around him. The Apaches were now careful what they said within his earshot.

But in many ways he wasn't like them. The relentless abuse had woven his body into nothing but hurt. The various knife, cane, and whip marks, along with the myriad of bruises, reminded him of drawings he'd seen of people dying of the plague. No doubt, he felt as bad as they had.

James listened to the camp. The warriors were staying close today. They sharpened axes, whittled new lances, and even strung bows.

Sudden whooping and hollering from one side of the encampment shook James. He peered through legs and strained against the horsehair rope, still unable to see what caused the excitement. He listened to the women around him. They spoke more freely and frequently than the men, and he received much more information that way.

Quick-to-Run, the young woman who paid him special attention, squatted at his side and wiped the sweat from his face. The soft, wet cloth she used tingled.

"What's going on?" James whispered.

She glanced over her shoulder at the throng of people. "Coyuntura has returned. He brings his wife and four others."

"Good God!" James sat upright, lifted his chin. "I'm free?"

The woman's eyes hit the ground. She shook her head, stood, and then disappeared into the crowd.

Questions bombarded his thoughts. If Trace had managed to get Coyuntura released, then where was his brother? Why hadn't he come back with him? Then again, he'd only been gone four days. Was that enough time for Trace to do his job?

James' spirit plunged. He was no longer needed, no longer a pawn in Cochise's master game plan.

Throughout the long afternoon, James waited, tied, while Coyuntura and Cochise spent most of the time in a wickiup. The rest of the tribe danced and drank special liquid made from agave. The men grew louder throughout the afternoon—many staggered and swore.

"Our land, our people forever!"

"Death to the Mexicans and white settlers!"

"May the gods keep our arrows straight and our warriors victorious!"

James kept a close eye on One Wing and the other Apaches as the cactus juice affected their judgment. More and more often a few of the tribesmen and older boys stumbled past.

Without warning, ten, maybe fifteen men turned and stared at him. Drums pounded, beating in time with James' heart. A throng of drunken Indians lurched closer.

James cursed his bindings. Right now he needed to run, to escape this intoxicated crowd. They'd literally pull him apart limb by limb before killing him. He recoiled against the cactus as best he could and searched each face rushing toward him, looking for the one sane Indian who would stop these vigilantes. He saw nothing but anger and hatred.

"You're lower than dogs, White Eyes."

Globs of spit hit his face, slid down his cheek.

193

"Son of a whore."

A moccasined foot plowed into his upper leg. Twice into his ribs.

"Old woman!"

Like an ax falling, the attack stopped as quickly as it had begun. James' eyes cleared enough for him to recognize Cochise standing between him and the frenzied warriors. Cochise's words were strong, quick, and definite. James watched the men's faces, caught a few words, then relaxed when the crowd turned around and staggered back toward the fire.

Cochise knelt by James. One Wing and Coyuntura towered over him.

"I have stopped my warriors from killing you for one reason only," Cochise said. "Your brother has not yet prevented the army men from killing my people and pushing us from our land." Cochise untied the rope around James' chest. "You have much courage, James Colton. A few of my braves could learn from you."

James swallowed the last bit of moisture in his mouth. His chest and leg throbbed.

"So, my brother's still alive?"

Cochise nodded and tugged James to his feet. "This is my brother, Coyuntura."

James stared at the muscled Apache. "Did Trace get you released?"

Coyuntura shook his head. "An army man. I was not aware your brother was sent to free me."

"Why'd the army do that?"

"Not the army." Coyuntura stared down into James' eyes. "One army man. I traded information about you and your brother for my freedom."

"Someone wanted to know about me?" James mentally listed the few people who would go to that much trouble.

Coyuntura nodded. "A girl in Mesilla."

James knew he hadn't heard right. He stepped closer to Cochise's brother.

"Lila? Lila asked about me? She knows I'm here...still alive?" James envisioned his love, the woman he'd rush back to marry...if he lived.

Coyuntura spoke to Cochise, then used his halting English on James. "She wants to retrieve your body to bury it in Mesilla."

James' world collapsed. Lila had felt enough heartache to last a lifetime, and now she thought he was dead. His shoulders sagged. Would she still want him?

No, he knew better. Battered, bruised, wounded, scarred, probably close to crazy, people would think he'd become an Indian. A crazy white Indian. No one would want him now.

Especially Lila.

Shoulders slumped, his chin close to touching his chest, James closed his eyes and massaged his forehead with his bound hands.

Cochise spoke again. "Your brother has been trailed to the Apache Springs stage station. He's made it that far."

James' eyes shot open at the mention of his brother. Maybe there was hope.

Cochise nodded. "One Wing will not kill you yet. He will follow my orders. But do nothing to anger him."

With that, the most powerful leader of the Apache nation turned and walked with his brother toward the fire.

# CHAPTER FORTY-ONE

The sun hung low on the horizon; gray shadows grew long. Clay, along with Sunny and the Medina family, stopped for the night. Their bodies ached from the miles they had covered. They'd hated leaving the security of the way station, but they knew it was only a matter of time before the Apaches returned.

While the surrounding rocks ignited with the orange and pink of sunset, Sunny made a small fire. Perla prepared beans and rabbit stew while the men unpacked and fed the horses. The hills faded from dark orange to blue to dark purple, and the seven people who were gathered around the fire ate.

Clay froze, fork poised halfway to his mouth. "You hear that, Sunny?"

"No. What?"

"That."

Clay lowered his plate and put one finger to his lips. Perla clutched the baby to her chest. Cisco moved in close to her. Sunny rushed several feet from the small fire, then hunkered down behind a boulder. He aimed his revolver. Clay ran to the side and crouched behind a tree. The older Medina grabbed both girls and hid behind a clump of mesquite.

Hooves on sand. Sagebrush rustling. Horse wheezing. A voice cut the stillness.

"Hello the camp! Smelled your coffee!"

Clay peeked through the lower limbs of a desert willow and saw the silhouette of a single man on horseback. Clay bent a branch for a better view.

The man, possibly white, definitely not Indian, appeared to be alone. Clay gripped his revolver tighter.

"Stop right there!" Clay said. "Get off your horse, step into the light where we can see you!"

The man's hands flew up. "I'm only lookin' for a cup of coffee.

Honest. Didn't mean to scare you."

"I said get off your horse, mister."

The man eased down, released the reins, and reached skyward.

Sunny stepped from behind the boulder and grabbed the man's holstered gun. Then he planted his own revolver in the man's back.

"Who're you? Why you sneaking up on us?" Sunny's voice rang strong, demanding.

Clay marched over, gun aimed chest high. "Answer or my partner'll drop you right where you stand."

Clay knew it would take a lot more than that to get Sunny to kill anyone, but the threat sounded real.

"I'm...I'm Priv...Patton, Bill Patton. Don't mean you no harm, mister. Just passin' through."

"Well, Mister Patton. Nobody's just *passin' through* these days. Too dangerous. Or ain't you heard about the Apaches?"

"Oh yes, sir. I've heard. Have first hand experience."

He nodded at Clay, then twisted around to Sunny.

"Don't move." Sunny jammed the gun harder against the man's back. The stranger faced Clay again.

Even by the low light of the campfire, Clay could see the man's face was much like Trace's—swollen and covered with bruises.

"Can I put my hands down?" Bill asked. "My ribs are still real tender. Believe me, I mean you no harm."

"Careful. Remember, my partner's right behind you." Clay eased down his revolver's hammer.

"Yes, sir." Bill lowered his arms. "I got discharged from the Army a couple weeks back. Matter of fact I remember you two at Apache Springs station."

"We were there." Clay cut his eyes sideways at Sunny.

"I remember your friend gettin' the boot by Bascom," Patton said, then jerked as Sunny's gun jammed farther against his backbone. "Anyway, I have somethin' I gotta do before I get any older. Gotta find some men. I hear they're bein' held by Cochise."

Silence. Bill turned to each man, including the Medinas.

"Maybe you've heard something about them? Two brothers. Drive for Butterfield. Everyone back in Mesilla thinks they're dead, but I know they're alive, captured by Cochise himself."

"How do you know all this?" Clay inspected this man. He

197

didn't look familiar, but there had been many soldiers at Apache Springs. In uniform, they all looked alike.

Patton's coat buttons strained. "I helped Cochise's brother, Coyuntura, escape from jail."

"What?" Sunny grabbed Bill's coat front. "He escaped?"

"Yep. I even opened the door." Patton stood a little taller. "Coyuntura told me that those two fellas was still alive in exchange for his freedom. Even told me where to find them."

Clay snorted, his heart pounding deep in his chest. "Good God!"

He looked from Bill to Sunny and back. Did this man really seal James' fate?

Sunny exploded. He jerked Bill around and shoved the revolver into his face. "You have any idea what you did? You signed our friend's death warrant!"

Clay grabbed Sunny's arm. "Before my friend here beats you to death, Mister Patton, you better start talking! Fast. Believable."

"It's true! I swear! I met the shotgun guard's sweetheart, and when she found out he was dead, all she wanted was to get his body back."

"Lila thinks James is dead." Clay looked at Sunny.

"You know her?" Patton's voice quivered.

Sunny pushed the gun under Patton's chin. "Keep talking."

"I was on guard duty and Coyuntura said he'd tell me 'bout the men if I'd get him and the rest of those Indians out of jail. That's when I found out those two men were still breathing."

"So Lila knows James is alive." Clay glanced at Sunny again.

"No. Coyuntura beat me senseless. I couldn't remember nothing 'til two days ago." He shook his head. "Wish I could go back and tell her he's not, but Bascom kicked me out of town. For good. And, I'd love to steal old Bascom's thunder, make him look like a fool to the General. Mainly, I just gotta do something to help those fellas escape."

Sunny lowered the gun and released Bill's shirt. Clay ran his hand down the cold metal of his gun, then holstered it.

"Good God, Sunny."

"What'd you wanna do now? Think we can find Trace and tell him?"

A shake of the head. Shoulders slumped. Clay stared into the ebony desert.

"Mister Patton," Sunny said, "any idea where Coyuntura might be right now? Did he say where he was heading to?"

"No. But he's had plenty of time to get back to Cochise's camp. I'm sure that's where he went."

Clay squeezed his eyes shut.

# CHAPTER FORTY-TWO

Bascom opened one eye and glared at the young officer touching his shoulder. Corporal Connor's words soaked into the canvas tent walls.

"Hate to wake you this early, sir. But, a civilian just rode into camp. Asked to speak with you."

"What about?"

"Wouldn't say, sir. Only that it's critical. Says his name's Trace Colton. Appears to be on the brink of exhaustion. Looks like he's ridden for days."

"Be right there." Bascom rose to his feet.

"Sir."

Corporal Connor disappeared into the growing dawn.

Lieutenant Bascom stepped from his beige two-man tent into the golden rays of what promised to be another breath-taking sunrise. Deep rose and light purple streaks lit the bottoms of clouds and danced across the gray-blue sky.

Trace stood next to the fire, sipping coffee, warming his hands with the tin cup.

The dark circles under Trace's eyes, the healing bruises and welts on his face, the look of panic—Bascom took it all in.

"What can I do for you?" Bascom asked.

They shook hands. Trace's voice was deep, graveled, as if he'd been denied water once too often.

"Well, sir, I was wondering about six Apaches who were captured some time back. Hoping you knew about them. I understand they're over in Mesilla in jail."

"Why are you interested, Mister Colton?"

"I have an urgent need to find Cochise's brother, Coyuntura."

Trace swayed. Bascom gripped his arm, steadying him.

"You all right?"

"Fine. Just haven't had much sleep lately."

200

"Your face looks like it met someone's fist a few times."

"Look, Lieutenant. I need to know about those Apaches. I gotta find Coyuntura. It's a matter of life and death."

Before answering this stranger, Bascom chose each word. "You appear to have been riding quite a while. Where'd you come from?"

Trace finished his coffee, then held out his cup for a refill. Warm brown liquid poured, he met Bascom's gaze. "Lieutenant, you're possibly the only man in the world who can save my brother's life."

Bascom pursed his lips and signaled for a cup of his own. He cocked his head.

What game was Washington playing?

The man standing before him swayed again. Exhaustion? Maybe, but more than likely just a good actor playing a part. Only man to save his brother's life? Please. That was laying it on thick, even for Washington. Bascom sipped his coffee.

"How so?"

"My brother and me were captured by Apaches, and now I've been sent to bring back Coyuntura. Trade him for my little brother. If I don't get that Apache and have you soldiers ride away, they'll kill James. Soon."

"Who's *they*?"

"Cochise."

Bascom's face wrinkled into a smile.

*This kid may be useful after all.*

"Get this man some breakfast," Bascom said. He turned back to Trace. "Soon as you eat, Mister Colton, we'll discuss the Apache situation."

Bascom marched off, but Trace ran after him. He grabbed Bascom's arm, spinning him around.

"He's held hostage, tortured every day. We gotta get him out now!"

"Touch me again and I'll arrest you for assault."

Bascom yanked his arm out of Trace's frantic grip. Trace shook, his face glowing.

"I need to know, Lieutenant, right now. My little brother's out there dying and you're more worried about breakfast?"

"I'm concerned about all the men out here. But right now, the only thing you can do is find some grub and eat. We'll talk later."

201

With a final glare, Bascom pivoted on his heels and walked off.

Trace called after him twice. No wave of the hand, no turning around. Just the retreating figure of a self-important man. The back disappeared around a supply wagon. Trace's shoulders slumped. He headed for the center of camp.

He found a space near the fire. Its heat felt good on this crisp morning as he sat on a rock. A young officer handed him a plate of salted ham and beans. Trace shoved a forkful into his mouth, not tasting it.

Exhaustion. Trace struggled to keep his eyes open, and he nearly pitched forward into the fire. A conversation behind him grabbed his attention. He glanced over his shoulder.

"I do that all the time," a young private said. "Break those *señoritas'* hearts. This last one in Mesilla, Perlita, even told me I was the only one."

"You haven't never even kissed a girl, Joe. Hell, you ain't had a bath since last Christmas." The second private thumped his friend's chest. "They won't let you get close enough!"

"Yeah? Just wait 'til we get back to Mesilla. You'll see."

The third private spoke over a mouthful of ham. "Might be a while. Connor says we gotta go capture Cochise first. Guess we gotta replace those other Apaches we lost. That detail sent out a couple weeks ago couldn't even find hide nor hair of them."

Trace set his plate on the ground and turned around, facing them.

"Like the world opened up and swallowed them whole." The first private swept his fork-held hand around the desert. "They're gone. Vanished. Pretty scary."

"You've been listening to Smitty's ghost stories again, Simon," the second private said and huffed into his plate. "All I know is once this Cochise is captured, we'll head back to Mesilla." He spoke to the first private. "That'll give you plenty of time to break more hearts, Joe. Maybe even get a bath."

Trace stood. "Excuse me, gentlemen. You're trying to capture Cochise? You had prisoners, but now they're gone? Who were the prisoners?"

The biggest of the three stepped back. "I don't know nothing 'bout escaped prisoners or where we're headed. I just follow orders. We was only funnin'."

These men weren't about to say much more. Trace tried a different tactic.

"Look, I don't care 'bout Cochise. I'm headed the other way, over to Mesilla. Are those women as good as you say?"

The second private produced a quick grin. "Oh, yes, sir. Not an ugly one in the bunch. Why, just the other week when we was there," he leaned closer, "one of them said more girls were comin' every day 'cause Mesilla's growing so fast. Pretty soon they'll be plenty of girls to go around."

"You were in Mesilla recently?" Trace glanced at the other soldiers. "Did you leave me any of those *señoritas*?"

"One or two. But you'll be all right. With all of us gone now, and gone so sudden like, I'm sure they're lonely." The short soldier raised both eyebrows. "If you get my meanin'."

"Thanks, gentlemen."

Trace handed his plate to a private, then turned away from the campfire. Something didn't sound right.

*If Bascom's chasing Cochise, where's Coyuntura in all this?*

"Now, Mister Colton, what exactly can I do for you?" Bascom's words rang strained, official, cold.

Trace eyed the man now standing in front of him. What was it about this person he just didn't like? There was no reason to distrust him. Bascom was, after all, the commanding officer of a large company of troops. He wouldn't have been put in such a position of authority if he had been untrustworthy. Trace had to have faith in somebody. He chose Bascom.

As Bascom listened to Trace's story, he rested one hand on his revolver. The other he clenched into a fist.

"Where exactly is Cochise, Mister Colton? We're in pursuit of him at this minute."

Trace envisioned his brother back at camp. What would the Apache do to James if Cochise or One Wing were captured? He swallowed hard and pushed conjecture aside.

Bascom raised his voice and repeated the question. "Where is he?"

*Should I guide him to Cochise's camp? One Wing'll kill James first chance he gets. But, Cochise promised his safety. What do I owe that Apache leader?*

Memories flooded his mind.

*Everything for saving James' life. How many times had One*

203

*Wing tried to kill him?*

"Lieutenant, I won't tell you where Cochise is. But I will tell you that if I don't find Coyuntura fast and take him to Cochise, my little brother's a dead man. May be already."

Bascom's face turned red. "I want Cochise and I want him now. You know where he is and you'll take me there!"

"Not until I have Coyuntura and your word you'll turn around and head home! This is Apache land. It belongs to them. Cochise'll not be put off his land and frankly, Lieutenant, I don't blame him!"

Bascom leaned in nose to nose with Trace.

"Look, Indian lover, this is United States territory, not Apache. Cochise is a dead Indian and when I catch Coyuntura, so is he. Interfere with me, you'll die, too."

"Where is Coyuntura?" Trace demanded. "Is he the one who escaped? Is that why you're after Cochise?"

Everything hinged on Bascom's answer.

"Coyuntura was small potatoes," Bascom said. "I let him go so he'd lead us to Cochise. It was planned from the start."

It all came crashing down. Coyuntura was free—James dead. Trace gripped the lieutenant's shirt and shook him until his hat flew off.

"You allowed Coyuntura to escape? Planned it? How could you? My brother's gonna die 'cause of you! He's gonna die!"

Trace's fist plowed into Bascom's cheek. He swung again and again before Corporal Connor and two others pulled him off of their bloodied commander.

Trace screamed words he hadn't used before, screamed at the coldness of the man in charge, screamed for the life of his brother.

Bascom swiped at blood streaming from his nose, balled his fist, then struck.

Trace crumpled into Corporal Connor's arms, and Bascom's words circled Trace like vultures.

"Cuffs and chains, Corporal. He'll tell us where Cochise is."

# CHAPTER FORTY-THREE

James glanced up at the sun. The days were longer and hotter now, and the work had increased two-fold since Trace left. James had never known loneliness before. From a family of four boys, James had taken his brothers for granted. They had always been there when he needed them. Especially Trace. But not now. No one was here now. There were still times at night James shivered in fear, in uncertainty.

He dropped an armful of sticks at the outside corner of a wickiup that housed the oldest woman in camp, and then he swiped at the sweat pouring into his eyes. A bent woman, eyes black as a stormy night, stepped from her shelter and spit staccato Apache words at James. This snarling old woman ordered him around like a slave, but hit him only on rare occasions. That was a blessing in itself. Although she was small, her hands were powerful.

The woman examined one of the swollen gashes on his body—forty-five of them now. Their throbbing woke him at night, out of the deep sleep an exhausted man deserved. Her gnarled hand traced the most recent welt on his stomach. She brought her eyes up to his.

"Pain."

Surprised at her English and what seemed to be sympathy, James nodded. "Yes, ma'am."

She shook her head, muttered what James figured could be oaths, then disappeared into her wickiup.

James' Apache guard pointed to another pile of branches. More wood to be broken into sticks for the wickiups or fires. This tribe moved so often and so fast that James wondered if any wood would be left in the desert in another year.

As he broke more long sticks for the wickiups, James speculated on that young woman, the beauty called Quick-to-Run. She often smoothed a salve made from ground golondrina weed and cedar on his back and chest, anywhere the whip had stung. Her fingers ran over his skin like water trickling over pebbles. He grinned at the memory of her touch, so soft and gentle. Just like Lila's. James frowned. Lila's memory faded into images of that Indian girl. Big, innocent eyes, raven hair, slim body. Her closeness stirred feeling deep inside.

He tried to push away the thoughts of her beauty, but they refused to recede. He stacked the branches and envisioned Quick-to-Run's body held against his bare skin, skin without welts and cuts. She would whisper words of love and he would kiss her, tell her of her beauty and his desire for her.

"Move, White Eyes!" A palm slapped his back. It burned like a cattle brand.

James picked up the sticks and limped across camp where another family was setting up their shelter. As if in a dream, he watched Quick-to-Run spread out a blanket in front of a wickiup no more than ten feet away. He knew to keep his eyes on the Indian guard at his side and his thoughts on his work. But damn, she was pretty! He swallowed desire.

* * *

Trace's eyes fluttered open. Was that a nudge? Something banged against his leg. One eye remained open, but the other was too puffy to allow much vision. Wooden crates. Boxes. Canon balls. A powder keg?

His eyes focused, and he read the labels. Ammunition. Bullets. Gun powder. Must be enough firepower to blow the entire Apache nation to California and back. He glanced into the sky, the sun making a run for the west. Where was he exactly? He studied his confines. Wooden sides, wood floor, open on top. In the back of a wagon? A war wagon?

His head thumped and his cheek throbbed like one of those cannon balls had slammed into it. Trace brought his hands up to massage his head. Iron cuffs rattled around his wrists.

"What the hell?" Trace focused on a private kneeling next to him.

The soldier stared back. "Sir?"

"What is this?" Trace shook his bound hands at the private. "What's going on? I'm not a prisoner."

The private scrambled out of the wagon. "Don't know, sir. Just told to watch you, make sure you don't try to escape. Bascom himself put those cuffs on you. Don't know nothing else."

"Get me Bascom. Now!"

Trace's voice rang out over the loud ramblings of the company. The men froze, plates in hand, forks halfway to their mouths. All eyes turned to Trace. He clambered over the side of the wagon and glared at the men. Dried blood tugged at his face, but he didn't care. After the last several weeks, it seemed his face wouldn't have been complete without a coating of dried blood.

The private stumbled back, then darted around the front of the wagon. Trace dogged the soldier through camp and found Bascom emerging from his tent, the private holding the cotton flaps open.

"Finally on your feet, I see." Bascom tucked his shirt into his uniform pants.

Trace thrust cuffed hands into Bascom's face. "What the *hell* is this?"

"You're under arrest," Bascom said.

"Arrest?" Trace's fuse was lit.

"Assaulting a United States Army officer." Bascom's voice hardened. "Boy, you can be shot for that."

"Assault? Arrest? Are you crazy? I came to you for help. What kind of officer are you?"

"A good one that won't allow a civilian to waltz into my camp, assault me, and then ride away unpunished." Bascom grabbed Trace's cuffed hands. "How do I know you won't use these fists against me again?"

"I'll use them against anything that stands in my way. I gotta save my little brother."

"Your brother's already dead, Colton. Or hadn't you figured it out? They killed him the minute Coyuntura waltzed into Cochise's camp. The best you can hope for is to retrieve what's left of his body."

Trace grabbed Bascom's neck. Even with bound hands, he squeezed until his knuckles turned white and Bascom's face flushed. Corporal Connor wedged himself between the men and pried Trace's fingers off Bascom's throat. Two other soldiers pinned Trace's arms.

"Say that again, you sonuvabitch," Trace screamed. "Say that

207

about my brother and I'll kill you. I'll kill you with these bare hands!"

Bascom smoothed his hair and turned to his corporal. "You heard him threaten me?"

"Yes, sir."

Bascom leaned into Trace. "Keep digging, boy. Soon you'll be six feet under. Planted right next to your brother." Bascom threw orders toward Connor. "Keep him under lock and key until this matter of Cochise is finished. After Cochise dies, we'll hang Colton."

"Sir." Connor saluted, a slight grin creasing the corners of his face.

Trace lashed out with every ounce of strength he possessed. "You can't hang me!"

"Can't, Mister Colton?" Bascom's voice turned deadly. "*Can't* is not a word in my vocabulary. *Can* and *will*, sir. You twice assaulted a US Army officer and threatened me with death. That's a hanging offense. Or firing squad."

"At least take me to a sheriff. Let him figure it out." Trace cocked his head toward Mesilla and strained against the soldiers' hands clamped around his arms.

Bascom snorted. "A backwards country sheriff? Not on your life!" He chuckled. "I'm the law out here and what I say goes. Better get used to it, boy. Because that's just the way it is."

Trace kicked out, but connected with air.

Bascom frowned. "Corporal Connor?"

"Sir?"

"Restrain this man any way you see fit. Leg irons are fine. Oh, and see that the prisoner gets grub. Wouldn't want him dying until he takes us to Cochise."

"I won't lead you there, Bascom. He'll kill James. You gotta ride away. Take your stinkin' army and get the hell outta here!"

Bascom stepped nose to nose with Trace. "Oh, I'll ride out of here, Colton—with Cochise head-down over a horse."

Trace fought to keep his rage under control. He relaxed his fists.

The grip and pull on his arms were strong; they reminded him of One Wing.

"Private." Connor's voice cut through Trace's thoughts. "Secure the prisoner to the wheel." He pointed toward the ammunition wagon. "Feed him, then station guards throughout the night." Connor sneered at Trace. "If he tries to escape, shoot him."

With his back jammed against a wooden wheel and tied so tightly that even breathing was difficult, Trace again vowed he would rescue James.

*Whatever it takes, James, whatever it takes.*

# CHAPTER FORTY-FOUR

Rotting meat. Stomach-turning stench. Buzzing flies. James swatted at one on his cheek, then ignored the rest crawling on his arm. His thoughts turned to Trace. Ten days had passed since his brother rode away and into...what? Freedom?

James adjusted his weight while he sat on the hard ground. The old woman next to him muttered to herself while her gnarled hands gripped the knife. Several young girls sat cross-legged in a circle, each with a deer hide draped across her lap. The women scraped and chatted. James scraped and listened.

As the lowest people within the tribe, it was their job to remove every scrap of meat left, then chew on the hide until it was softened enough to be made into clothing or shoes. The increasing heat added to the nauseating odor of the deer's flesh. Since he'd been old enough to shoot a rifle, James had killed and skinned his share of game, mostly rabbits and deer, but this process, chewing the hide, left only disgust for the chore. But, he buried his feelings and did what he was told. He focused his thoughts on something beautiful—Quick-to-Run.

Without thinking about her, Lila's face materialized onto the deer hide. He frowned. What was she doing here? A shake of his head. Better question—what was he doing thinking of that Indian girl? He reminded himself that Lila was the woman he wanted to marry. Lila—the woman who kept his yearning for freedom alive. But then again, she thought he was dead.

*She's right. The old James is dead. I won't be going back.*

Maybe he should stay with the Apaches.

Iron claws dug into his shoulder, and James' heart pounded. Time for the daily whipping. Five more lash marks to add to his collection. Would he die today? Would this whipping end him? Every minute proved harder and harder to get through. Maybe dying would be easier.

He sorted out his survivors. Trace was now free and would live. Lila would mourn him for a while, but then she would move on, marry, and have a family. Maybe she already had. His younger brothers and parents—they would mourn, too, but they'd continue with their lives. Ma would be devastated, but she would keep on going for her family. That was the way it had to be.

One Wing hovered over him. James cringed, put down the flat rock used for scraping, struggled to his knees, then pushed up to his feet. One Wing's wide hand encircled his upper arm.

"Please, One Wing." James shook his head. "No more. I'm not doing anything wrong." His pleas fell on unsympathetic ears as One Wing led him across camp—toward the saguaro.

James glanced behind a wickiup and spotted Quick-to-Run. The water jugs she carried sloshed their contents. She flashed a quick smile, then looked away.

He half turned to One Wing. "Not again. Please."

James wanted to tug on the Apache's arm, explain to him, rationalize with him that now he—James Francis Michael Colton—was broken. Tamed. He wouldn't run away, wouldn't even try to escape. He'd accepted the idea that he was part of the tribe—forever.

"No need for the whipping, One Wing. Please…no more."

One Wing sneered. "What a woman. You cry like a baby. You're not a man. I don't know why I keep you alive."

"You don't understand," James said. "I'll make you a deal."

The Apache stopped at the cactus and stared into James' eyes. A scowl wrinkled his forehead. "You—want to bargain with me?"

James nodded and forced air into his lungs. "No more beatings or whippings. I'll stay here, grow strong again." His shoulders straightened, his broken ribs screaming at him. "I'll become an Apache."

Silence.

James studied One Wing's face for a hint, any indication of his thoughts.

*Yes? No? Right or wrong. There it is. Cards on the table.*

He cut his eyes sideways, seeking Quick-to-Run. She could make him happy…at least sometimes forget about his former life.

One Wing's eyes scanned James from moccasins to eyes. He snorted. "What makes you think we'd ever allow you to stay here? Live here? Fight alongside us?"

211

"I'll learn Apache ways," James said. "I already know some of your language. I'm strong. I'll be a warrior. Anything you and Cochise want."

"Why would we want you? You're nothing. Nothing but a broken White Eyes who cries at the whip."

The scar on One Wing's cheek crinkled with a sneer. Had James overstepped his boundary? Did he really like this woman enough to willingly stay? Why would she want him?

The way she moved, the easy but confident stride in her walk. Her fleeting smile. Her skin against his. Warmth flushed his entire body.

"I will counsel with Cochise."

Had James heard right? One Wing agreed to speak with Cochise? Maybe, just maybe, he could make plans for his future. His future here as an Apache. He blinked and sighed. It could be worse. He could be dead.

One Wing tied James' hands over his head, his body backed against the cactus. There was no shirt to remove; the last shreds of fabric had ripped away during a beating days before. The short needles stung his bare back.

One Wing held up the whip. James closed his eyes and mouthed a silent prayer.

# CHAPTER FORTY-FIVE

Clay, Sunny, the Medina family, and Bill Patton stood in the morning sunlight. Their campfire sputtered dead with the water poured on the coals, while the horses flicked their ears as if somehow knowing it was time. Time to leave and get on with their lives. The desert beckoned.

Clay shook hands with the older Medina, then turned to Cisco. "You should be safe enough now to go on to Mesilla alone," Clay said. "You've got as much ammunition as we could spare and plenty of food."

"*Gracias, Señor* Clay." Cisco gave a quick nod and helped his father onto the horse.

"Mister Patton assures us, as best he can, that the road is clear." Clay glanced back over his shoulder. "Apaches probably haven't hit this far yet. The San Simon stage station is half a day's ride. With luck you should be in Mesilla in three days."

He patted the sorrel's neck and ran his hand over the shiny coat. Sunny shook hands with Cisco and smiled at Mrs. Medina. "You have the name of our friend in Mesilla?" he asked.

Perla nodded, a tear glistening in her eye.

"Good. I'm sure Lila will put you up at her place until you get settled. She might even help your husband find a job. And please tell Lila that James is alive and we'll bring him back soon as we can."

Perla nodded again.

"Tell her to wait for him." He pulled in air. "He's gonna need her."

"*Sí, señor.*" She stared into Sunny's eyes. "You've both done so much for us, I'm afraid we'll never be able to repay you."

Clay's mouth curled into a grin. "Just keep those beautiful *niñas* safe and that'll be thanks enough." He looked at the two girls, winked, then looked back at Mrs. Medina. "You should be in

213

San Simon by nightfall. Say howdy to Mister Romero for us."

Clay bent down, pecked her cheek with a quick kiss, then turned to Sunny and Bill.

"Gotta go, men. Time to find Trace, and tell him about Coyuntura."

The three men mounted, waved a farewell, and galloped east toward Mesilla.

\* \* \*

Twilight cast rose-purple shadows on the mesquite bushes, while the sandstone hills glowed. Clay stood up in his stirrups, a feeble attempt to unknot the kink in his back. This was the end of their second day of hard riding. The three tired men had split up earlier in the day, hoping to cover more country. Alone, Clay had traveled a mile south of the main road, where he spotted what appeared to be Trace's tracks. He ran his fingers through the indentations in the sand. It looked like his friend had ridden into some sort of camp.

Clay shot once into the air, signaling Sunny and Bill to join him. While he waited, he inspected the hoof prints. The two men galloped in, reined up fast. Their feet hit the ground before their horses had stopped.

"I'm sure it's Trace," Clay said. "His horse's the only one not shod. That's an Indian pony."

"Right. But whose tracks are these? There's lots of them." Sunny squatted by a small circle of rocks, then stuck his hand in the middle of the ashes. "It's been a while since anyone's cooked here. Ashes're cold."

"US Army, gentlemen," Bill said. "I'd know these markings anywhere. Looks like your friend met up with Bascom."

"Bascom again?" Sunny gritted his teeth. "Why couldn't those Indians have killed him when they had the chance?"

Clay walked over to his horse, then jerked his thumb over his shoulder. "I'm gonna ride on west, see which way Trace went. Wanna camp here tonight?"

Sunny nodded. "If you're not back in half an hour, we'll both come lookin' for you."

"All right, Mother." Half a smile planted itself on Clay's face. Sunny. Rock steady. What would he do without him?

214

True to his word, Clay was back at camp twenty-two minutes later. He joined his partners at the small campfire.

"Looks like Trace joined them," he said. "No more tracks heading toward Mesilla. Suppose they told him about Coyuntura?"

"I'm sure Bascom rubbed his face in it." Bill gazed into the fire. "Wouldn't be surprised if your friend was…how do I put this? Forced to go with them."

"You mean like under arrest or something?" Sunny's angry eyes turned on Bill. "That low-down, worthless, son of a—"

"Sunny, we don't know anything right now," Clay said. "Could be he's just riding along with them. Trying to convince Bascom to turn around and go home."

Sunny cut his eyes toward Clay. "Even if the army retreats, you think Cochise'll release James?"

"Said he would." Clay shrugged. "Don't know what else we can do."

Sunny tossed his coffee at the flames. "Dammit, Clay."

"Yeah."

215

# CHAPTER FORTY-SIX

Each time Cochise strutted past, James held his breath, hoping to get an answer to his proposal. Now, more than ever, all he could think about was Quick-to-Run. He saw her everywhere—fixing meals, toting water, playing with the camp children, sewing garments, and developing into a very sensual, very desirable woman. James fixated on her beauty and gentleness. He'd be happy with her if Cochise would just give permission. Permission to join the tribe, be a white Indian. Someday, he would marry her.

Allowed to work unrestrained, James pushed a small boulder closer to a narrow stream and nodded at the two waiting Apaches. Since declaring that he'd become an Indian, he'd still been whipped, but during the day, his hands were no longer bound.

A glance into the west. The sun rushed toward its rapid plunge into the unknown. Soon, darkness and refreshing cool would spread over the desert like a gentle hand, smoothing out the wrinkles of life. He looked forward to this portion of the day, when the work was finished until light peeked over the eastern horizon. A bowl of stew and sometimes bread awaited him. Sleep, the escape from reality, lay ahead.

James held a thin pole that one of the Apache women had handed him. She threaded tanned deerskin over it. He counted the number of moves they'd made since the days warmed. This tribe didn't stay in one place very long. They erected wickiups and entire camps more easily than the US Army put up a single tent. One minute—nothing but flat desert, and the next an entire village was up and running. The Army could learn a thing or two from these Indians.

Sudden whooping and hollering spun James around. He straightened up and peered across camp.

A group of Apaches surrounded someone struggling. James squinted, but the setting sun blinded him. He peered around the swarm of people, but he couldn't see who was there.

His Apache guard grunted. James recognized the command. He'd come. Holding his ribs, he limped toward the group while his guard trotted toward the growing crowd.

They stopped on the edge of the mob. James peeked between bodies and around clumps of people.

It was an Indian woman. He recognized the warrior holding her, too. Standing Pony. More brutal than his brother, One Wing. Standing Pony was the one who'd beaten Trace unconscious just because he'd dropped a freshly skinned rabbit into the dirt. That Apache had also taken over the whip a time or two when One Wing was busy elsewhere. Bile threatened to rise, but James pushed it down.

"What's going on?" James turned to his guard.

"We took a girl from the Pima tribe."

"Pima?"

"Our enemy."

James glanced at his Apache guard. "What's gonna happen to her? She gonna be a captive, a slave, like me? Is she taking Trace's place?"

The guard shook his head. "Watch."

Cochise brushed past James' shoulder and swept into the center of the crowd. Murmurs and chanting died as the leader held up his hand. His eyes swung over his people.

"This is a time of victory," Cochise said. "The Pima have raided our camps, stolen our horses, our women. Now, we have taken one of theirs."

The tribe, too many for James to count, erupted into whoops of delight and taunts. Cochise held up his hand again.

James elbowed in a little closer, wedging himself between two women.

Cochise plucked the young woman from Standing Pony's grasp. The stoic expression on her face remained unchanged as she stared into nothing.

*She's no more than thirteen, fourteen at the most. What's gonna happen to her?*

James glanced back over his shoulder at his guard. The lust etched on his face spoke volumes. There was no doubt what this Pima girl's fate would be.

Cochise's words radiated across the desert sand like water

irrigating a dry field. "The Pimas must know we are strong, powerful. Therefore, their woman will marry someone outside her dirty-eyed tribe. Someone who will shame their pitiful people, bring disgrace and humiliation to them."

Cochise twisted his body from side to side as his gaze met the eyes of every man in the crowd. "Who better than a captive white man?"

Powerful fingers clutched James' upper arm and squeezed as Cochise's eyes rested on him. James stared at his guard, not understanding what Cochise meant. He faced forward again and recoiled against the staring Apache faces. After what seemed an hour, James focused on the towering leader of the Apache nation.

Cochise raised his long arm and pointed at his captive. "James Colton. I have selected you to marry this girl, take her to a wickiup, make her a wife."

Mouth open, numb, James' broken body was yanked and tugged through the crowd until he stood next to Cochise. Both men faced the Chiricahua people.

Cochise grabbed James' left hand and the girl's right. He placed James' hand over hers. Then he nodded at the tribe's shaman—their healer, their religious man. Cochise removed the red woven band from around his head and wrapped the two joined hands.

James shook his head and wrenched his hand from the cloth. Although his words were soft, he knew the entire camp heard everything. "I've asked to be part of your tribe, Cochise—if you'll have me. And I will marry. But not this Pima captive. I will marry Quick-to-Run."

Images of the bloody rancher woman, Lila, and Quick-to-Run melted together. He jerked back.

Cochise grabbed James' hand and tied the binding tighter. He shook his head.

"No. You serve me better as a captive white man. Dark Cloud will marry you now, or my warriors will kill her by the time the sun falls behind that mountain. She will suffer much more than you have, James Colton."

*Cochise doesn't lie.*

James looked from Cochise to Dark Cloud.

"She must make you desire her," Cochise added. "Make you take her as a woman. She knows this."

218

"No, Cochise!" James grabbed at the Apache leader's arm. "No. I'll serve you better as a warrior. I'll fight beside your men, marry Quick-to-Run, give her many sons. The tribe will grow." Panic fought its way from his stomach up to his throat. "Let another warrior marry this Pima."

Cochise shook his head, then pointed to the shaman.

"Wait, Cochise!" James played his last card. This was the only bargaining chip he had, and it wasn't much. "One Wing has a ring of mine. He's kept it woven in his hair since I first came here. Let me give it to Quick-to-Run as a token of my love...and my promise never to leave."

Apache eyes turned to One Wing, who held up a long strand of his hair. Still woven near the end hung a gold band.

"Mine," he said. "We do not want White Eyes fighting beside us, marrying our women." One Wing pointed at James. "Just your presence disgusts me."

All eyes returned to Cochise. The intensity of their stares reminded James of his first few days in camp.

Cochise regarded James, and then moved back to allow room for the shaman.

James hung his head. If he went through with this, he could never marry Quick-to-Run. Her tribe would never allow him to marry twice. Hell, if he married this Pima woman, he couldn't marry even Lila. Would she find out? And did an Apache marriage hold in the white world?

But if he didn't marry this trembling Pima, she would meet a death only imagined in horror stories. He knew. He'd felt the tortures, the terror, the unbelievable agony the Apaches could inflict.

*What choice do I have?*

Dark Cloud's eyes flitted to his, and then returned to the ground.

*I've never been with a woman.*

James again located Quick-to-Run. The sadness clouding her beauty hung over her like death. He felt the exact same way. So close.

Lilting Apache chants interrupted his thoughts. The shaman behind them sung, then shuffled around in front and sprinkled water on the new couple. James stole glances at the girl whose hand trembled under his and wondered what she thought. Her future, even dimmer than his, lay in his hands, literally. He nodded to her, squeezed her hand lightly, vowing he would protect her.

Many minutes of chanting, prayers, and gestures to the sky passed while James and the girl stood in front of the entire tribe. Quick-to-Run's eyes stayed downcast throughout the entire ceremony

At long last the shaman lowered his hands and unwrapped the binding.

Cochise stepped next to the medicine man and addressed the new couple. "With your union, we have embarrassed, humiliated, and disgraced the White Man and the Pima. Dark Cloud marries the defeated enemy, a man who carries open whip marks, bruises on his body...a man broken. You, James Colton, you married your enemy's enemy. What kind of man have you become?"

Cochise glanced up at the setting sun. "When the sun rises over those mountains, you will have sealed your marriage. Now take her to the wickiup near mine." Cochise pointed to his right and stared into the newlyweds' eyes.

James led his new wife toward the shelter. Oaths and scurrilous names were hurled in their direction, but he ignored them. He planted his arm around the girl and nudged her forward.

# CHAPTER FORTY-SEVEN

Apache Pass, its stately granite steeples flanking both sides of the road, signaled a welcomed landmark for Clay, Sunny, and Bill. The sun's late afternoon glare bathed the rocks and plants in light. Overhead, the fading sky was dotted with white clouds, but there'd be clear skies tonight. Nothing would block out the millions of stars.

They reined up and gazed at the valley ahead. Clay leaned over and patted his sorrel's neck. Tired. With all the riding they'd done, Clay knew his mount couldn't outrun a friendly swarm of bees right now, much less an angry band of Indians. He was used to the strong stagecoach mules, crossed between Mexican and Missouri stock, and he sometimes forgot the horses weren't as tough.

Clay's gaze took in the cactus, rocks, clouds, sky—the hundreds of square miles.

*Somewhere out there is James and Trace. And that Bascom.*

Clay reeled in his frustration and spoke over his shoulder. "My rear end's nearly flat, Sunny. And my horse's about done for today. Camp here tonight?"

Sunny stood up in his stirrups and pointed southwest. A column of dust way off in the distance blotted out part of the landscape. "Look there." He squinted into the sun. "Suppose that's them?"

Bill also stood in his stirrups. "Too far away to tell. Could be."

"Could be Indians." Sunny sat back in his saddle and frowned at Clay.

Silence. Somewhere nearby a rabbit skittered around a creosote bush. A family of doves flew past, one of them calling out. After several starts and stops, Clay broke the silence.

"Guess my horse has an hour left in him. What'd you say we

221

ride closer? If it is Indians, they're on their way back to camp. They usually don't raid at night, you know."

Sunny raised his eyebrows. "I don't like that usually part. What if they're a tribe that does?"

Clay thumped Sunny on the back and gigged his horse. "Only one way to find out."

Within an hour, Clay, Sunny, and Bill stopped near an outcropping of boulders and peered into the fading desert. Clay shielded his eyes.

"It's the army all right," he said. "Too many to be a raiding party. And look there." He pointed. "A flag. You know any flag-carrying Indians?"

Sunny shook his head.

"We're definitely gainin' on them." Bill peered into the dusky desert. "But my horse needs a rest and my belly's growlin'. They'll be stoppin' soon, too. We can meet up with them tomorrow."

Clay nodded, his own belly grumbling. "Fine. Tomorrow it is."

"Then what?" Sunny turned his eyes on Clay.

Clay met his friend's hard stare. Good question.

* * *

Trace turned in his saddle and spotted the three riders before the army scouts did. The noon sun cast no shadows on the men as they rode up from the east. He recognized two of them. Clay and Sunny. But who was the third? Couldn't be James—the rider was too small.

While his horse plodded along with the other army mounts, he pushed his hat farther up his forehead and studied his cuffed wrists.

How many days had he been gone from Cochise's camp? He'd lost count. Could it be as many as ten?

Trace glanced again at the three riders, escorted on both sides by two soldiers. His friends rode closer.

The soldier who escorted Trace looked behind, then shrugged. "Ain't Apache, that's a fact." He turned his eyes forward. "If they ain't Indians, then it's none of my business who they is."

Sunny, Clay, and the third man trotted to the front of the column. Clay flashed his broad smile as he passed Trace. Sunny nodded, but the stranger just stared at him.

They intercepted Bascom. He raised a hand and turned to Corporal Connor. "Company halt."

Connor repeated the order. The entire company of fifty-five men and four wagons stopped.

One of the scouts saluted Bascom.

"Who'd you find, soldier?"

Before the man could answer, Clay spoke up. "Lieutenant Bascom? Remember us? Clay Arrington and this is my partner, Sunny Williamston. I think you know Mister Patton."

Bascom bristled at the sight of Patton. "You've been discharged. I told you to leave."

"Sir, I'm...I'm with them." Patton cocked his head toward Sunny and Clay.

Bascom turned his attention to the other two men.

"What are you doing here?" he demanded. "Last time I saw you was at Apache Springs."

"Yes, sir, it was," Clay said. "We're still looking for one of our friends. Found one, but the other's still missing. We think we know where he is and we're hoping you'd help us."

"Look, son. I'm in the middle of this Apache uprising. We've got to get to that outcropping up ahead before dark. Ride along if you want to." Bascom barked an order to Connor, then regarded Sunny. "Last time I saw *you*, you were sprawled in the dirt."

He kicked his horse into a trot.

Clay looked over at Sunny and lowered his voice. "Now ain't the time, Sunny."

Sunny gripped the reins, his knuckles turning white. The last soldier in the long column of men rode past. Wagons loaded down with weapons rattled.

* * *

Two miles east of the Apache Springs stage station, Bascom stopped the troops and ordered camp set up. Trace, under watch of his guard, unrolled a woolen blanket. That was where he'd sleep tonight.

He perched on a rock near the campfire, stick in hand. He stared into the fire and watched death and destruction claim the life of yet another twig. Wasn't that the way life was? In the end,

223

there's only death.

A firm hand on his shoulder tugged him out of his gloom. He peered up into the face of his friend. Clay stuck out a hand, the grip strong, reassuring. Sunny introduced Bill.

Trace couldn't help but grin at his friends. "Damn, you're a sight for sore eyes," he said. "Thought you were heading toward Mesilla."

"Thought the same thing about you." Sunny eased his lanky body down to a rock. "The Medinas decided they could go the rest of the way alone." He produced a sideways grin. "Besides, we didn't want you havin' all the fun."

Clay sat cross-legged on the ground and Bill leaned against a boulder. The two privates guarding Trace eased away in their own conversation. One rolled a cigarette and stepped into shadows.

"Army won't go home, I take it," Clay said.

Trace shook his head. "Bascom's as dense as an adobe fence. Can't make him understand. He's determined to get Cochise, no matter what the cost."

"Lotta men gonna die."

Trace nodded and tossed a stick into the fire.

"What's going on, Trace?" Sunny tapped Trace's handcuffs. "Why'd they arrest you?"

"Guess Bascom doesn't like being hit." Trace grinned at the memory. "Or strangled."

Bill whistled. "I'm surprised he let you live. I know Bascom. Used to be a private in his army. Got kicked out in Mesilla."

"Sorry to hear that...I guess." Trace studied his hands and winced as the metal cuffs bit his skin.

Sunny snapped a stick and poked the fire. "Suppose we'll find James tomorrow? Gotta be getting close."

Visions of James as a kid back home popped into Trace's mind. He watched his favorite brother play with the new litter of kittens discovered behind the privy. He was gentle, kind-hearted. James loved life. And now, he was gone.

"Gotta tell you 'bout Coyuntura." Bill's voice pulled Trace back into the present.

"Cochise's brother," Trace said. "Escaped from jail. I heard."

"You already knew?" Sunny frowned.

Trace gave a quick jerk of his head. Something burned in his throat. "Guess that pretty much nails the lid on James' coffin."

"Not necessarily." Clay glanced into the evening sky, then back at Trace. "They may not need him to trade for Coyuntura anymore, but Cochise also wants the army to leave, so until that happens, maybe that old Indian's keeping James alive."

Trace lowered his eyes and spoke over the pain. "I should've stayed. Should've been me to take those whippings." Memories overwhelmed him. "I'll never forget the look on James' face when One Wing…" His cuffed hands gripped his head.

Clay reached over and placed his hand on Trace's back. "It'll be all right. James will be all right. You gotta believe."

"No." Trace glared at Clay. Had everyone gone stupid? "James is dead. Once those Apaches caught whiff of this army, they killed him. That was the deal Cochise made. He always makes good on his promises." His hands shook. "I let James down."

He buried his face in his hands.

Clay's hand on his back, Clay's sympathy, made it difficult for Trace to continue. Trace took a deep breath and raised his head.

"Only thing I can do now is get his body, bury him out here. I'll find a shady place, looks out over the valley. Put a nice marker on it." He swiped at a tear. "He'd like that."

Trace knew he could say anything to these friends, anything. They wouldn't judge. "Wish it was me who was dead."

Clay tightened his hold on Trace. "Don't think like that. You gotta keep good thoughts. We'll find James. Alive. You're not alone any more."

Trace met the stares of his friends and nodded.

# CHAPTER FORTY-EIGHT

A chilly wind accompanied the sun as it peeked over the eastern horizon. Clay stretched the kinks out of his saddle-sore body, ran his hand through his red hair, and eyed his sleeping friend. Bill Patton was gone, his bedroll already rolled and packed on his horse.

Clay nudged Sunny with his foot and waited for the snores to stop, the eyes to open. A couple minutes passed before Sunny mumbled anything intelligible.

"Up and at 'em, partner," Clay said. "Time to get James back." He sniffed the air. Bacon and coffee. Someone was cooking breakfast.

"Where's Bill?" Sunny stood, smoothed his mustache, and ran his hand through his tangled black hair. He adjusted his hat, then stretched and yawned.

Clay shrugged. "Guess army grub's still calling." His stomach rumbled. He nodded toward the group of soldiers breaking up camp several yards away. "Maybe they have some leftover grub so we don't have to cook."

There was no sign of Trace. Before Clay and Sunny made it across the entire encampment, Bascom met them near a group of soldiers.

"This just may be your lucky day, boys," Bascom said. "Our scouts tell me that Companies B and D, First Dragoons, are two hours away. With all that firepower, we'll take out Cochise today. You'll get to see first hand your army at work."

"You're gonna take out Cochise's entire camp?" Clay's surprise turned to anger. "What about James, our friend in there? When you start shooting, he'll be the first to die."

Sunny bristled. "Dammit, Bascom! Might as well pull the trigger yourself."

"I just may. Look, I'll tell you exactly what I told Mister

226

Colton." Bascom eyed Clay. "Once Coyuntura waltzed back into Cochise's camp, that prisoner was a dead man."

"You told him that?" Sunny stepped within inches of Bascom. Clay grabbed Sunny's arm, tugging him back.

"Yes. And I'll tell you this." Bascom shook a pointed finger in Sunny's face. "Interfere with army actions, either of you, and you'll find yourself cuffed and arrested just like your friend there. He's gonna hang. Care to join him?"

Bascom's eyes flared.

Clay stepped between Sunny and Bascom. "Where's Trace at? Can we talk to him?"

"Say your good-byes." Bascom nodded toward a wagon several yards to the west.

Clay nudged Sunny toward the wagon. "Keep your temper. Too much is at stake right now." Clay glanced over his shoulder. "I'd sure like to teach that Bascom some manners myself."

"You gotta be human to learn manners." Sunny wrenched his arm out of Clay's grasp.

Trace stood by the wagon and rubbed his wrists. He nodded at Corporal Connor speaking to him.

Sunny and Clay waited until Connor walked away. Sunny glared at the junior officer's back, then looked at Trace.

"You all right?" Sunny asked.

Trace held up his freed hands. The deep pink rope scars ran around his wrists like a chain.

"I'm going back in," Trace said, "see if I can get James' body. And if we're lucky, maybe I can get Cochise to leave without anyone else dying." He sighed, then shrugged. "Got nothing to lose now."

Clay noticed a sadness that drilled to Trace's core. How in the hell could Trace ever recover from a loss like this? His only salvation would be if James was still alive. But what were the chances of that? Practically none. After turning all the information over, Clay finally had to agree with everyone else. No hope of finding James alive.

Trace's words interrupted Clay's thoughts. "Bascom said he'd drop all assault charges if I get Cochise to leave this area and move to a reservation. Since I already know Cochise, he said I'm the one. Guess it's worth a try."

Clay frowned. "Bascom won't consider pulling out? Even backing away to give you a chance to get James?"

227

"No. Fact is, he's going in with me." Trace wagged his head. "If I don't get back, tell Teresa that I loved her and wished we could've got married." He looked from friend to friend. "You'll tell her?"

Clay nodded. He wouldn't tell Trace that Teresa was in Santa Fe and might never return. That information wouldn't help Trace right now. He'd tell him some other time. He shook Trace's hand.

"You'll tell her when you ride into Mesilla—soon."

Bascom, his horse's ears flicked forward, rode over to Trace. "Now, Mister Colton, when we get to the camp, I'll tell Cochise that two more companies are on their way. If Cochise won't surrender and agree to move off this land and go to a reservation, he'll have a real fight on his hands. He and all of his tribe will die. You tell him that."

"Women and children, too?" Trace frowned. "There's a lot of them. Not doing harm to anybody. Those children—"

"Grow up and attack our soldiers."

"But—"

"Unfortunate casualties of war, Mister Colton."

Sunny straightened his shoulders and pulled in air. Clay shook his head in a silent warning. He knew what his best friend was thinking and what he wanted to do. This still wasn't the time to argue.

Trace turned to his friends. "Funny how life turns out, isn't it?"

With that, he stepped into the stirrups of the army mount, kicked it in the sides and rode off before either Clay or Sunny could say goodbye.

# CHAPTER FORTY-NINE

James swallowed the last bit of stew on his plate and glanced at the sky. The sunrise was stunning this morning. Golden orange and light yellow rays danced on his face as he enjoyed the warmth. The wind had a slight spring chill to it. How long had he been with the Apache now? No real way of telling, but he knew how long Trace had been gone.

Exactly two weeks. He had the marks to prove it.

He watched the women and children of the camp go about their work. James again thought about family. His three nights with Dark Cloud made him realize how much he'd like to have a wife and family. He straightened his shoulders. He had a wife now, not one he'd chosen, but a wife nevertheless. Someone to love and protect. Would they produce children? Funny the turns life makes, he thought.

Careful not to open any healing wounds, and using all the strength he possessed, James handed the plate to a child. The Apache boy produced a shy grin. The campfire, warming James' body, sizzled and popped as one of the women roasted a rabbit, the aroma wafting over the camp.

A long look to his right, then to his left. Where was Dark Cloud? He hadn't seen her since early this morning when he'd been tugged to his feet and pushed outside by Standing Pony. James thought about his wife pressed against him, the trembling woman he held and comforted until dawn these last few nights. Consoling her actually helped him. Although any contact with his body brought agony, somehow, he could bear her touch.

The first night, she had finally fallen asleep in his arms after consummating their marriage. Both embarrassed and unpracticed at love making, he had spent an hour patting her shoulder while she fought tears. Without warning, One Wing had stormed into the wickiup and threatened death if James didn't take her right then. It was awkward at first, but soon Dark Cloud and James discovered they needed each other. There was comfort in that.

After One Wing left, she had submitted willingly and almost seemed to enjoy it. An animal instinct stirring deep inside, James admitted he'd enjoyed it, too.

Guilt roared. Shouldn't have been with her. Shouldn't have married a Pima. Shouldn't have been attracted to that Apache, Quick-to-Run. Should have stayed true to Lila.

Quick-to-Run knelt by his side. She spread the golondrina salve on his newest cuts, careful to navigate the welts and raised bruises. Her eyes darted from his gaze.

"I'm so sorry." James' words drooped in the air as the burning and stinging of his wounds receded. "Would you have married me?"

She nodded and pulled him forward, smoothing the concoction over his lower back.

"Why?"

Quick-to-Run scooped a second handful of medicine from the bowl and ran it down his arm. "You have much courage, strength, and conviction. Although you carry scars and are the enemy, I am not afraid of you." She stopped rubbing. "You make a good husband."

"Thank you." He flinched as she smoothed salve on his face, the latest whiplash still stinging on his left cheek. "Have you seen Dark Cloud?"

Quick-to-Run placed the bowl on the sand, then looked down. "One Wing took her into the desert this morning, James. I'm sorry. She is gone."

"What? What'd you mean *gone?*" He jerked back, several cuts opening and bleeding. He winced.

"She won't return." Quick-to-Run looked away. "One Wing and Standing Pony killed her."

"What? They what?" James struggled to his feet. "I did what they asked!"

Words soft, Quick-to-Run explained. "They were going to anyway. She had no chance. Everyone but you knew that. Cochise now has humiliated the Pima and they will retaliate on you, first. They will kill you as soon as they can."

Good God! First the Apaches, and now the Pimas.

*Poor Dark Cloud. Her body so tiny in my arms. She was*

*gentle, made me smile, feel good again. Should've protected her, should've—*

Moccasined steps drew near. James recognized One Wing's distinctive footfall.

"Come." One Wing yanked on James' arm.

James pulled his captor to a stop and glared into his eyes. "Sonuvabitch! You killed her! Why? We did what you wanted. Why'd you do it?"

"We kill dogs in our way. We used her, got what we wanted." One Wing tugged James closer. "She was not needed any more."

*But I needed her.*

James stumbled forward.

Pushed and pulled through groups of Apaches, he dodged insults and jabs before stopping at the edge of camp. Wedged between One Wing and Coyuntura, his eyes tracked right and left. Twenty, perhaps thirty warriors crowded behind and to either side.

Two figures appeared on the horizon.

James tried to make out who was either brave or foolish enough to ride this close to camp. Who would be insane enough to get this close to Apaches? He squinted.

*Pimas, already?*

Something snapped. Trace! Had to be. No one sat a horse like his big brother. That certain carriage of his upper body was a dead giveaway. This ordeal was near an end. One way or the other, it was almost over.

\* \* \*

Trace reined up after riding across the wide meadow, Bascom at his side. Trace scanned the warriors, hoping to catch a glimpse of his brother and praying he was still alive.

Bascom nudged Trace and pointed to a man sagging in an Apache's grasp.

"That him?" Bascom asked.

Trace squinted against the sun, then recognized his brother. "Yes, sir, it is! Damn! He's still alive!"

It took everything he had not to run across that meadow and grab his little brother, hold him, feel the life in him. Instead, he shut his eyes.

231

*Thank you, God.*

He couldn't stop the grin spreading from ear to ear, relief flooding his entire body.

"Let's go, Colton." Bascom dismounted and waited for Trace to do the same. Then they marched toward the Apaches.

Two factions. A hundred yards apart. Coyuntura emerged from the gathered Indians and paraded across the meadow. Trace noted the similarity between Cochise and his brother. They walked the same with that confident stride, their shoulders held with pride.

The men met and stood a few feet apart. Bascom snorted.

"Coyuntura? So, we meet again."

"Lieutenant Bascom. Lose any more prisoners lately?"

Bascom had met his match. Trace looked past Coyuntura at James. Was he really still alive? It was too good to be true. He looked almost dead, though. Wouldn't take much to finish him off. Even from this distance, Trace could see the red lines covering most of his chest. Was that one on his face?

Bascom straightened his shoulders, took a deep breath, then remembered to introduce Trace. "Coyuntura, this is Trace Colton, brother of your prisoner."

Coyuntura studied the former captive.

"I see James over there. How is he?" Trace asked.

"Just like all you White Eyes—in our way."

Bascom's eyes swept over the crowd of Indians. "Where's Cochise? I must talk with him."

"Mexico."

"Listen, Coyuntura. I have many soldiers all around here, guns and rifles pointed at your head as we speak. You must convince your brother to give up, bring all of his people to live on a reservation. That is the only way I'll allow you and your tribe to live."

Trace held his breath while Cochise's brother considered Bascom's offer. A slow smirk lifted one corner of Coyuntura's face.

"What makes you think I'll allow you and your tribe to live?"

Bascom's eyes narrowed into slits. "We have more guns than you, especially since it looks like many of your warriors are in Mexico. More of ours are on the other side of this hill."

Coyuntura gazed at the sky. White clouds skittered by on the high winds while a hawk circled breakfast. The Indian shook his head.

"I do not trust White Eyes."

"Come with me to my camp, bring several of your warriors, Coyuntura." Bascom cocked his head toward the army encampment. "We'll parley, have all the details worked out by the time your brother returns."

"I still do not trust you, Bascom, but I know my brother respects the captive. If that is what he wants."

Trace nodded. "Could bring peace to everyone."

"All right. I will come with three of my braves to your camp."

"I'll get James." Trace stepped forward.

"No." Coyuntura shoved his hand hard against Trace's chest. "He stays with the Apache. If I die, he dies."

Trace's heart thumped in his throat. "May I talk to him? Make sure he's all right?"

Coyuntura studied Trace from arm's length, then nodded.

Trace covered the yards in seconds, but he slid to a stop at the sight of the deep cuts and welts covering James' body.

James' bare chest glistened with blood and long puffy furrows of split skin. Instead of embracing his brother, Trace peered into James' brown eyes, took in relief edged with worry. He gripped James' arms.

"You all right?"

Trace knew his brother wasn't all right, would never be, but had no idea what else to say.

James nodded, tears in his eyes. "Thought I'd never see you again."

"Told you I'd be back." Trace cradled his brother's face and frowned at the blistered red line running across his left cheek. "Soon, James. It'll be over soon. Just gotta hold on a little longer."

"I'm trying." James' words were so soft Trace strained to hear them. James hung his head and spoke into his chest. "I got married."

"What?" Trace leaned his ear close to his brother's face. "You what?"

James nodded. "Married."

"No, you didn't."

"They killed her."

233

"No, they didn't. Lila's still alive in Mesilla." Trace stared into his brother's brown eyes. "James, do you know where you are?"

Coyuntura stepped next to Trace, pointed and spoke to a few of his warriors. Three of them held up their lances and walked into the meadow.

The tug of the Indian's grip. Trace balked at the nudge.

"Take James back with you instead of me," he said. "Trade us. I'll stay here with One Wing."

Coyuntura shook his head. "You made a bargain. You will see it through."

Trace's shoulders slumped. "Dammit, James. I'm sorry. I'll be back soon. I promise."

He stepped back.

James strained against One Wing's hold on his arm and grabbed the front of Trace's shirt.

"Don't leave, Trace. Please. God, don't leave me again." Panicked fingers clutched the fabric like a lifeline.

"Soon." Trace gripped his brother's hand and squeezed. "I'll come back soon."

"They're gonna kill me. Pimas are gonna kill me."

Trace hung his head, staring down at his feet. If he looked at James he'd never leave. Instead, he pried the frantic fingers from his shirt.

He glared at One Wing and pushed his face nose to nose with the Apache's. "Touch my little brother again, I'll bring this whole damn army down on your head. There won't be enough of you left even for the dogs to bury." He glanced at his brother. "And that's a promise."

Trace spun around and trudged back to Bascom with Coyuntura and three Apache warriors at his side. Rage kept the tears from flowing.

# CHAPTER FIFTY

*Walk away, Trace. One foot in front of the other and walk away.*

Trace sang the mantra over and over until he stood next to Bascom. Guilt rattled in his chest, but he'd had no choice. Maybe by the end of today, James would be free, Cochise and his tribe would be headed toward a reservation, and Bascom would leave. It was a lot to wish for, but he needed that thread of hope.

Trace, along with Bascom and the Apaches, met Corporal Connor at the encampment, then followed him to Bascom's tent.

Inside the tent, Trace eased down to a gray blanket covering the dirt and folded his long legs while the four Apaches sat near him. He winced at his bruises and strained muscles, but with the image of James' agony in mind, he brushed aside his own pain.

Bascom perched on a three-legged canvas stool that tottered back and forth each time he moved. Although precariously perched at best, Bascom still sat above everyone else in the tent, reigning over his kingdom.

Hours dragged. Neither side would negotiate past agreeing that too much blood had already been shed.

By the time the noon meal had been served and consumed by the rest of the company, Trace, along with five other soldiers and Apaches, emerged into the sunlight. Bascom spoke to Connor standing guard outside the tent. Uninterested in the conversation, Trace headed for the campfire and the remaining food.

Bascom accepted a plate and turned as two Army scouts rode into camp.

"Lieutenant Bascom." The men saluted the commander.

Bascom returned the salute. "What?"

"Companies B and D, First Dragoons approach from the west, sir. They should be here within a half-hour."

"They were supposed to be here an hour ago."

"Cannon wagon wheel broke, sir."

"Bring the commanders to me as soon as they arrive." Bascom turned his back on the scouts. He glanced down at his Indian guests. "Enjoy your meal. It may be your last."

Without uttering a word, all four Indians stood and walked away, toward the tent.

"Trace?"

He turned at a familiar voice and noticed his two friends loping toward him.

"You saw him?" Clay's green eyes grew wide, the eyebrows arched. "Alive?"

Trace nodded.

"How is he?" Sunny asked.

Trace met their stare. "Badly beaten and whipped, but still alive." The words sounded too hollow. "Think he'll be all right."

He knew he was lying. But what else could he tell these friends?

"Thank God!" Sunny patted Trace on the shoulder.

"What'd I tell you?" Clay beamed, but grew serious as he studied Trace's drawn face. "What else?"

The plate in Trace's hand rattled. Trace brought his gaze up to Clay's. "James thinks he got married." He pinched the bridge of his nose. "And he thinks he's with the Pimas. His mind's snapped."

Clay gripped Trace's arm and glanced at Sunny. "He's just confused is all. Get him away from here, some real food and sleep, he'll be all right."

Trace nodded. His friends meant well, but they couldn't understand what both he and James had gone through.

James was broken.

"What did Bascom and Coyuntura decide?" Clay looked over his shoulder at Bascom.

"Coyuntura won't make a decision without Cochise. And Bascom wants an answer now. Let's just hope the big man himself gets back from Mexico soon. This is a boiling pot ready to explode."

Sunny turned to Clay. "Wonder where Patton is. Haven't seen hide nor hair of him. Suppose he's all right?"

"Yeah," Clay said. "I wouldn't worry about him. Probably found some of his army friends holed up playing cards."

Trace stared into the distance. Heat shimmered across the

desert like water trickling over pebbles. A flock of crows punctured the blue sky.

"How can we help?" Sunny asked. "What d'you want us to do?"

Trace raised one shoulder. "Wish I knew." He hung his head. "You should've seen the look on his face when I had to leave. Stabbing him in the heart would've been easier. I offered to stay and take his place, but they wouldn't let me."

"I know it's hard," Clay said. "But you did what you had to. James knows that." He nodded toward the food. "You need to keep your strength up...for James' sake."

By the time Trace had finished picking at his noon meal, Lieutenants Murray and Anderson rode into camp. They spotted Bascom and saluted, then dismounted and followed Bascom into his tent.

Trace groaned up to his feet and ambled over to the tent. He knew he couldn't be much help, but at least he'd know what was going on. The sergeant at the tent held up his hand.

"Sorry, Mister Colton. No one else allowed in."

"What?" Trace looked over his shoulder at Clay and Sunny, hoping he hadn't heard correctly. "What? I can't get back in?"

"That's correct, sir. I have strict orders. No one else allowed." The sergeant raised his shoulders. "Sorry, sir."

The afternoon dragged by while Bascom, the two additional Dragoon commanders, and Coyuntura spoke in Bascom's tent. Trace paced the length of the camp, keeping an uneasy eye on the tent flap. Something didn't feel right. It was taking much too long. And why hadn't he been allowed into the tent?

Shortly before sunset, an army scout galloped into camp. Bascom stepped from his tent and returned the salute. "News, Private?"

"Sir. Cochise has just returned."

"How many men with him?"

"Maybe twenty."

"Thank you private. Return to your post."

The man saluted, but stayed where he was. "Sir?"

Bascom glared at the soldier.

"Thought you'd also want to know. Those Indians brought back a lot of things taken from ranches—dresses, chickens, many rifles." He winced. "And many scalps."

237

One side of Bascom's mouth twitched. "It's war, Private. People die."

"Yes, sir." Saluting again, the young soldier executed a smart about-face, mounted his horse, and galloped south.

This was it. Time for action. With Cochise back and the army here, James was as good as dead. Trace stepped in front of Bascom before he could retreat to the tent.

"I'll ride into camp and get Cochise to come back with me before he kills James."

"No."

"No? Dammit, Bascom. With Cochise back and you here, the first thing that's gonna happen is James dying. Cochise doesn't make empty promises."

"You don't listen, boy." Bascom shook his head. "I said no. I'm placing the other companies around this entire valley. Can't do that before morning." He scowled at Trace. "You'll have plenty of time to say goodbye to your brother before I hang you tomorrow— if he's still alive."

"Hold it!" Trace grabbed Bascom's sleeve. "I did my part. I brought the Apache to you. I can get Cochise. That was our deal. I'm not under arrest any more."

"You're under arrest until I say otherwise," Bascom said. "Just so you don't play hero and ride into Cochise's camp and spoil my plans, you'll be cuffed to this wagon wheel again. One wrong move, Trace Colton, you'll hang right here."

He spun around and marched away.

# CHAPTER FIFTY-ONE

The voice in James' ears made no sense. Were they words or just sounds? His eyes opened in the bright morning light. He blinked at Cochise's face just inches from his.

"It is time." Cochise untied his shaking hands and pulled him to his feet. "Come."

James resisted the pull. "Are you gonna kill me now?"

What was Cochise thinking? James searched the man's face. Unreadable, as usual.

"I know the army is here," James said, "but so is Trace. Before you kill me, please...please listen to his words."

Cochise's eyes narrowed, and his mouth turned down. "The army must listen to me. I will not take my people to a reservation, I will not allow White Eyes on my land." His grip on James' arm tightened into a stranglehold. "I will keep my people free."

"Killing me won't keep you free. It'll give the army one more reason to wipe out your tribe. I don't want that, Cochise."

"What do you want, James Colton?"

James stared up into the chief's eyes. "Just for everyone to live free. Not have to die." He ran his hand over the most recent welt on his stomach. "Truth is, Cochise, I'm afraid of dying."

Cochise loosened the grip. He held James' shoulder with his other hand.

"You are wise for someone so young," he said. "You have honor, you do not lie. That is important to me." He released James' shoulder, then pulled him toward the edge of camp. "If you die today, you'll die a brave man—a white warrior."

*A warrior.*

Cochise had paid him the greatest compliment possible, but still, James was afraid. He limped through the village with Cochise. Words and sounds mixed together in a riot of noise. Nothing made sense.

One Wing joined them, and the three men marched to the edge of the camp and faced the wide meadow. One Wing's fingers grasped James' left arm, making bright white dots on the skin. James' right arm, held by Cochise, just tingled and grew numb.

The men waited.

Silent and slow, several riders appeared in the distance. James couldn't identify any of them except his brother. He didn't care who the others were. He just knew Trace was nearby. A cold shiver hit him.

What if Cochise makes Trace watch him kill me?

White dots spun in front of James' eyes.

*What if Cochise kills Trace first?*

He had to force himself to breathe until the dots faded.

The men dismounted on the far side of the meadow, a little closer than the day before. Cochise's grip on his right arm tightened. James tried to pull away, but Cochise's strength buckled James' knees. His world turned blazing white as he hit the ground.

"Stand!" Cochise's low voice slammed James' face.

Like a small child, James felt himself jerked up and planted on his feet again.

*Do that again, and Cochise will kill me.*

James locked his knees.

James and the two Apache leaders waited for the soldiers to come closer, to cross the open field. When they didn't, Cochise released James' arm and marched forward.

Behind him, James heard the warriors ready their bows and arrows. He glanced over his shoulder and watched the Indians tighten their grips on their lances. A few Apaches had donned war paint, faces streaked with ribbons of red.

*Like blood.*

\* \* \*

Bascom pulled his shoulders back and stood as tall as possible. He decided that if he moved or even flinched, this imposing Indian might think he was weak, someone to be defeated. He had to look tall and powerful, as the most famous Apache leader in the Southwest strode across the meadow toward him.

Cochise stopped inches away. The Apache leader stood at least six foot five. A good four inches taller than Bascom. For a few

240

seconds, Bascom couldn't find the right words.

"Cochise, I am Lieutenant George Bascom, United States Army. Your brother and three of your warriors are back at my camp. While you were in Mexico, we made a plan, an agreement, for peace between the Americans and the Apaches."

Bascom's mouth dried as he studied the Indian. His ticket to a promotion and a command of his own army post was less than three feet away. He had to be careful. All Apaches, he knew, especially this one, were smart, clever, cunning. He had to say the right things to lure him.

Cochise turned his eyes on each of the men standing before him. His gaze rested on Trace.

"You bring army men although you promised to keep them away. I should have killed your brother upon my return." His hand caressed the handle of a knife slid in his waistband. "Your brother suffered greatly because you were not as fast as the wind."

"I rode as quickly as I could, Cochise," Trace said. "Please don't kill him. Your brother has returned. We can parley, talk with the army. Make an agreement."

Not to be upstaged by a mere stagecoach driver, Lieutenant Bascom wedged into the conversation. "He's right, Cochise. No need to kill that young man right now. You can always do it later."

Trace glared.

Cochise's mouth turned up slightly at one corner. He spoke to Trace and Trace alone. "James is strong, like you, like my son. What do *you* think of this peace plan?"

"If it brings peace to everyone, Cochise, and stops the killing, you know how I feel. It's worth a chance."

Bascom held his breath. He straightened his jacket and held out his hand to the Apache. "Let's give our word and go back to camp where your brother and friends wait. We'll draw up the final plans there."

Cochise turned back to One Wing, held up his hand, and motioned.

Before anyone moved, an Apache brave galloped across the meadow toward the small group.

"Cochise! Cochise!" The warrior launched himself off his pinto and gestured. "Your brother." The Indian spoke over short gasps. "Coyuntura is dead. Hanged at the army camp!"

"What?" Cochise frowned at the messenger. "Are you

241

certain?"

"Yes. I saw him and the others hanging from oak trees on the other side of this pass."

He pointed north.

Trace turned to Cochise. "I didn't know." He shook his head. "I'm sorry."

Cochise let out a war cry, a whoop. Apaches sprung up from behind every rock and clump of bushes. Arrows and bullets flew, soldiers shrieked attack orders, men fell to the ground clutching their wounds.

Like hordes of angry wasps, soldiers and fierce Apache warriors attacked. They covered the hills. Soldiers and Indians alike screeched, shot, and charged—right where Trace stood.

* * *

*James.*

The first person to be killed. Trace knew One Wing would hold him up as an example. He'd slit his throat before anyone knew what happened.

Gun whipped from his waistband, Trace bolted through the throng of warring people. He ran fifty yards before he spotted One Wing and James, fighting.

One Wing slammed James to the ground, then raised a knife over his heart. Even from a distance, Trace read pleasure on the Indian's face.

Trace screamed. He wouldn't get to his brother in time. It was too far, and there were too many arrows and crazed soldiers to dodge. The odor of gunpowder attacked his nose. Bullets popped around his ears.

Three running steps, then Trace tripped over a fallen soldier. He hit the ground, but he leaped to his feet just as an Apache lunged at him, knife in hand. A bullet sent the Indian flying forward and into the desert sand. Trace spun and took off for his brother again.

"No!" Trace hollered as he ran. "No!"

He stretched out his arms as One Wing thrust the blade down toward his brother's bare chest. James scrambled backwards.

Someone tackled One Wing. The knife flew out of his grasp as the men hit the ground and tumbled over and over.

James lay motionless.

Trace ran harder.

One Wing fought back like a bear attacked by a mountain lion. He clawed, bit, twisted, but Bill Patton was stronger. Both men scrambled to get the upper hand.

One Wing kicked his attacker's legs; Bill hit the ground. Then One Wing jumped on top, but Bill rolled him over, pinning his arms and body against the rough sand. He struggled and cursed, but Bill used all his weight to hold him down.

A fist. Barreling toward One Wing's face. He jerked, but with his hands pinned, he was defenseless. The impact jarred his teeth, and blood pooled in his mouth.

Bill punched One Wing again and again, until his fists hurt. One Wing tried to throw him, but Bill was determined to do something right in life. He lifted his clenched fist one last time.

Suddenly, Bill sucked in a gasp, his last breath, and rolled off of One Wing, carried by the force of the lance embedded in his back.

\* \* \*

James' world tilted as he rolled back and forth, fighting to sit up. The knife scrape across his side burned, but he knew he had to ignore it. He prayed an ounce of strength was left in his body. As if in answer to his prayer, he spotted a knife near his leg. He picked it up.

One Wing struggled to his knees, then crawled to James.

"Nothing will keep me from killing you now, White Eyes. Too bad you'll bleed only once more." He fell into James and shoved him back to the dirt.

Even though his head slammed against the ground, James maintained his focus on One Wing. The Indian's breath in his ear, the curses in his face, fueled the rage burning inside James.

James plunged the knife into the Apache's neck.

One Wing's body jerked. James pulled the blade out and thrust it in again, deeper.

*The beatings.*

James yanked out the knife, then shoved One Wing off of him and perched on top.

*The whippings.*

James raked the knife across One Wing's chest, slicing skin. *Endless torment.*

James leaned back and balled his fist. It connected with One Wing's cheek. Blood splattered both men's faces.

*Trace. Dark Cloud. Agony. Humiliation.*

One Wing moaned.

"You sonuvabitch! Son...of...a...bitch!" James stood and kicked One Wing. Foot to ribs, foot to face. One Wing brought his hands up as though to cover his eyes. Instead, he reached out, grabbed James' leg, then pulled.

James crumpled to his knees. One's Wing's feeble effort gave James the chance to plant a knee in One Wing's chest.

James lifted the knife shoulder high. One Wing closed his eyes. A final breath escaped his lips.

"Don't die on me, you sonuvabitch! Face me like a man!" James dropped the knife and clutched the front of One Wing's shirt. He pulled the limp body a few inches off the ground.

"Sonuvabitch!"

He glared at One Wing, released the shirt, then closed his eyes. All his energy, every last bit of effort was gone. He couldn't even move his eyelids. Sleeping or dying would be fine now.

James Francis Michael Colton collapsed into the sand.

* * *

Sunny shouldered his Hawken and aimed at an Indian a few yards away from Clay. He fired. The Apache spun once and hit the sand. Between the screeches and screams, men running, and rifle smoke, Sunny lost sight of Clay.

Then he spotted Bascom.

Bascom wasn't more than thirty yards to Sunny's right. Sunny gripped his shotgun stock, then sighted down the barrel.

"Bang!" Sunny spoke the words as he envisioned that lieutenant flying backwards, blood soaking his shirt. He lowered the weapon and thought again.

*No, I'm not a killer. But, damn, I owe him.*

Sunny marched closer. He watched Bascom shout orders, then hide behind that boot-licker, Connor.

*What'll it be? Rifle butt between the shoulder blades? Bullet to the calf? A good rap on the head?*

244

"Sunny!"

He heard his name, recognized Clay's voice.

*Not now, friend. I made a promise I intend to keep.*

"Sunny?"

Ten yards now separated him and that *pendejo* Lieutenant. Dodging soldiers and Indians, Sunny sidestepped fallen warriors.

"Sunny!"

Something about Clay's voice, the way he called his name, made Sunny stop. Something was wrong. Definitely wrong.

Pivoting on one foot, Sunny spotted Clay sprawled on the ground, clutching his leg. Blood soaked his pants. Even from twenty yards, Sunny saw the pain on his friend's face, the tanned skin paling, the arrow at attention in his left thigh.

"Hold on, I'm coming!"

Sunny ran around three groaning soldiers and slid to a stop at Clay's side.

\* \* \*

An Apache rolled over. Trace cocked his revolver and aimed at the Indian's face. As he did, he realized this man was the only Apache who'd been halfway decent to him and his brother. His wife had even sneaked extra food to them a time or two.

*He might be an Indian, but not an enemy.*

He eased down the hammer.

Trace searched the sea of bodies for his brother. There. Blanketed in blood.

*Please be alive. Please be alive.*

Distance covered in seconds, Trace skidded into the sand and knelt. He rolled James over, then pulled him up, propping his brother against his knee.

"James?" He brushed away sand and hair plastered to James' face. "James?"

James clutched his brother's sleeve. "Alive?"

"Yeah."

"Free?"

"Yeah."

Apache screams. Rifle shots. Trace flinched when an arrow landed a few feet away.

James opened his eyes and swiped at a bleeding cut on his lip.

245

He pushed away from Trace, then crawled to One Wing.

"James?" Trace knelt beside his brother and the dead Apache. "We gotta get outta here. We're right in the middle. Liable to get shot by the army or the Indians. Or both."

Without a sound, James raked his fingers through One Wing's blood. He examined it in his hands, then smeared it down One Wing's face with his fingers. The blood ribbon started on One Wing's forehead and ended at his chin.

James sat back. Despite swollen lips, a semblance of a grin warped across his face. James pulled the knife out and gripped One Wing's hair. The black strands hung in his fist like ebony ribbons.

"James, don't do this." Trace reached out and touched his brother. "Let it go."

Trace's eyes stared at James. What was his brother thinking? Images of the scalping twisted Trace's stomach. "Don't do it, James. Please."

Silence from his brother.

James wrapped the hair around his hand and yanked. Just like the rancher woman's, One Wing's head flopped up and rolled to one side. James brought the knife shoulder high, then plunged it down toward One Wing's face. It slashed through the black hair.

James held up the braid and with it, a wedding ring.

A deep breath. Trace eased the knife from his brother's hand.

Mute, James unwrapped Lila's ring and threw the hair into the Sonoran Desert. He cradled the gold band in his palm and ran his finger over it.

Trace moved in front of James, put his arms around him, and drew him against his chest.

Both men wept.

# CHAPTER FIFTY-TWO

Clay lay on the ground, the wound in his thigh oozing blood. He clutched his leg and rocked side to side. "You see Trace or James?" he asked.

Sunny glanced to his left and spotted the two brothers sitting, Trace holding James. "Both alive, Clay. They're all right. Let's worry about you." He ripped part of the material exposing the entry wound.

"Is it bad?"

"Just a splinter." Sunny flashed a quick smile at his friend. Somewhere to his left, a cannon roared. He ducked as if it sailed overhead. Indians screamed. Or were those soldiers?

Sunny tried to sound calm. He sure didn't need Clay passing out right now. "First, we'll get that arrow outta there, then head for higher ground." He gripped the wooden shaft. "This is gonna hurt."

"Already does."

"Hold steady, partner."

Clay gritted his teeth. Sunny rocked the feathered rod back and forth. Clay grabbed Sunny's leg and squeezed. One yank. Another. Something snapped.

"Damn!" Sunny held up the rod. "Arrow shaft broke off, Clay." He held up the bloodied end. "You all right?"

Clay grimaced and nodded.

"I'll get you over there by those trees, you can rest in the shade. You'll be fine."

Another cannon blast. This time closer. Sunny flinched. "Sonuvabitch!"

He studied Clay's gray face. Judging by the way Clay held his stomach, he was about to vomit.

Sunny helped Clay to his feet, then wrapped an arm around his waist. He guided him several yards out of the battle and settled under a cottonwood.

Clay leaned back against the trunk. He ran his hand across his eyes. "What's going on, Sunny? I can't see too good from here."

"Bascom's shouting orders to Connor. That coward's hiding behind his corporal." He squinted into the meadow. "Good Lord, Clay. Bascom's standing on top of a rock and grinning. Just like Napoleon at Waterloo!"

From where he sat, Clay could see Cochise. He pulled on Sunny's pants leg and pointed. "Looks like that Indian's hurt." A red stream ran down Cochise's arm while he shouted orders to his warriors. "He's determined to win."

"They both are."

Sunny wagged his head and knelt by Clay. His friend's hands shook, and all the color had drained from his pinched face.

"You're turning a strange shade of white. Even your freckles are gray. How're you feeling?"

"Fine." Clay grabbed at his leg and grimaced. "I lied. Hurts like hell."

More Apache screams. Soldiers hollered orders. Softer now.

Sunny slid an arm around Clay's shoulders. "Take a couple deep breaths. That's it. Don't pass out on me. We'll get that arrow head outta your leg real soon."

"Gotta help Trace. Get James out." Clay closed his eyes and clutched Sunny's shirtsleeve. "It's getting quiet. I'm dying?"

"Nah, you're too ornery for that. Fighting's about done is all."

\* \* \*

James heard his brother's name called, then felt Trace's grip relax around his chest. He pushed away from Trace and opened his eyes. To his right, he spotted a man loping down a low hill toward him and his brother.

Trace patted him on the back. "Someone you know's here."

The man trotting over looked familiar, but James couldn't put a name with the face. Not a soldier. Definitely not Indian.

Trace stood as the man reached them. James noted the relieved look on his brother's face as he gripped the stranger's forearm.

"You all right?" Trace asked.

The man nodded, then knelt by James.

Trace glanced over the man's shoulder. "Where's Clay?"

*Clay. Familiar name.*

The man jerked his thumb over his shoulder toward the edge of the meadow. "Took an arrow in the leg, but he's all right. Bleeding's already stopped. He's resting under a tree over yonder."

James watched this man turn his brown eyes on him. He'd seen him somewhere before.

"Thank God you're alive, James. Too mean even for the Apaches?"

The stranger reached out, but James recoiled. The hand retracted, then curled a couple of times. The man raised thick black eyebrows that matched his thick black mustache.

James stared at the stranger, this person who'd come from another time, another place.

Another life.

"So that's where Patton went." The man eyed the stranger who lay dead near One Wing. The stranger who'd died trying to save James. Who now lay on his side, eyes wide open.

"Why'd Bill jump in like that?" Trace followed the stare.

The man wrenched his gaze from the dead ex-soldier and the Indian. He turned back to Trace. "Guess he felt responsible, figured out he shouldn't have opened that jail door."

Trace nodded. "Just saved James' life, though."

"Who's he?" James tugged on Trace's shirtsleeve and swung his gaze from man to man.

"Sunny Williamston," Trace said as he clutched Sunny's shoulder and shook it. "Ride shotgun for Butterfield. Just like you. Remember you and me'd ride into Mesilla or Tucson and play poker with him and Clay? We'd have a drink or two? The four of us."

James stared at Sunny and listened to his brother's words. They made little sense. All he could do was shake his head, hoping to knock memories back in place.

Trace leaned closer to Sunny. "He and Clay rode a long time to find you. James, this is one of our best friends. Sunny."

A glimmer of recollection wedged into James' brain. He'd heard that name before.

Sunny extended his hand again. This time James reached out, then noticed the drying blood covering his palm, caking on his fingers.

Without saying a word, each man stared at James' bloody hand.

# CHAPTER FIFTY-THREE

As James rode through the outskirts of Mesilla, his gaze swept over the faces staring at his rag tag party. Everyone froze, open mouthed. He recognized no one. Where were his friends, people he knew? He was a stranger in town.

He regarded some of the people, nodded at two. A few women recoiled; one even grabbed her child as James rode by.

*Do I look that bad? Do I look Apache?*

Sunny led the procession past the plaza and halted in front of the doctor's office. James focused on the door. Behind it lay help.

After settling inside, Trace limped back and forth in the small examining room and watched the doctor work on his brother. Clay waited in a chair in the outer office, his injured leg propped up. And Sunny, with the knife wound to his shoulder already well healed, scouted around town.

Trace's gaze alternated between his brother's face and battered body. How many bones were broken? How in the hell had he survived?

James lay motionless, but he tried to answer questions, his voice gravely from too much abuse. Memories. Trace gritted his teeth and focused on folding then refolding the shirt James had borrowed from Sunny.

Dr. Logan studied the thermometer and raised his eyebrows. "Uh oh."

Shirt forgotten, Trace laid his hand on James' forehead and frowned. The warmth bordered on hot, too hot.

"Doc?"

A shake of the head, then Dr. Logan pulled up a chair, perched on the edge, and glanced up at Trace. He cleared his throat. "Several of those lesions are infected. I'm not surprised." He leaned forward, closer to James. "I understand a couple of the Indian women rubbed a salve, a poultice on your cuts. Do you know what it was?" Dr. Logan frowned into his face. "James? You hear me?"

James' eyes softened. "It was Quick-to-Run. She was so beautiful." He looked up at Trace. "I wanted to marry her, not—"

"James," Trace said. "Stay with us. We're here in Mesilla. Doctor Logan's gonna fix you up." He snapped his fingers in his brother's face.

James' brown eyes traveled up and met Trace's. For a brief moment, the hair, his posture, something about the way he spoke… Had James actually become Apache?

Trace vowed to bring his brother back.

He turned to the doctor. "I don't think he knows what the salve was, and I sure don't." He clenched his jaw.

*I should know.*

"Whatever it was, probably saved his life," the doctor said as he nodded at James' whip marks. "Kept most of them from getting infected, anyway." He poked at several swollen, crimson streaks. "These are bad enough."

Trace gripped the doctor's arm. "He gonna be all right?" A long silence and stare from Dr. Logan ignited Trace's fear. "Doc?"

"If we can get this fever down…" Dr. Logan wiped James' face with a damp cloth, then patted the lash mark on the cheek. He dunked the cloth in a bowl of red-tinged water. "It's hard to say, what with everything that's happened, but he's young. He was real strong before…"

Trace listened to the doctor, but the words were muffled, muddled. He hung his head.

"Trace?" James held his bandaged ribs.

Careful not to jar James, Trace eased down to the edge of the bed, his own injuries reminding him he wasn't close to being healed. Their eyes locked. Was his brother back into the present?

James tapped Trace's leg. "I'll be fine, don't worry. You're as banged up as me. We'll both get all right."

Trace nodded. "I know."

His brother's black and blue eyes, the purple fist marks on his face, spun Trace's stomach. Hard to imagine James healing from all this.

The doctor patted Trace's shoulder and tugged on his arm. "Let's attend to you now, Mister Colton. I'll bet your injuries are just as severe as his."

251

"They're not. I'm staying here."

"Look, he's not going anywhere," the doctor said. "I gave him laudanum, he'll sleep. That's the best thing for him right now."

James attempted a grin. The distortion turned his face into a grimace.

Dr. Logan pointed. "You'll be right across the hall in my other room."

"All right." Trace stood. "Holler if you need me, James."

His brother's eyes closed.

* * *

Half an hour later, Sunny appeared in Trace's doorway. He walked across the room, turned a chair around, then plunked his body into the seat. His arms hung over the back.

"How's James?"

What could Trace tell his friend? That James may never recover? Never be strong? Certainly never be the man Sunny remembered from before.

"Trace?" Sunny sat up straighter. "How is he?"

"Doc here says fever's too high, but...I don't know." Trace winced as the sutures tugged at a cut on his back. The doctor's needle poked him again.

Sunny pried off his hat and ran his hand through his black hair. "We've been in town what, two, three hours now?"

Trace nodded.

"I've looked everywhere for Lila. Can't find her."

Stinging turned to burning across his back. Trace jerked and glanced over his shoulder.

"Hold still now," Dr. Logan said. "Your brother didn't squirm half as much as you are."

An embarrassed nod, then Trace turned his thoughts back to Lila. "Did you ask around?"

Sunny nodded. "Nobody's saying. But they do say 'welcome back' and 'glad you survived'. A few of the women said they'd be over to see you two in a few days. Promised apple pies and casseroles."

"Can't wait." Trace's stomach growled. "What about Teresa? Did you see her?"

"She's in Santa Fe staying with relatives. Supposed to be

back in a couple weeks. The lady at the boarding house said she'd send Teresa a message, tell her you're here."

Even though his whole body hurt like it'd been punctured with Lucifer's pitchfork, Trace relaxed as the doctor wrapped wide strips of cloth around his sore ribs.

Sunny's lips drew tight.

"What else?" Trace waited for an answer.

Sunny stared at the wall, then let out a long breath.

"Dammit it, Trace. The Medinas. Those sweet little girls, that baby, Missus Medina." His knuckles gripping the back of the chair turned white. "Every last one of them killed at the San Simon way station."

"Apaches?"

"Yeah. Heard it over at the Mercantile."

Trace closed his eyes. Incessant drums. Apache war chants. Thundering raids. Arrows. Lances. Screams. Trace gripped his head and rocked back and forth.

A hand on his shoulder, a voice in his ear.

"Trace?"

The drums faded.

"You all right? You're shaking." Sunny patted Trace's arm.

A nod. Trace swiped at sweat beading on his forehead.

*If only I could wipe away the memories as easily.*

"The Medinas." He swallowed. "Clay know?"

"Takin' it real hard. Blames himself. Sure was fond of those little girls."

Dr. Logan finished tying the bandages around Trace's ribs. "What a damn shame. Imagine—a whole family." He frowned up into Sunny's face. "San Simon. That's east of Apache Springs, isn't it?"

"Yeah."

"Then count yourself lucky. Apaches just missed you."

Trace had to agree with Logan. They were all lucky. Damn lucky.

"Extra lucky, Doc. Since Cochise let James go, Bascom had to let me go, too. No hanging, no execution…just freedom." Life was once again looking up.

The doctor set the rolled gauze on the bedside table, then patted the bed. "Rest here, Trace. For a few days, anyway. We'll get real food down you, get those ribs and bruises healed. I'll give

253

you some laudanum for the pain. When you're ready, I'll have supper brought in."

"Thanks, Doc."

Trace lay back on the cotton mattress, the tiny lumps flattening out with his weight. As much as he resisted, Trace closed his eyes.

* * *

The next days blurred by for James. All he remembered was his brother talking to the doctor, alternating with Clay and Sunny sitting by his side. He'd open his eyes, and like magic, there they were. Then the next second they were gone.

Trace sat with him all the time. Or so it seemed. When James wasn't sleeping or answering Dr. Logan's questions, James and Trace would talk. Many words were spoken, but not much was said. James was still numb. He knew that in time he'd figure it out. But not now. Only one question plagued him.

Where was Lila?

Lila. After a lot of words, lots of thinking, lots of putting memories in their place, James replaced Quick-to-Run's face with Lila's. But sometimes when he didn't focus, Lila's face would vanish, and Dark Cloud's would take its place. Dark Cloud, his murdered wife. Dark Cloud, the woman who got him through those last horrific days. Dark Cloud, his savior.

Or was Lila his savior?

Or was it Quick-to-Run, with her soft hands and soothing salve?

He was still confused sometimes, and just last night he hadn't been able to tell Trace who was who. But, today he was getting better. Most of the time he knew it was Lila he was waiting to marry and that Quick-to-Run was still alive back in Cochise's camp.

Dark Cloud, however...

Thoughts of Lila flitted in his mind and he struggled to keep them there. Didn't she know he was back? Didn't she want to come see him? Why hadn't she rushed to his side the moment he arrived in Mesilla?

He reached for the tiny tied package sitting on his bedside table. Its red ribbon. The ring inside. Every time he looked at it, he smiled. As soon as Lila appeared, he'd give her this gift, this token of his love. Maybe they could get married right here in the doctor's office.

He clutched the ring to his chest.

* * *

James listened to Trace and the doctor in the next room. Sounded like his brother spoke over mouthfuls of food. A fork clattered against a tin plate. Must be breakfast.

"How's my brother doing, Doc? I'm worried about him."

True concern peppered each word. Did Trace know something he wasn't telling?

"He's been through a helluva ordeal," Dr. Logan said. "If Sunny hadn't told me that he was James, I wouldn't have recognized him. Didn't believe it at first. Took him for a half-breed Indian. Fact is, I didn't recognize you either." A long pause and sigh. "His injuries are severe. But, his fever's down. His body's trying to heal. Trace, he can only concentrate on getting well. Give him time. He's just gotta sort it all out."

Silence.

The doctor's voice dropped. James listened harder. "Just like you. You know, any time you'd like to share your stories, I'm here."

"They're too jumbled up, they just hurt right now."

James squeezed his eyes shut. He felt the exact same way.

"But when it's time, I will."

A bell jingled. James cringed. Had he heard that before? He relaxed.

*It's the front door. I'm not in Cochise's camp any more.*

Trace limped into James' room and leaned against the door jam. "Morning." Trace held out the coffee cup in his hand as an offering.

"No, thanks." James patted his healing split lip. He pushed himself up and sat propped against several pillows.

Trace pulled up a chair, then sat facing James. "You're looking better. You know, with your hair cut now and several baths, you kinda resemble my little brother again."

James straightened his shoulders and sat up taller. He stared into his hands, then brought his eyes up to his brother's. "Did I

255

imagine One Wing and Cochise?" His finger traced the healing wound on his cheek. "Was it real?"

Trace lowered his voice to a whisper. "It was real all right. Damn real."

"Then...did Lila find out I got married? Is that why she hasn't come to see me?" James stared at the ribboned box waiting on the table. "I knew I shouldn't have been with...married Dark Cloud."

"The way you told it, James, you had no choice. You saved her life—at least for a few days." Trace gazed at a spot above his brother's head. "If it really happened."

James' eyes narrowed. "I told you—"

A figure appeared in the doorway. The doctor walked in, a folded piece of paper in his clutches. "This just came for you, James."

Dr. Logan extended his hand.

James opened the note, read twice. He closed his eyes and crumpled the paper. Without speaking, he handed it to Trace.

Trace unfolded it, read, then looked at Dr. Logan.

"It's from Lila. Says she's going away. To think." Trace paused. "Seems the reason she was gone when we got back... She was on her honeymoon. Married the sheriff."

He handed the paper back to James.

Fingers stiff, James crumpled the edges of the paper, then wadded the entire note into a ball. With white-knuckled fists, he hurled the bad news across the room. It bounced off the adobe wall, rolled back, and stopped at his feet.

James planted his foot on it and crushed down.

# About the Author

"I don't believe in reincarnation," says author **Melody Groves**, "but tendrils of the Old West keep me tied to stories yet untold. As long as I can remember, I've lived in the Old West, walked the plank streets, listened to the clip clop of horses trotting out of town, the occasional gunfire of cowboys whoopin' it up, or a sheriff going toe to toe with an outlaw."

For years, she denied this connection, but the people, the stories, the tendrils kept pulling. She lives, she says, not only in the real West, but also in the Old West. Groves is a member of New Mexico Gunfighters, a group of Old West re-enactors who perform skits and shoot outs in Albuquerque's Old Town every Sunday. Therefore, she knows what it's like to face down a sheriff or to stand with her "gang" and harass the "law." Her .22 Ruger single-action six has been busy—shooting hundreds of times—almost as often as she's "robbed" the bank! A performance highlight came in the form of performing as Morgan Earp at the famous shoot-out in Tombstone's OK Corral. As a writer, she uses those experiences to enhance her western fiction stories.

Groves grew up in Las Cruces, New Mexico, in the far southern part of the state, and rode horses and explored the desert. Heading for a jaunt in rodeo as a barrel racer, her life sidetracked when she moved to Subic Bay Naval Base, Philippines. As a teenager during the Viet Nam War, and only 800 miles from there, her life experiences were drastically different from her friends' back in the States, her barrel racing career extinguished.

She returned to attend college at New Mexico State University, earning a bachelor's in education. After moving to Albuquerque, she worked for the public schools and earned a master's degree in education. While sitting with students in front of her, Groves says, her mind raced with shootouts, dastardly outlaws, and women and men who wanted to tame the West. "Finally," she says, "I allowed the tendrils to take hold, the stories to unfold, and my pen to take flight." She quit teaching and now writes full time, magazines, screen plays as well as books.

A contributor to *True West, New Mexico Magazine,* and *albuquerqueARTS*, Melody Groves is the publicity chairman for Western Writers of America, the public relations chairman of SouthWest Writers, member of New Mexico Gunfighters Association, and a member of the New Mexico Rodeo Association.

Groves' first non-fiction book, *Ropes, Reins and Rawhide: All About Rodeo,* explains the ins and outs of rodeo. It is designed as a "how to watch rodeo" book, complete with 93 photos.

***Arizona War*** is one of the stories in her Colton Brothers Saga, published by La Frontera Publishing.

# Ordering Information

For information on how to purchase copies of Melody Groves's *Sonoran Rage, A Colton Brothers Saga, No 2*, or for our bulk-purchase discount schedule, call (307) 778-4752 or send an email to: company@lafronterapublishing.com

## About La Frontera Publishing

*La frontera* is Spanish for "the frontier." Here at La Frontera Publishing, our mission is to be a frontier for new stories and new ideas about the American West.

La Frontera Publishing believes:
- There are more histories to discover
- There are more tales to tell
- There are more stories to write

Visit our Web site for news about upcoming historic fiction or nonfiction books about the American West. We hope you'll join us here — on *la frontera.*

### La Frontera Publishing
*Bringing You The West In Books* ®
2710 Thomes Ave, Suite 181
Cheyenne, WY 82001
(307) 778-4752
www.lafronterapublishing.com

# OldWestNewWest.Com

It's the monthly Internet magazine for people who want to explore the heritage of the Old West in today's New West.

With each issue, **OldWestNewWest.Com** brings you new adventures and historical places:

- Western Festivals
- Rodeos
- American Indian Celebrations
- Western Museums
- National and State Parks
- Dude Ranches
- Cowboy Poetry Gatherings
- Western Personalities
- News and Updates About the West

Visit **OldWestNewWest.Com** to find the fun places to go, and the Wild West things to see. Uncover the West that's waiting for you!

# www.oldwestnewwest.com

La Frontera Publishing's eZine about
the Old West and the New West